SUNFLOWER

D.L. BROOM

A Wild Ink Publishing Original
wild-ink-publishing.com

ISBN: 978-1-964885-23-0

To Ward, Clay & Max

Your love & support

has made this dream

come true

Chapter 1
Ivey

Walloon Lake, Michigan

I joylessly jerked my roller bag down the hall of my Aunt Lauren's lakeside cottage—the site of my summer exile. Conspiratorial giggles floated from the kitchen as I backed through the bedroom door. My mother and my aunt had already broken into the wine and were probably trading stories about the good ole days. My mood lifted somewhat when I took in the guest room, all scattered florals and plaids in shades of pale blue and yellow. Oversized pillows in coordinating fabrics covered the comfy-looking queen size bed. The thick, white shag carpet made me smile. I'd always wanted a shag carpet, but my mother said it was too much upkeep and that I had a disturbingly seventies style. I kicked off my trainers, plopped onto the bed, then dipped my toes into the carpet's downy fibers. My stubborn resolve not to enjoy a minute of this trip to Walloon Lake, Michigan, dissipated a bit.

Was it always this quiet around here?

I remembered the lake being full of sounds when I would visit as a child: dogs barking, boats revving, children laughing. I slid off the bed, hoisted my bag up on the comforter, then wandered over to the window, cranked it open, and looked out over the gravel road to the water. It was that golden time of day when the sun's softening pink rays lined the blue and white sky, reflecting off the sparkling teal of the lake.

Not that I care. Just because Walloon is beautiful doesn't mean I have to like anything about being here.

My grandparents' house was on the other side of Walloon Lake—that's where my mother and Aunt Lauren grew up. I used to love exploring their house and backyard with my sisters. The Corbett home was a big rambling old place that'd been in the family forever. Pops, who owned the local Ace Hardware for forty years, had enjoyed updating the place before he and Nan moved to Sedona, Arizona, last year. When Nan fell about six months ago, my mother made plans to visit them this summer to give Pops a caregiving break, subjecting me to this banishment. I'd much rather be back home in Florida, hanging out with my besties, Clara and Kelli, and working at our favorite boutique. But since I'm the youngest of three girls, I have no rights and have been foisted on any relative at any time. My perfect older twin sisters, Daisy and Rose, would never have been forced to trash their summer plans. Case in point—they are in DC for a Leadership Conference.

I'd started to unpack when my phone played Clara's ringtone. I flopped on the bed and opened Facetime. Both Clara and Kelli's adorable faces lit up the screen.

I cuddled into the freshly scented comforter. "Hey! What's up?"

Clara smiled and waved. "Hey, Ivey! It looks like you've arrived safely."

Kelli made faces behind Clara's back.

I giggled. "Yes, I'm here. Kels, be careful! Your face might stick like that!" I propped the phone against a blue vase on the nightstand, then rolled onto my side. "I'm so happy to see you both. Thanks for checking on me. My sentence is about to start, I guess."

Clara pursed her lips and wagged a finger. "Now, now. Positive thinking, girl. Show us around."

I loved my girls for trying to cheer me up. "Room tour, room tour!" Kelli piped up in the background.

I didn't want to let them down, so I crawled off the bed, collected my phone, then panned around the room. They oo-ed and ah-ed as I narrated with a terrible English accent. "And here is the closet, voila, enough room for my evening gowns and furs with large, mirrored doors upon which I will gaze at my beauty. Oh!" I had an inspired idea. "One sec!" I exited the room and sneaked down the hallway toward the back door, hoping not to alert my mother and aunt as to my whereabouts; I'd had enough of them.

I heard Clara's dorky laugh. "Wow, you're laying it on thick, weirdo," she said.

I brought the phone up to my face and shushed her. "I have something very special to show you."

The back door creaked as I pried it open. I looked back down the hall checking, once again, that I hadn't interrupted my mother and aunt's conversation. I heard them chittering, so I figured I was cool. I tiptoed out of the house and around to the grassy side yard.

"I must give the fans what they want." I cleared my throat theatrically. "And the pièce de résistance!" I lifted the phone to show the girls the gleaming lake from outside of Lauren's cottage. "The view!"

Clara gasped, then passed her phone to Kelli.

"Ivey, what a gorgeous place!" Kelli exclaimed. "You have a dock right there? Does your aunt have a boat?"

I flipped the camera screen back to myself and wondered aloud. "Hm, I'm not sure, but I'll ask."

What was that? Stay the course, Ivey. Remember, you do not want to be here.

As I stood in the yard chatting with the girls, a huge gold SUV rolled to a stop in front of Lauren's house. An incredibly good-looking guy jumped out of the driver's side. His face was hard, his full lips were flattened into a straight line as he stomped around the vehicle and pulled the passenger side door open so hard it bounced back on its hinges. When the car door started to close, he halted it with his slimly muscular torso.

I froze in place, wondering what might happen. My curiosity was legendary, at least, among my friends.

"Ives?" I heard Kelli ask. I plastered myself against the side of the house, hopefully out of eye and ear shot. "Oh, I'm sorry," I whispered into the phone, looking up into the leafy trees swaying above the house. "There seems to be some drama out front."

Chapter 2
Ivey

"What's going on?" Clara's voice sounded far away as I pressed the phone against my chest.

I peered around the corner and flipped the camera back so the girls could see.

I heard the guy yell at whoever was in the SUV. "Well, I didn't ask you for a ride!" He slammed the passenger side door closed, then turned away, pulling his phone from a back pocket. He started madly texting while his jaw clenched.

"I don't know, but that guy is very pissed," I mumbled.

The SUV backed up, circled around, and pulled away heading toward Main Street. I assumed the passenger scooted into the driver's seat unless there was someone else seated further back. Darkly tinted windows kept me from seeing if the driver was a male or female. Not that it is any of my business, I reminded myself.

As I stood at the side of the house, holding up my phone like a paparazzo, I wondered why this guy got out right in front of Lauren's. Then he looked up from his cell as if he sensed my thoughts, so I dropped my phone to my side and pressed my back harder against the house.

"Hey! We can't see anything!" Clara complained, the phone's speaker muffled against my leggings.

Kelli added, "Let us see; let us see!"

"Shhh!" I aimed my phone back at the boy when he lifted his cell to his ear.

"What the hell?" he barked. "You just pulled away!" He paused and listened while running a hand through his longish black hair. "No! Leave me alone!" His voice was deep and menacing.

I shivered and my stomach did a flip-flop, making me nauseated. The guy reminded me of someone that I didn't want to recall.

"You know who he looks a little like?" Clara remarked, as if she'd read my mind.

I switched the screen back to my face and grimaced at her. "Maybe a passing resemblance."

The guy started speaking Spanish, and although I had no idea what he was saying, I guessed he was blessing out the SUV driver. Why did I assume he was shouting at a girl?

Come on, Ives, you know why you think that way.

I took a deep breath, pulled the phone back into my chest, and escaped toward the back door. Once inside, I tiptoed down the hall and slinked into my room.

"I gotta go. I'll hit you both up later!" I blew the screen a quick kiss and disconnected.

Chapter 3
Ivey

I tossed the phone on the bed and peeked over the window sash. The guy was still halfway up the path to Lauren's door. He'd returned to intently texting with his nose practically touching the screen. Now that I was safely inside and he couldn't see me staring, I noticed how his slouchy jeans skimmed his narrow hips, and his worn tee-shirt stretched nicely across his chest. He did remind me of my ex-boyfriend, Oliver, physically at least. The temper was familiar too. I heard a burst of laughter from the kitchen. I felt my heartbeat in my ears because it finally occurred to me. The guy wasn't pausing to finish a text— he was coming to Lauren's door.

My first thought was how hideous I must look. A quick glance in the mirror justified my concern. No makeup, my light brown hair flying in all directions, and smelling like an airplane cabin was not how I wanted to meet anyone. I heard the tell-tale knock at the screen door, then I tiptoed to the doorway to listen.

"Rafe! Come in, come in," I heard my aunt say. "Carrie, here's the man himself."

I stood stock-still waiting for the—

"Ivey! Come say 'hello' to Rafe!"

I tapped my forehead on my room's doorjamb. "Crap, crap, crap," I muttered, then louder answered, "Coming!" I fluffed my hair and adjusted my hoodie. This is as good as it's going to get. I made my way to the kitchen, my heart beating wildly.

Rafe towered over the breakfast bar, his phone tucked away, holding a large glass of lemonade. I caught my breath.

Seriously, it's not like he's Harry Styles—get a hold of yourself.

Aunt Lauren waved me into the kitchen with both hands. "Ivey! This is Rafe Torres. He's going to help us at the Sunnyside this summer."

Rafe's eyes met mine. My stomach dropped to my feet. His bright, white smile contrasted beautifully with his light brown skin. His eyes were a soothing deep mahogany. Rafe's shaggy, black hair curled under his slightly large ears.

Clara would think that he's too skinny, but, man, it worked for me, despite my better judgment.

I'd figured that Aunt Lauren and I would be the only ones manning her summer pop-up shop at the Walloon Market. My parents had used the money I'd make working with my aunt to justify the loss of my hometown job at Maylene's Boutique.

"Hi, nice to meet you." His voice was light and smooth. It was hard to believe he had been bawling someone out five seconds ago.

Oliver could do that too. Switch gears in a flash.

"Hey." I looked at the hardwood floor like an idiot. I felt warm in my belly but freezing cold along my skin.

Lauren beckoned with another wave. "Well, come here, girl."

I shuffled toward the breakfast bar, gravitating to a stool next to my mother. She subtly reached out and put her hand on my back, tracing circles with her fingernails. My mother knew I got super nervous around new people; she was trying to be kind and comforting.

"So, Rafe, my sister tells me that you're putting up some shelves at the store, right?" Mom asked him.

"Um, yes, Mrs.?"

"Des Jardins, but please, do call me Carrie."

Rafe flashed a movie-star grin at my mother then took a sip of lemonade. "I got the brackets up. I'll get to the shelves in the morning, but I wanted Lauren to know that I've finished for today." He handed her a ceramic sunflower keychain labeled "Corbett Farm" which is my aunt's primary business, a sunflower farm.

"Thanks." Lauren took the keychain and dropped it into a nearby bowl. "I appreciate it." She turned to me. "Rafe's father has managed my flower fields for the past three years. I'd be lost without his expertise."

Rafe nodded at Lauren, then glanced at me. His eyes seemed even rounder and sweeter, which I knew was impossible.

"Oh, cool. Sunflowers are my favorite," I squeaked out.

Rafe smiled. "They are cool. Well, thanks so much for the drink, but I need to get home. See you in the morning?" Rafe kept his eyes on me.

I'm so sure he's enthralled with my obvious wit and intelligence.

It's not that I cared, exactly, but we were going to be working together the whole summer. I didn't want anyone thinking I'm a loser.

"Absolutely, we'll be there," Lauren spoke for both of us. "What'd ya think, nine-thirty, Ivey?"

Since my breathing had finally returned to normal, my voice was steadier. "Sure, whatever works for you."

Rafe took one last lemonade gulp then set the glass on the bar. He turned toward the screen door. "Bye now." He gave a backwards wave.

After Rafe had left the house, Mom and Lauren fixed all four eyeballs squarely on me.

"Well," Mom said, with an annoyingly smug smile. "It's too bad that young man is so darn unattractive." She patted my back again.

"Mother!" I groaned, as I pulled away dramatically.

My aunt chuckled. "He's a great kid. Smart and responsible. And not too bad to look at." She seemed to be enjoying my discomfort as much as my mother. Neither woman, obviously, had heard his disturbingly angry phone call.

"I need to finish unpacking," I said. "I'll get some dinner in a bit."

"Well, I'm ready to eat." Mom raised her wine glass, and the sisters' clinked glasses.

I hated them both.

Chapter 4
Ivey

Ivey: OMG! He does look a little like Oliver, but who cares? I'm not on the Bachelorette.

Clara: I only saw him for a sec, but he looked hot.

Kelli: deets gf!

Ivey: he's nice looking and taller than me—not that I am interested in the least.

Kelli: ok… more deets!

Clara: what's his name?

Ivey: Rafe Torres—kinda cute name

Clara: soooooooooo cute!

Kelli: why did he come by your aunt's?

Ivey: He was dropping off Aunt L's keys from the store.

Clara: Wait a minute, is he working—

Kelli: at the store?

Ivey: Yeah, he's hot and all but—

Clara: Ok this is serious. Take a breath, you must appear unaware of his man-tractive-ness.

Ivey: duh!

Kelli: make sure you wear some makeup Ives. Maybe some light powder ;)

Ivey: Thx Kel, But I have no intention of making a love connection.

Clara: Ok ok ok But it's ALL summer! You should have some fun too!

Kelli: Wait a sec! Do u think ur aunt planned this?

Ivey: hmm hadn't thought of that… maybe. Ha.

Kelli: I'd talk to her.

Clara: Kelli, pls!!

Kelli: What? I'm trying to help.

Clara: Ives, there's nothing wrong with giving Rafe a chance. He isn't Oliver.

Ivey: Stop! will ya? I gotta get some dinner-Luv ya!

Kelli: good luck! Luv ya2

Clara: luv ya gfs!

I sat up on the bed, clicked off my phone, and reached for the charger cord on the nightstand. My stomach churned up. I hadn't eaten anything since that bagel at the Tampa airport. The soda I'd grabbed when I'd arrived at Lauren's had soured in my belly. I knew I had to get up and make nice with my mother and aunt to feed myself, but my body felt heavy as a boulder. I rubbed my temples. I'd hoped to keep my head down and get through as much of this summer as I could without drama—especially guy drama.

I'm being so stupid. Rafe's conflict with… whoever… is his deal—not mine. I have to remember what Clara told me about listening to my intuition. I can't even solve my own problems, let alone anyone else's. But what made him so angry, earlier? I wonder if he's that short-tempered with everyone.

I took some steadying breaths, peeled myself off the bed, and finished unpacking my bag. Rafe's image wormed its way into my brain despite my best efforts. I needed food.

Chapter 5
Ivey

When I returned to the kitchen, Mom and Lauren had moved to the adjacent den with a second bottle of wine (the first one peeking out of the recycling bin) and the Eagles' "The Long Run" playing through a tiny Bose speaker on a side table.

"Ivey! Did you get unpacked all right?" My aunt's voice was slurry, and her curly blond topknot had shifted to the side of her head. "I hope you like the room."

I had my "happy girl" face back on. "It's so cute. I love it." Despite the put-on levity, I did love the room.

"I'm so glad you like it! I found the comforter and pillows online—and on sale!" Lauren winked at my Mom, and they did an air high five. My God. "Just grab a plate there by the coffee maker and serve yourself."

I did indeed grab a plate, not surprisingly decorated with a giant sunflower. Aunt Lauren sure did stick with a theme. I scooped a heaping portion of delectable fettuccini on my plate and attempted to retreat to the tranquility of the bedroom, but my mother interrupted me.

"I hope I didn't embarrass you around Rafe," my mother said from her perch on the sofa. She giggled and took another sip of wine.

"Oh, of course not, Mother. I love meeting boys in front of family while I look and feel disgusting." I stuffed a forkful of pasta in my mouth.

"Come sit with us!" Lauren patted the love seat cushion next to her. "I want to hear all about your life: your school, your friends, but—" She glanced at my mother. "You're both probably too exhausted to talk, and if I remember correctly, my sister can be incredibly annoying on trips." Lauren tipped her wineglass at Mom.

"You're hilarious, sissy." Mom laid her head back on the leather sofa cushion. "Mmmm, I could just fall asleep right now."

"Oh, dang! Let me put some sheets and towels in the office for you, Carrie. I meant to do it earlier." Lauren popped up and headed to a closet off the den. I settled down with my food.

My mother, miraculously, found a second wind when Lauren disappeared into her office. "Honestly, Ivey, are you going to be surly all summer? Your aunt's rolled out the red carpet for you. I haven't seen her this excited since, before, well—in years." Mom's eyes darted to a framed photo of Lauren and her ex-husband, Michal Lyska. I wondered why Lauren had the photo so prominently displayed when, according to my parents, Uncle Michal had abandoned her five years ago. But Mom had made it glaringly clear that I was not to ask Lauren anything about my uncle as we drove from the Traverse City Airport.

Earlier that day, Mom and I had exited the airport, rented a tiny Ford EcoSport, and took off for the ninety-minute drive to Walloon. Mom proceeded to, for the millionth time, hammer into my head that bringing up Aunt Lauren and Uncle Michal's marriage and divorce was verboten.

"Please do this for me, honey." I felt the stress radiate from her, but Mom kept her eyes firmly on the road ahead.

"Okay, okay! I've already agreed not to talk about him. God, Mom! If you're so worried about my loose lips, you should have let me stay home with Clara's family." I turned to the window with a huff.

Mom sighed, then breathed in sharply, as if she was going to say something else, but stifled it.

I felt a sick satisfaction that I'd managed to shut her up.

Mom's eyes were wide, and her brows furrowed. "Well?" she said. "Are you going to perk up?"

I balanced my plate on my knee. "Yeah, of course. Tired, I guess."

"Well, for goodness sakes, stop schlumping around and engage in conversation!" Mom said, sharply.

"Yes, ma'am!" I sat up straight and saluted like a soldier.

Mom's grim expression softened. She scooted across the sofa closer to me, placing her hand on my plate-free leg. "As far as Lauren is concerned, you *want* to be here this summer. She'd have never gone for this idea if she thought you were reluctant to come."

"Mom!" I cried out. "That is so unfair. To her and me."

Mom panic-looked toward the hallway. "Shhh! She'll hear us."

I dug my thumb and forefinger into the bridge of my nose but lowered my voice. "So, not only did you and Dad force me to come here, but I also have to put on a show all summer?"

My mother pulled her hand from my leg, then rubbed her temples. "Leaving you in Florida, alone, was not an option. You get that, right?" When she looked back at me, her eyes pleaded. "I'm not asking you to be dishonest with your aunt, just give her a break. Lauren doesn't deserve your misplaced anger."

All the blood rushed to my head and thundered through my ears. I wanted to scream. I wanted to jump up and flail around like a lunatic. "Misplaced anger? Really, Mom? I had a job all lined up at Maylene's, and Clara's mom agreed that I could spend the summer at their place. I'd say I have every reason to be angry."

Mom sighed. "Okay, you're right. We're both tired, so—"

"You know that's not it." I set my plate on the coffee table; it clunked as it hit the glass top. I lifted it to make sure nothing had cracked. "Why wouldn't you and Dad let me stay with Clara?"

Mom looked toward the hallway again. I guess she was worried that Lauren might walk in and see us not being perfect mother and daughter. "As much as we love Clara, we didn't feel comfortable leaving you for over two months with another family."

"I know, I know." Exhaustion cascaded over me, making my mouth dry and my throat scratchy.

Mom gathered a pillow to her chest. "Well, I can't make our reasoning any clearer."

I twirled some pasta on my fork, trying not to give her the satisfaction of my complete attention. "Yeah, well, Clara's family is amazing and it's not fair."

"Fair or not, you're here, and I'm sure you'll be the mature and kind young woman I know you can be."

Lauren sailed back into the room. "You're all set up, Carrie!" She talked way louder than she needed. It made my head hurt. "And Ivey, I put some extra towels on your bed. Make sure you tell me if you need anything else." She sat down on the loveseat, jostling me.

"Thanks so much, Auntie." I gave her a peck on the cheek and a hug. "I think I'll take a quick bath and get some sleep."

Lauren kept me in the embrace longer than I expected so her gardenia scent enveloped me. "I'm so thrilled you're here. I love you so much for coming to visit," she whispered in my ear.

I gently pulled away, picked up my plate, and rose from the loveseat. "Love you, too. See you in the morning."

"I'll say goodbye before I leave tomorrow. Have a nice bath, honey." Mom called after me.

I nodded, then dragged myself to the bathroom with two mysteries banging through my brain. Who was Rafe so angry with earlier, and what was the deal with Aunt Lauren's divorce that freaks my mother out so much?

Chapter 6
Ivey

Ten minutes later, I was neck-deep in chamomile and lavender-scented bubble bath, a bath pillow snuggled behind my head and a hydrating face mask soothing my parched skin. I practiced the belly-breathing Clara, Kelli and I learned in our Saturday morning yoga class. I'm not sure it was relaxing me, but it sure was making me dizzy. My phone vibrated. I dried my hands on a convenient hand towel and grabbed it from a tiny tub-side table. Dad.

"Hey, Dad," I answered. Thank God he didn't try to Facetime—awkward!

"Hey, Birdie. Mom said that you got to Lauren's safely. How are things going so far?"

"Yeah, we got here just fine." Be positive, Ivey. "You got Daisy and Rose to their conference?"

"Sure did. I'm hanging out at the D.C. Sheraton, enjoying a room service burger and fries."

I heard a baseball game in the background. "Sounds good. Aunt Lauren made fettuccine alfredo for dinner. I wonder if someone told her it's my fave?"

He laughed. "I'm sure your mother had something to do with that. How is Lauren?"

"She's good. I'm exhausted. I was about to go to sleep."

"Birdie." Dad hesitated. "You know how much your mother and I appreciate you agreeing to visit with your Aunt this summer."

"Dad, please don't—"

"No, honey, listen." Dad's voice was deep. "We know we can always count on you to do what's best for the family. Your mom had this trip to your grandparents' planned for a long time. Then your sisters got this incredible opportunity."

Blah blah. "I know, Dad. You don't have to tell me again." I sighed.

"Maybe next summer you can join your friends working in town." He paused. "Your mom did remind you not to bring up Michal, right?"

Oh my God.

I shot up from my prone position in the bath and my sheet mask slipped off and plopped into the water. "Dad, if I hear that again, I may pop a vein. I will not mention Uncle Michal."

Dad's tone mellowed. "I'm sorry—your mom's very worried about upsetting Lauren."

I couldn't get off the phone soon enough. "I hear you, Dad. I gotta go. Love you!"

"Love you, Birdie. Keep in touch, and, maybe, reach out to your sisters?"

Deep breaths, belly breathe, Ivey.

"Yeah, sure. Talk soon." I ended the call before my Dad asked me to kiss my mother and aunt good night. I checked the time on my phone display. It was only around seven-thirty, but I definitely didn't want to get into any kind of extended conversation with Daisy or Rose. I shot them both texts saying:

Ivey: Mom & I in MI, have fun in D.C.!

Duty communication finished—good girl Ivey strikes again. I dropped my phone on the thick bathmat. I smoothed the excess moisturizer from the sheet mask down my neck, then dipped my hair back into the warm water, swishing it back and forth. My thoughts turned to Rafe Torres. He sure gave me all the "feels," but I wondered how we'd get along as co-workers. The only real working experience I had was selling Girl Scout cookies and school wrapping paper.

I closed my eyes and took a few more deep breaths, hoping I would be able to fall asleep. All my nerve endings had fired off today. My buttons had been pushed left and right by my mother and now, my dad.

Did I pack my Melatonin gummies?

I looked around the bathroom frantically. Ah! My make-up bag sat on the back of the commode. I grabbed it, unzipped, and dug through all my toiletries. Thank God! I found the purple and white bottle under everything else. I must have packed it first thing. Whew!

At least, I could count on my subconscious to look out for me.

Chapter 7
Rafe

Rafael Lucas Torres walked along Main Street from Lauren Corbett's house to his place on Clarion Street. As he turned the final corner, his family's two-story contemporary came into view. The ever-burning front porch light welcomed him. It was a warm evening, but a light breeze made the walk refreshing. He yanked open the rusty screen door, the tell-tale creak announcing his arrival. The mouth-watering scent of homemade macaroni and cheese wafted from the kitchen. He thought about the thinly sliced smoked ham his mother added, and his stomach clenched—he was starving.

Rafe's latest encounter with Hattie Foster, when she showed up and offered him a ride, had zapped all his energy. His stomach agreed.

"Mijo, dinner's ready!" Rafe's mother, Gabriella, announced from the home's rear kitchen.

Rafe strode down the cramped paneled hallway. "Be right there, Mamá!" A quick glance into his brother's empty room made him pause for a few seconds. When he entered his own room, Rafe thought about Lauren Corbett's niece. He was into Ivey's disheveled appearance. She was super cute in her oversized hoodie, with no makeup (that he could tell), and light brown, shoulder-length hair tucked behind her ears. He thought most girls spent too much time on their makeup and hair (or maybe just one specific girl), but Ivey had an open, natural look, especially her pale green eyes.

Rafe stripped the sweaty t-shirt off his body, then pulled on his favorite old Detroit Tigers sweatshirt. The neckline sagged and there was a hole in the left armpit, but it felt like a second skin, like the shirt equivalent of home.

When Lauren had mentioned needing some help at her store, his father had insisted Rafe take the summer work she'd offered rather than joining his pal, Morgan Turner, working at Mariachi's Mexican Restaurant. They had argued, but Rafe eventually had relented. Bottom line— money was money. Despite a bit of Morgan's harmless ribbing, Rafe made peace with the Sunnyside job. Now that he'd be seeing more of Ivey, he thought it might make working at the Square worth his while. Meeting someone new was suddenly quite appealing.

Rafe heard his father's F-250 pull onto the newly paved driveway as he finished off a massive serving of mac and cheese. Rafe's mother rose from her meal to prepare a plate for his father. She scraped the shell shaped noodles out of her well-worn cast iron skillet, then plopped the gooey mixture on a bright yellow plate.

Rafe glanced at the kitchen clock, noting his father was about thirty minutes later than usual. He looked at his mom. "Dad keepin' tabs on Tonio?"

Gaby turned from the stove. "Let him tell us if he wants to, okay?" She raised her voice. "Marco, come get it while it's hot!"

Rafe's father entered the kitchen. "Smells fantastic. I hope this one left enough for me." He tousled Rafe's hair, then kissed his wife on the cheek. He pulled out a chair and settled his six-foot, sturdy frame at the table. "So, how did things go today at the Sunnyside?"

Rafe's mom set the steaming plate of mac and cheese in front of him.

"Gracias, carina," he said, pouring water from a nearby cut-glass pitcher into a matching glass.

"I got all the brackets hung and waited for the shelving to be delivered." Rafe smoothed his curls down over his ears. He hated when his dad messed up his hair. Other people thought it was endearing—Rafe knew different. It was to make Rafe feel like a little boy. "I'll get it finished tomorrow, so Lauren and Ivey can start bringing in the inventory." He leaned back and hovered on the back two legs of his chair.

Rafe's mother had finally settled down to eat her meal. "Rafe, how many times have I asked you?"

"Oops, sorry, Ma." Rafe gave his mother an exaggerated wide-eyed look of innocence. He righted the chair on the linoleum.

She wiggled her finger at him. "That look is not going to work forever, Mijo," she replied, with a mock-serious expression.

Rafe winked at his mom. "You always say that."

"You baby him too much, carina." Rafe's father finished his water.

Mama smiled. "Well, he is my baby boy." She reached over to pat Rafe's hand.

Rafe's father changed the subject "Ivey? Oh, that must be Lauren's niece. How old is she?"

"Well, Dad, I talked to her for about two seconds, so I don't know."

His father set down his fork. "Rafael, I was simply making conversation. Don't be a smart aleck."

Rafe grunted when the phone in his pocket vibrated. He held it under the table hoping to avoid alerting his father. Morgan.

"Son, you know the rule about phones at the table," his father warned.

Rafe couldn't get a thing past him.

"I know, Dad. I'll text him later." He stuffed the phone in his pocket. "I'm sure he's gonna tell me all about his job at Mariachi's."

"Well, good for him."

"He's gonna make a ton of cash with tips," Rafe said, poking the bear a bit.

His father was non-plussed. "Perhaps."

The family lapsed into an edgy silence. Forks tapped on plates, as Rafe stared down his father, who ignored his son's provocative posturing.

Rafe "blinked" first. "Well, I'm going to take a shower and crash. I told Lauren I'd be there at nine-thirty." Rafe pushed back his chair, picked up his plate, and deposited it in the sink. "Night!"

Chapter 8
Rafe

After showering, Rafe pulled on pajama pants, then fell on his bed. He heard the not-so-hushed voices of his parents in the kitchen.

"—not in his usual hangouts," said Marc.

"Maybe he's got a job," Gabby responded, her voice hopeful.

Marc growled. "—sick and tired—"

Not wanting to hear any more of his parents' conversation, Rafe rolled off his bed and gently shut the door.

He'd made a concerted effort *not* to think about Antonio lately.

As little boys, only twenty months apart, they had been best friends—riding bikes and building forts in the backyard. Rafe always depended on Tonio to be his sounding board and his first line of defense. People had called them the Torres "twins," but that was ancient history.

Rafe turned over, then punched his pillow when a particularly precious childhood memory invaded his thoughts.

Antonio had come up with the "Summer Supply List" after Rafe's last day of fourth grade. Second only to their Christmas list, the SSL became a carefully curated collection of essential items for a perfect guys' summer. The list included snacks like taco-flavored Doritos, sour cream & onion Utz potato chips, and peanut butter-filled pretzels. Also listed were favorite Fanta sodas—grape for Rafe, and orange for Tonio. The rest of the SSL included things needed for backyard projects, science experiments, and world-changing inventions. They even had an old Radio Flyer wagon to hoist their summer booty around.

A text message brought Rafe's attention back to the present. He rifled through the bed sheets to find his phone.

Morgan: wat up?

Rafe: not much u?

Morgan: just finished training at Ms

Rafe: all good?

Morgan: yeah, lotsa work, how about u?

Rafe: tired, doing some shelving for the store

Morgan: come to Ms after work la noche de mañana?

Rafe: Hey-like the lingo, man! I'll try to stop by

Morgan: okay c ya

Rafe: c ya

Rafe wasn't sure why he hadn't mentioned Ivey. He had a good feeling about getting to know her, but he wasn't sure if he wanted to get his friend's opinion yet. Morgan had never been shy about his particular dislike for Hattie. The summer was just beginning, and who knew if he and Ivey would have anything but a part-time job in common. Rafe heard the creaking screen door open, just as his eyes closed. He grabbed his noise-canceling headphones and went to an ASMR app on his phone.

It was about to get loud in the Torres house.

Chapter 9
Ivey

I woke up at 8:30 am the following day, checked my phone, laid like a petrified log under the comfy duvet for ten perfectly timed minutes, then rolled myself out of the bed. I wondered what it would be like to just pop up in the morning. After tons of sleepovers, I'd learned that Kelli literally bursts awake. It was a bit terrifying. Clara and I would "mole" under the covers, hoping Kelli'd forget we were even there.

Dang, I already missed them. I especially missed Clara's impeccable style and Kelli's funny bone. A gnarly pit formed in my belly as I recalled telling them about my northern exile as we finished lunch the last week of school.

The three of us had been sitting outside the cafeteria, when, Clara Casperson, the fashion editor of the Brandon High Banner and master debater, tugged on my sleeve. "Ives, isn't Michigan where people can't drink the water 'cause it's all polluted?"

"Yeah," Kelli Winter nodded. "I remember that! Wasn't Mr. Bonito talking about that in Current Events last week?"

I tilted my head and flattened my lips. "You guys are boneheads. That's in Flint, which is one city in *all* of Michigan. That's like saying Miami is all of Florida."

Clara flipped her shiny black pony. "At least I was right about the state…" She raised her diet Dr. Pepper can.

Kelli giggled and stuffed a sweet potato fry into her mouth.

Clara playfully pinched my arm. "Still, why do you have to be gone the whole summer?" Her voice was high and whiny.

"Ow!" I pushed Clara's hand away. "God, it's not my fault! I can't help that my parents are forcing me to go." I sounded even whinier than Clara. The whole situation made me feel like a toddler being pulled from a hot stove.

Kelli reapplied her pink lip-gloss and admired herself in a mirrored compact. "Maylene was counting on you for the summer. No offense, but your parents suck."

I clicked my tongue. "I know. I talked to her last night. I was really looking forward to the forty percent discount—"

Clara interrupted. "Ah, forty-five, Ives."

I palmed my forehead. "Dang, are you serious?" I love the clothes at Maylene's. I put up my arms in surrender. "Well, I'll text and FaceTime you both—it'll be like I'm home the whole time." I tried to sound bubbly as I stood up from the stone lunch table, picking up my lunch tray. "This chicken is truly disgusting."

Kelli held up a pukey green plastic bowl half full of fries. "That's why I only get these."

Clara rose from the table, gripped the waistline of her short kilt and tugged it around so the leather buckle faced the front. "Hmm, maybe you'll meet someone interesting. I'm sure there's a boy or two in Michigan." She wiggled her eyebrows up and down. "Maybe help you forget someone?"

My shoulders drooped when I thought about my breakup with Oliver. "I can't even think about boys. I've just gotta get through the summer without boring myself to death."

I couldn't help smiling, thinking about my crazy friends. I slicked my hair back with coconut conditioner and exited the shower when that old familiar stomachache flared up. Little had I known that I'd meet Rafe mere minutes after arriving in Walloon. As I brushed my teeth, acid crawled up my throat, threatening to gag me. I shook my head like a wet dog, looked into the bathroom mirror, and said aloud, "Get a hold of yourself!"

Starting a new job did explain my nerves, but this was too much! Why was I fooling myself? It was seeing Rafe that was churning up my gut.

I'd have to focus, breathe, and try not to be a complete idiot around him. You'd think I'd never met a cute boy before. Truthfully, I hadn't met a boy who made me *this* nervous. Not even Oliver. With that, I gave my hair a quick blow-dry and pulled it into a high pony. I applied some powder, a bit of mascara, and lip gloss, then studied my reflection.

Crap! Is that a zit?—NOT okay! I grabbed concealer, wishing I had Kelli's talent for covering pimples. I spritzed on the Chloé perfume my parents had given me for my sixteenth birthday last month, took another deep, cleansing breath, then joined Lauren in the kitchen.

Aunt Lauren glanced at the kitchen clock above the fridge. "Hey there, right on time! Coffee?" She looked bright and sunny in a white eyelet swing top, light wash denim crops, and rhinestone sandals.

"Oh no," I replied. "I'm not much of a coffee girl. Any OJ?"

"Of course, in the fridge, on the top shelf; official Sunnyside cranberry scones if you're interested."

I grabbed an individually wrapped scone from the piled-high plate on the breakfast bar. "Thanks. Travel cup?" I picked at the cellophane around the scone.

"Cabinet to the right of the stove. Let me feed Peppercorn, and we'll be off." Lauren pulled a plastic container from under the sink, opened it, and scooped some food pellets into a tiny dish. She made a kissy noise as she placed the plate on the floor. I heard clicky little footsteps coming towards us.

"Aw, I didn't know you had a kitty." I kneeled to pet a grey and white feline gobbling her food.

"I call her my part-time cat." Lauren stooped to pet her as well. "Peppercorn just showed up one day, and I couldn't help but feed her. Margie, next door, takes the dinner shift." The cat took a break from her feast to flip over and encourage more attention. "She can be bashful around new folks, but she likes you!"

The cat purred while I rubbed her belly and threaded my fingers through her fur. "What a sweetie."

"Well, your mom made it to the airport. She texted me a few minutes ago."

I looked up from the cat. "Oh, good, I vaguely remember her coming in and saying 'bye."

As Lauren stood up, she grunted softly when her knee made a click. She sipped her coffee, then said, "You don't want to be here this summer, do you?"

Chapter 10
Ivey

Lauren leaned against the kitchen sink, cradling her coffee cup, her eyes wide and twinkling.

My stomach churned back up. I closed my eyes and hung my head—maybe OJ had been a bad idea.

"Wow," I mumbled. "Did mom say something?"

Lauren didn't seem angry. When I opened one eye and peered at her, she looked amused. "No, she didn't have to." She moved toward me, putting a hand on my shoulder. "Ivey, I was a teenager not too long ago. I figured you would've preferred to be home with your friends—remind me their names?"

"Clara and Kelli." I nodded nervously, like a bobble-head toy.

Lauren lifted my chin gently. "Please don't be embarrassed. I get it. Let's make the best of the situation, okay? You let me know when you need time to yourself, and we'll go from there."

My eyes betrayed me by filling with tears. "I'm so sorry. You must think I'm the worst brat."

"Of course not. Listen, your mom's 'big sister' genes kicked in hard when I was born. She's always tried to protect me from any disappointment or hurt, and I love her for it. But, sometimes, it's made it difficult for me to stand on my own two feet." The twinkle briefly faded from her eyes. "Carrie thinks I'm tragically lonely and need a chaperone."

"I don't think Dee or Rose inherited those genes," I said, more pitifully than I meant to sound.

Lauren was quiet for a few more seconds. "I'm sure your sisters love you very much."

"Yeah, but I wouldn't say they look out for me, though. They have each other, and I'm just an inconvenient extra body in the house." I took a quick look at my phone—just as I expected, no response from either sister to my previous evening's text. "Are you tragically lonely?" I asked before I realized that my question might lead to the verboten Michal discussion.

Lauren set down her mug and took my hand. She didn't look the least bit bothered by my question. "I'm not." She grinned. "Just the normal kind of lonely. Now, let's make a pact. Repeat after me. 'I, Ivey Flora Des Jardins—'"

I gently pulled away and wiped my eyes. "You don't have to do this, Aunt—"

"Ivey? Repeat after me, now," she insisted.

"Okay, okay." I raised my right hand. "I, Ivey Flora Des Jardins."

"Do solemnly swear." Lauren was sure enjoying this.

"Do solemnly swear."

"That I will have the best possible time this summer."

"That I will have the best possible time this summer." I set the dregs of my scone down and stuffed my hands in my pockets.

"And I love my aunt the best of anyone. Amen." Lauren laughed at herself like a goofball.

"And I love my aunt the best of anyone. Amen. I think you mixed up a prayer and a pact, y'know?" I smiled. I like goofballs.

Lauren waved off my comment and started for the door. "Let's get to work—don't want to keep Rafe waiting."

Quite right. I certainly didn't want to keep cutie boy waiting.

Chapter 11
Ivey

"Wow! Aunt Lauren, it feels amazing out here!" I glanced at my weather app, which registered 78 degrees and super low humidity.

Lauren smiled broadly, extending her arms out like a tour guide. "Yep, can't beat summer in the Mitten."

We walked over to the public dock across from the house. The shimmering lake and azure-blue sky reflected off each other. The three-dimensional clouds from yesterday had returned, floating lazily up above us. The harbor bustled with boats, large and small—primarily white, with silvery chrome and gleaming glass. Families were chatting, children giggling and happily screaming as they prepared for a lake day. If you could smell sunshine, it would smell like that—freshly cut grass, pollen-laden flowers, and crisp cool water. It's not a beachy smell; it's clean and invigorating.

Thanks to the scone nibbles, the nervous butterflies had somewhat subsided—whew! After briefly pausing to appreciate all the activity, we turned toward the main road.

"You've had the summer store three years now?" I asked.

"This is the third season, and I've broken even for the past two years, but with your help—" she elbowed me, playfully "—we'll make lots of money!"

"Yikes, pressure much?" I grinned.

We arrived at the Square and passed under the Shops of Walloon banner at the entryway.

"How come the shops don't stay open all year?"

"Well, there was quite a bit of discussion about that exact subject at our town meetings. There just isn't enough traffic to support year-round shops." She gestured toward a small parking area on the right. "Plus, most shop owners, me included, have other businesses to run. Here we are!"

We stopped in front of Lauren's booth, which was adorable, all done up with bright yellow fabric draped over the creamy white wood frame.

"Oh, the sign will definitely draw people in!" Glorious sunflowers on either side of the words and a bright aquamarine background made the sign pop.

Lauren beamed. "Thanks so much! I think it's about time you just call me Lauren. Especially since we're going to work and live together."

I winced. "Seriously? That is going to be too weird."

"You can phase it in slowly if you want." Lauren rubbed my back, then whispered, "You have no idea how excited I am to have you here."

"Me too," I whispered back, noticing Rafe as he stepped down from a wooden ladder propped against the right side of the booth.

He wiped the sweat off his forehead. "Does it look straight to you?"

Okay, usually, I would find that gesture truly disgusting, yet, when Rafe did it, my knees turned to jelly.

"Looks perfect to me," Lauren cocked her head and placed her hands on her hips, studying the sign.

"Yeah." My voice came out stupidly high.

"Okay, gather round, you two." Lauren gestured us toward her. "Opening day is Saturday, so we need the shelving behind the register finished and stocked by Friday afternoon. Rafe, do you need Ivey's help with the shelves, or can she and I get some merchandise from Linda Myers?"

Did I want Rafe to say he needed help or not?

He looked down at his feet, then over to me. "Um, I may need a spotter when I get to the top shelves."

"No problem, Ivey can help me bring over a few things, and then she can make sure you don't fall and sue me for everything I'm worth. See you in a bit!"

Rafe nodded. "See ya." Before I could respond, he disappeared behind the yellow curtain separating the sales area from the stock room.

Chapter 12
Ivey

Lauren and I walked back onto Main Street. "Who is Linda Myers?"

"Oh, Linda owns a shop just up the street. Her store stays open all year, so she didn't want the hassle of a summer booth. She's crazy about sunflowers too, so I stock some of her collectibles. I wouldn't have much of a store if I only sold sunflower stems and seeds."

It was so cool that the store owners helped each other. "I hadn't even thought about that," I said.

We turned off the sidewalk onto a smaller road.

Lauren continued. "The Sunnyside's been a real work in progress. The first year, I only sold flowers, seeds, and baked goods. I was lucky to almost break even. I sat in the booth feeling like I was wasting my time that summer." She looked up, shading her eyes as a plane whooshed by. "The next year, I added the fridge for soft drinks and bottled water, so the baked goods sold better. Linda came in halfway through last summer and asked if I would stock her artist friend's watercolor canvases. The art went fast, so I asked for more this year."

"Lauren!" bellowed a plump, older lady with a bubble of platinum blonde hair. She stood on the porch of her store that was housed in what looked like a converted gas station. There was a nondescript sign beside the glass door that read, "Decor and More."

"Hey, Linda! How are you today? This is my niece, Ivey."

I extended my hand, but Linda pulled me into an embrace. "Oh, Ivey, the last time I saw you, you were in a stroller. I know your grandparents."

I didn't remember this lady, so I was embarrassed by the hug but appreciated the sentiment. I wiggled away and smiled sheepishly. "Thanks. Nice to meet you."

Linda Myers stepped back into her shop, making room for us to enter. "Well, come in, come in. I have my trusty wagon packed."

Lauren and I returned to the store dragging the wagon stuffed with boxes of 4x6 and 5x5 watercolors by artist Stassi Sumter, along with wooden craft items, all embellished with one or more sunflowers.

I brought the boxes into the stock room just as Rafe was about to start on the two highest shelves in the front. I joined him after stowing the art, positioning myself at the bottom of the ladder, prepared to—what? Catch him if he fell?

Please, God, don't let him fall. That is so *not* how I would ever envision touching him. The angry expression on his face yesterday flashed through my mind, hardening me to today's seemingly nice guy persona. Oliver could do that too—until he couldn't.

Rafe looked down at me from his perch on a stainless-steel ladder. "Oh, hey, thanks for the spot. Could you hand me one of the shelves, then just hold 'er steady?"

"Of course," I handed him a white plank. I noticed the view from the bottom of the ladder was not bad at all.

Think, Ivey, say something intelligent.

I took a deep breath and took the verbal plunge. "So, have you lived in Walloon for a long time?"

"Yeah, since second grade." He glanced down. The ladder wobbled when his weight shifted.

I gripped the ladder until my knuckles whitened. "Oh God, be careful!"

He regained his balance. "I'm good. What about you? Lauren said you're from Florida?" He focused on the brackets and balancing the shelf.

"I live in Florida now, but I was born in Texas. My Dad's in the Air Force, so we've moved around."

He slipped the shelf onto the brackets with a click. "That sounds so cool, moving around the country."

"It was hard to leave Texas, but I like Brandon."

"Your mom and Lauren grew up here, though, right. Can you hand me the other one?"

"Sure." I hoisted the shelf up to him. "Yeah, my grandparents lived over on Merritt Street."

"Oh yeah, your family used to own the Ace Hardware." He balanced the second shelf. "I was down there this morning." The plank clicked when it attached to the metal bracket.

Wow, this is a scintillating conversation.

I watched Rafe as he pulled a level out of his back pocket and checked the last two shelves. He nodded, pocketed the tool, and started down the ladder.

I scooted back, so as not to crowd him when he stepped off. "Oops, sorry."

"No worries, thanks for the spot." He grinned and he wiped his hands on his jeans. "What's next?"

I chewed my bottom lip. "I'm not sure. Lauren's going down to the farm to check on the flower supply for Opening Day. Why don't we unwrap the wagon stuff?"

"Lead the way." He gestured toward the storeroom.

Chapter 13

Ivey

I was alone with him. I wasn't exactly worried, but having seen his temper, I couldn't help being on alert. I'd like to think Rafe was as self-conscious as I was, but he seemed totally at ease. Come to think of it, I'd probably have been more comfortable if I were home as well.

We settled on the floor of the storeroom and began to unwrap Stassi Sumter's art.

"So, do you and your friends spend a lot of time on the lake?" I asked.

"We used to. Most of us work during the summer now unless we play sports. My friend Morgan is working at a restaurant. I'd hoped to work there too, but my dad didn't want me working anywhere with a bar, which is stupid. I'm seventeen, so I couldn't serve it anyway." His expression darkened for a moment but brightened just as quickly.

Something in common! "That's crazy!" I started. "I'd planned to work at a clothing store with my friends when my parents made me come—" I hesitated, worried that he might take offense at my not wanting to be in Walloon.

He made an exaggerated thinking face, stroking his chin like a man contemplating the universe. "I'm so shocked that you didn't want to fly miles away from your home and friends to work in a town where you hardly know anyone? How unadventurous of you."

I felt the heat rise in my cheeks. "I've been mopey about it, which is pretty immature."

He nodded. "I get it. I didn't talk to my dad for two days after he nixed my working at Mariachi's—it was embarrassing 'cause I had to call the manager and tell him I couldn't take the job. Then Morgan busted my chops…" He glanced down at the artwork he was unwrapping.

I pursed my lips. "Yeah, I had to do the same thing. It was awful! My girls were cool about it, though."

"Well, Morgan is a dipsh—oh, sorry!" His light brown cheeks flushed.

"No problem," I assured him. "I didn't realize how obvious I'd been around Aunt, oh, I mean, Lauren, about being forced to come here. She mentioned it this morning, but she totally understands."

"Lauren's cool. My Dad respects her, and he's not the easiest guy, so she must be chill."

We returned to unwrapping. The sound of packing tape ripping reverberated around the stockroom as the conversation sank like an anvil through wet cement.

I couldn't stand it. "So, do you have any brothers or sisters?"

"Yeah," Rafe responded quietly. "Older brother, Antonio." His deep brown eyes looked pained.

"I have older twin sisters, Daisy and Rose."

Rafe's face brightened up. "I see what your parents did there with your names. Are they botanists or gardeners?"

I grinned. "Oh no, my mom liked the 'floral' theme. Y'know, with Des Jardins— of the gardens, in French."

Rafe pulled the shrink wrap off a canvas with a snap. "I didn't even connect the last name. Cool, cool. Why aren't your sisters here, too?"

I grimaced. "They're at a student leadership thing in D.C. It was this huge deal at our school that Mr. Moultrie got both in, but it upended our family's summer." I was bumming myself out.

Rafe shrugged his shoulders. "Sounds to me like you got the better end of the deal. I've had friends go to those things, and its tons of classes and meetings. Not my scene at all—but, hey, some people love that stuff."

I gently set a painting on the pile, then reached for another. "Believe me, Dee and Rose do." I clucked my tongue against my teeth. "They'll have all-new ways to boss people around."

Rafe laughed, a deep masculine laugh. "You don't seem like a bossy type."

"Nah, but you just met me, right?" I tried to look mysterious by raising one eyebrow. I think they both went up.

"Whoa—I better watch out this summer, huh?" His face was so sweet, almost like a hunky Snuggle fabric softener bear. I found the change delightfully assuring.

I gave him my best innocent face, hoping I didn't look constipated. "I'll have to get your recs on stuff to do around here."

"You'll definitely have to hit Mariachi's if you like Mexican food. Maybe we could—"

A high-pitched "Yoo-hoo! Anyone here?" coming from the storefront cut him off. A tiny, bracelet-clad hand pushed aside the yellow curtain, and in walked a drop-dead gorgeous girl wearing a bright orange and green tracksuit.

She looked around the storeroom with a disdainful expression but quickly snapped on a fake smile as she glided over to Rafe, draped her arms around him, then kissed him on the cheek. "Oh my God! Rafey! I'm glad you're here!"

I sat there with a half-wrapped sunflower canvas in my lap, my mouth sagging open. This tiny person sure filled up the room.

The girl turned to look at me as Rafe tried to stand up and peel her off.

"Hattie," he said, gruffly. "What are you doing here?"

Could this Hattie be from the Escalade?

"Oh, Rafey, don't be such a downer; I'm just here to see what you're up to." Her eyes were firmly set on me. "And who is this?"

I set the canvas aside and popped up to look her in the eye, but she was several inches shorter than my five-foot six. "I'm Ivey, Lauren's niece." I offered my hand for a shake. "And you're a friend of Rafe's?"

Rafe had disengaged Hattie's arms from his torso, but undaunted, she snaked her arm around his waist.

Her fake smile turned ice cold. "Ivey, dear, I'm Rafe's girlfriend."

Chapter 14
Ivey

A wave of embarrassment started from my scalp and flew down the back of my spine. My summer flashed in front of me—this super petite, posh princess traipsing into the store, summoning Rafe with her stupid siren song. Did I completely misjudge what I had seen and heard yesterday? Maybe they were just that couple who fights. Why do I feel so disappointed?

My hand hung out there as Hattie looked like I had the Ebola virus. "Oh, nice to meet you." I squeaked. She finally shook my hand, touching the least possible surface area. I shuddered.

Rafe pushed off Hattie's remaining vise-like grip. "She is not my girlfriend." His voice was as stony as his expression. No longer Snuggle bear, for sure.

Hattie poked out her bottom lip. "Rafey, that is so rude!" She stamped her foot.

He took a couple of steps back out to avoid her grasping claws. "And please stop calling me that. You broke up with me, remember?"

Hattie brushed back a bit of her glossy black bob. "Oh, that? Who cares?"

I stood there with my eyes wide, watching the drama unfold. I probably looked like a homeless person next to Hattie. My ragged jeans shorts and sweaty tank top hanging limply off my shoulders.

Rafe's brows furrowed. "I think Hank Purcell cares."

Hattie waved a hand dismissively. "Oh, pooh. I prefer to stay friendly, and Hank agrees." Hattie sauntered around the storeroom, touching several items, and squishing up her face. "Do people want all these sunflower things?"

I felt a surge of defensiveness. "This is the third summer for the store, so, yeah, people seem to like all the sunflower things."

Rafe covered a snort with his hand.

Hattie looked me up and down, her tiny nostrils flaring. "Well, I was just trying to make conversation." She picked up a honey-scented candle in a glass jar, sniffed, then winced theatrically. "Hm, I don't get the attraction. What on earth is this?" She removed a feathery item from a cellophane bag.

"It's a dreamcatcher," I looked at Rafe incredulously. "It's one of our best sellers." Well… it could be!

"Whatever. Stace is probably waiting for me. Bye, *Rafe*." She squished up her face again. "Uh, nice to meet you, Irene." She glided out of the storeroom.

"It's Ivey!" I yelled after her.

Rafe stood there, grinning from ear to ear, his hands shoved deep in his pockets. "One of our best sellers, huh?" He glanced at the dreamcatcher. He chuckled.

I shrugged, proud of myself. "She's a real charmer—I totally get why you went out with her." I crossed my legs, sinking back down to the floor.

"Ouch!" Rafe clutched his chest, faking a heart attack.

I smiled up at his antics, so incongruous to his behavior the previous day. I wanted to grill him about the scene in front of Lauren's, but I remembered that he had no idea that I knew anything about that interaction. I quickly realized how creepy and stalkerish it was of me to have cowered behind the house. We had all summer for me to learn more about him, so I struggled to find a way to segue back to Rafe nearly asking me to have Mexican food with him. Not sure I should even go if he did ask me out.

He joined me on the storeroom floor, and we got back to unwrapping merchandise. Another awkward silence fell over us.

I wondered if he remembered what we were talking about before Hattie's rude interruption.

Lauren entered the storeroom carrying, and dropping, several bulging shopping bags. For such a small person, she made an awful lot of noise.

"Excellent! Looks like you two have been busy bees!"

Busy bees, my God.

Rafe spoke up. "We're just about done here—what's next?"

Lauren dropped the remaining bags. They clunked on the wood floor. One tipped over, and a brushed grey metal container rolled out and across the floor. "Son of a biscuit!" Lauren cried. She chased the wayward item and snatched it up.

Rafe and I looked at each other, then broke out laughing. "Such language! My poor ears!" I giggled.

Lauren pursed her lips and set the container right side up on a nearby table. "Hush! Look at the cool flower bins I found. They'll class up the booth, don't ya think?"

I nodded. "Oh, definitely."

Rafe cleared his throat, having recovered from our burst of laughter. "Very Joanna Gaines."

He knows who Joanna Gaines is? I didn't expect that!

Lauren glanced at her Apple watch. "I knew I hired Rafe for a good reason! I've got several more bags of merch in the car. Once we get those sorted, we can start stocking the shelves."

"Gotcha, boss!" I winked, seriously, I winked.

Rafe started toward the storefront. "I'll go get those bags for you."

I stared after him. Get a hold of yourself, Ives. You need to stop objectifying this guy. Well, maybe for one more minute. I tilted my head to get a better look, then stood up.

I scurried over to help Lauren stack the metal bins. "You know what might be super cute?" I lifted one of the bins and inspected the surface. "I could make some little chalkboard labels to sort the flowers by name or color—whatever."

Lauren smiled. "Great idea!"

I shrugged. "It's not a biggie. I'm sure Rafe will have tons of good ideas, too."

Lauren got scarily serious. "Ivey, look at me." Her eyes were wide and her hand now on her throat.

I straightened up like a tin soldier.

Her eyes bore into mine. "Always, always accept praise! Don't be self-deprecating. When you have an innovative idea, own it." Her whole vibe was heavy.

"Uh, sure, um, thank you?" My voice was raspy.

She softened immediately. "Oh heavens, I didn't mean to get all intense on you. Here, give me a hug."

I did, hoping that was it for the "teachable moment."

I was wrong.

As I pulled from our embrace, Lauren's hands found my shoulders and stayed there. "Listen, I love you, and I know that you are special and will do such great things—"

"Aunt—" I tried to stop her. This was so embarrassing! What if Rafe walked back in?

She held up a finger. "Okay, okay, just promise me you'll take credit for your skills, and don't let anyone diminish what you bring to the table."

I squared my shoulders, lengthening my neck. "I will. I promise."

Lauren stepped back, releasing me, then clicked her tongue. "I've got a few more errands to run." She fiddled with her smartwatch. "I'll set a timer, so I'm back by three-thirty. You good, here?

"Absolutely, we'll unpack everything, then start filling the shelves out front."

"Great, be creative! I'll see you guys in a bit."

Rafe passed by Lauren as she left the storeroom. I heard them exchange a few words, and he came through the curtain, carrying four enormously packed bags.

"We have our work cut out for us," he grunted.

Yes, yes. We do.

Chapter 15

Ivey

Over that next week, the three of us fashioned a killer booth if I do say so myself. Channeling Lauren's passionate speech about accepting praise for my ideas, I gave myself several metaphorical pats on the back as we worked. My label idea rocked. Not only did the chalkboard labels coordinate the flower stems, but Lauren used them as price tags. I loved it when things matched—not too much—just enough. Rafe ended up adding a few more shelves, so we could display more of Stassi Sumter's watercolors.

I was hip-deep in sunflower stems, sorting them into the proper bins, when a willowy young woman came sailing into my space, side-swiping me and crushing some innocent sunflowers.

"Oh my goodness!" she exclaimed once it registered that the air in front of her was occupied by a solid form (that being me, of course, and the flowers). "I am so, so sorry! Girly-girl, are you okay?" She took a dramatically deep breath, gathered the voluminous folds of her colorful caftan, and helped me up.

Once up, I salvaged the remaining flowers. "I'm fine, no problem. Are you okay?" I wasn't being rude attending to the merchandise—I wanted to save Lauren another trip to Corbett Farms.

The young woman threaded her long fingernails through her wavy, chestnut hair. She gathered it in a gigantic ball at the back of her head and fanned her neck. "Whew! I'm runnin' around like a looney tune today! Is Lauren here? I'm Stassi Sumter, by the way."

It took a minute for me to connect the name with the watercolorist. Plus, she was so much younger than I expected. "Oh, yeah! I'm taking some lessons from you soon—I love your art!"

Stassi dropped her hair and grinned. "You are too sweet! Wait! Are you Ivey?" She pointed at me like I was a prize petunia at the county fair.

"Yeah, I'm Ivey, Lauren's niece." I wiped my hands on my dusty jeans and went in for a handshake.

"It's so great to meet you, finally!" She gave me that hand-on-top-and-bottom kind of shake. "Lauren's been all 'Ivey this' and 'Ivey that' since you decided to visit. She's thrilled to have you here in Walloon." Stassi settled into a standing position after so much pure motion, then looked around the booth, nodding approvingly. "The space looks fantastic, and I love how you've arranged the pieces on the shelves—so much easier to see than on a table!" She clapped her hands.

I knew I could put way too much stock into my first impressions of people, but I got a good feeling from Stassi Sumter—a warm feeling. She paced around a bit more, then turned back to me. "You have a good eye for merchandising. It'll be a blast working with you!""

"I'm so glad Lauren asked you about the lessons—it was my mom's idea."

Why did I feel the need to say that?

She gave me a grave expression, her head tilted. "I hope you want to take lessons, Ivey."

My body tensed, and I bounced on the balls of my feet. "I do! I do! I've been painting for a couple of years now, mostly acrylic." I pulled my phone from my back pocket and tapped to access my photos. "Would you like to see some of my work?"

Stassi scooted to my side. "I'd love to!"

I handed my phone over and watched her scan the files, her smile widening with each swipe.

"These are lovely, Ivey! Have you tried watercolors before?" Her eyes fixed on my phone.

I excitedly rubbed my hands together. "I have, but nothing formal. Nothing memorable enough for me to save."

Stassi handed me my phone. "How about we start the week after next—Tuesday?"

My heartbeat faster and I grinned like goof. "That'll work for me."

"Perfect." Stassi playfully poked my arm. "Onto the main reason for my visit. I have the wrought iron table and chairs that Lauren wanted to use for the summer. They're out in the truck." She scanned the area once again and pensively scratched her chin. "Hmmm, I wonder where she may like them?"

My excitement over the art lessons felt great, like I could lift a car. "Let me help you bring the pieces in, and we'll figure it out."

She nodded, and I followed her out to a sparkling new-looking Toyota 4Runner. I let out an unintentional laugh.

"What?" Stassi clicked her key fob to open the vehicle's rear.

I suppressed a giggle. "I pictured a beat-up pick-up with wooden railings or a VW van. You have such a boho vibe."

Stassi laughed heartily, throwing her head back. "I do give that impression, don't I?"

I stood alongside her and reached for a delicate-looking, but surprisingly heavy loden green iron bistro chair. "I think you have amazing style. Not trying to be a creeper."

As we both hefted the chairs into the front of the Sunnyside, Stassi said, "Not at all—it's great to have a fan!"

Rafe walked out of the backroom. "Whoa! Ladies, can I help with anything?"

Stassi and I looked at each other and answered in unison, "Yes!"

Chapter 16
Ivey

The Shops of Walloon Opening Day started out slowly. Lauren paced around the booth, sat on a bistro chair, got up less than two seconds later, and paced again. She repeatedly tapped on her Apple watch as if time had suddenly stopped. Rafe and I leaned on the check-out counter, watching Lauren's silent come-apart. Rafe kicked me gently with the tip of his cross-trainers.

"Stop," I whispered, not really meaning it.

He kicked me again, then looked in the opposite direction. "What? I'm not doing anything."

Over the last two weeks, I had come to realize that my first impression of Rafe Torres being anything like Oliver Trammell was completely off base. Yes, Rafe did have a temper, but I had not seen a bit of it, other than an occasional dark look when his father or Hattie popped into conversation, which hadn't happened often—thank heavens. The only thing he shared with me was that he dated Hattie for about six months, but she cheated on him with Hank Purcell (naturally, on the football team), so they had broken up. Hattie, apparently, had her sculpted fingernails in just about every social situation in Walloon Lake, along with every guy she had ever dated. According to Rafe, that is.

I leaned closer to his ear. "Seriously, should we try to look busier? Lauren looks majorly stressed."

People milled about the Market booths, just not that many people. Lauren prowled back and forth, which wasn't very welcoming—not that I was Miss Retail Expert.

Rafe looked at his phone, "It's only ten-twenty. If I wasn't working, I'd be asleep."

I thought about my snuggly bed at Lauren's place. "Yeah, me too."

Our neighboring booths, Barry's Woodworks and Tootsie Toes, each had a single casually browsing customer. Lauren had commented earlier in the week that she liked Barry Tobin's and Sarah Klonski's stores flanking hers. The first layout for the Market had the Walloon Farmer's Co-op next to the Sunnyside, and Lauren persuaded the town council president to reconsider. "Since we have some similar merchandise," she had told them, "both booths would suffer. Why not spread the love—literally?"

She'd made a good point. The farmer's co-op had shifted its booth to the end of the boothes. It all worked out beautifully since the co-op decided to add a BBQ smoker. Being right next to the parking lot kept the cooker's smoke from overtaking the whole Market. Thinking about barbeque made my stomach growl.

I pushed myself up from the counter. "I have an idea! Hey, Lauren!"

She looked up from her watch and plastered a weary smile on her face. "Yeah, everything's fine."

I came out from behind the counter and patted her on the shoulder. "You don't look so fine. How about Rafe and I slice up some scones and walk around with samples? Maybe that'll bring people in?"

She popped up from the chair and raised her arms. "Excellent idea!"

I laughed. "I've heard the way to people's hearts is through their stomachs."

Lauren looked relieved. "Let's do it!"

Rafe had disappeared into the storeroom, then returned with two plates and a plastic knife. "It's not fancy, but it'll do for now."

After we piled the plates with scone pieces, I went left and Rafe went right, each of us offering morsels, then guiding folks to our booth. The Market got steadily busier, and by noon, we ended up with more customers than the three of us could handle. It seemed like everyone was buying gifts, so I perfected my cellophane, brown paper, and raffia wrapping skills. We only had one iPad with a card scanner, so Rafe fetched and toted things for the customers, and Lauren rang the purchases up as I wrapped.

Lauren tap, tap, tapped on the iPad. "Ives, can you grab some more votives for Mrs. Cleary?"

I was glad to get a momentary break from the crowds. "Of course." I took my time digging the votives out of a box at the back of the storeroom. When I came back through the yellow curtain, I saw Rafe high fiving a skinny guy with saggy black cargo shorts, a Led Zeppelin tee-shirt, and a bright blond buzz cut. He looked a bit like Machine Gun Kelly to be honest.

Rafe made introductions. "Hey Lauren, you know Morgan, right?"

"I sure do. Hi, Morgan! How's your summer so far?" She looked up as she gathered items for Mrs. Cleary, a sweet lady with bright red hair and a leashed Yorkie at her side.

Morgan grinned brightly and looked around the space. "Things are good, Ms. Corbett! The store looks great." He picked up a package of shortbread and moved toward our tea table. "My mom sent me down for tea and cookies before you run out."

Rafe pulled on his friend's arm. "Morg, this is Ivey."

I set the votive pile down when a couple of the tiny candles broke free and rolled across the counter. I grabbed at them like a spaz.

"Awesome to meet ya," Morgan smiled. "I hope this guy isn't too much trouble for you, ladies." He glanced at Rafe.

I was about to respond when Lauren piped up. "He's been fantastic, and if you decide to stop slinging hash this summer, I can find some work for you too."

Morgan selected a tin of Lemon Verbena tea and brought the items to Lauren to ring up. "Yeah, I'll keep that offer in mind."

I noticed that unlike MGK, Morgan had an engaging smile that in no way looked disturbed or tormented. "Need those wrapped?" I asked.

He shook his head. "Nah, save a tree. I'm on my way home. So, Ivey, it's super nice to meet you."

"Same here!" I liked him—good vibes.

After Morgan paid, he and Rafe walked out of the store, chatting. They seemed so comfortable with each other, laughing and playfully punching each other on the arm. I thought wistfully about my friends wondering what they were doing right that minute back home.

Chapter 17

Ivey

A crash, glass breaking, and frenzied screaming stopped my musings about home. Lauren shot from behind the counter, yelling, "Stay here!" at me. Rafe and Morgan followed as she ran to the center of the Market. My body moved like a slug, but I quickly spotted the refrigerator wide open, with iced tea and soda bottles smashed on the wood floor. I grabbed a broom and dustpan from the corner and crouched to clean up. Well-meaning customers offered to help, but I warned them off.

"Thanks, but back away, I'll get this!" I was glad I had worn Converse trainers instead of flip-flops.

"My word, what on earth happened?" asked a customer with a spiky blonde shag and tennis outfit. She had some of Stassi's canvases in her arms.

"A kid stole some drinks then ran off," grumbled an older man behind her.

I stood up, straining to see over the crowd. Shoplifters? On the first day?

I dumped the mess in the trash bin and then rubbed in squirt of hand sanitizer.

"Are you ready to check out?" I had just tallied up the tennis lady's purchase when Lauren stomped back into the booth dragging a very small, very unhappy boy by the elbow. Both Morgan and Rafe had equally sorrowful boys in tow. The mewling and moaning from the alleged culprits hushed the tittering customers.

Lauren brandished her cellphone. "Stop fussing, Reynie. Your parents are going to be extremely disappointed." She looked back at Rafe and Morgan. "Bring them back here—I'm calling their families. Ivey, you okay?"

"I'm good, did they—?" But she'd disappeared behind the yellow curtain.

"These monsters almost outran us," Morgan said to me. "Thankfully, we know all the shortcuts!"

Rafe nodded at Morgan, but he looked tired and a bit "over" the whole scene. Rafe coaxed the boy he held into the storeroom.

I could hear the youngsters pleading with Lauren. It was all, "Please don't call my mom!" "We're so sorry!" "Please, ma'am, we won't ever do it again!"

Five minutes later, I had a chance to go to the storeroom to check out the drama. What a scene! The three little boys sat on upside-down metal bins, in a straight row, like men before a parole board. One hiccupped, one wept, one was stoic, but they all looked miserable. Lauren stood in front of the boys, arms crossed, tapping her foot. Her piled-up hair had fallen in her face after chasing the little buggers.

I sidled over next to her, mustering a solemn expression. "So, what are you going to do with them?" I tapped my foot and looked from boy to boy.

Lauren took me by the elbow, then addressed Rafe and Morgan. "Would you guys keep an eye on the kids while I chat with Ivey?"

Rafe and Morgan settled tiredly on nearby stools. "No problem," said Rafe.

Chapter 18

Ivey

There were only a few customers in the booth at the time, so Lauren and I highjacked the bistro chairs for our chat. Lauren slumped over the table, her back heaving. I thought she was crying, so I rubbed her back, hoping to sooth her.

"It's okay, I cleaned it up. There's no harm done."

Lauren peeked up, and she was giggling. So much so that tears streamed down her face.

I pulled my hand from her back—stunned. "What is going on?"

She dabbed at her eyes with a tissue and sat back with a sigh. "We are so lucky that Rafe and Morgan were here. Those munchkins got more than they bargained for." She shoved the tissue into a pocket. "Having the older boys chase them down scared the living heck out of them. I've spoken with their parents, and I have their blessing to make the boys sweat a bit."

"Do you know their families?" I settled on the opposite chair.

"Oh yes, they're summer folks but they've come to Walloon for years. The boys are Reynolds and Patton Wheeler and Ben Eisner."

"Hmm," I fanned my sweaty face with my hand.

Lauren leaned over the iron table. "I see that brain working—what is it?"

I squirmed in my seat, uncomfortable with Lauren's eyes on me. "I don't know. Stealing isn't cool. I don't care how young they are, and I can't imagine Mom and Dad taking something like this casually. We all worked hard to get the store together." I shook my head. "Maybe I'm judging too harshly, but I've seen lots of people at school who don't own up to their mistakes. I know it's because their parents let them get away with tons of stuff."

Lauren thought for a minute, then she stood up. "You make a good point, Ives. Consequences! Suggestions?"

I glanced at the fridge. "Well, I already cleaned up the broken bottles, so maybe have them unpack some merchandise and sweep up the store? Oh, and restock the fridge."

Lauren clapped her hands. "I agree! Let's get those little boogers working!"

The boys enthusiastically helped once they learned that their world would not end. I had no idea what would happen once they got home, though. The kids had put sincere effort into sweeping up, unpacking items and they even wrote Lauren an apology note.

"Aww, thank you, boys!" she said, when Reynie Wheeler handed her the note. "Next time you want a drink or something, you just ask, and we'll see what we can do—deal?"

"Deal," the boys chorused.

Reynie and Patton's mother arrived, talked with Lauren for a few minutes, then took the children home.

Chapter 19
Ivey

A half an hour before the Market shops closed, Lauren and Rafe were off to pick up flowers from Corbett Farm, and I was helping the last few shoppers. The Market hummed, but in a quiet, pleasant way—not harried and intense like earlier. The perfect kind of busy, in my opinion. I had finished wrapping an 8 x 10 canvas for Mrs. Patterson (the perkiest eighty-six-year-old I'd ever met) when Hattie and a posse of similarly dressed girls swept into the store. Now, I'd encountered my share of mean girls. It's a rite of passage, like getting chickenpox or gagging on your first cigarette, but Hattie's vibe felt different—darker and *much* more personal.

Hattie ran her finger along one of the display tables like a mini-Cruella de Vil in designer jeans. "Well, hello, Ida," she said, oozing barely concealed contempt. All she needed was a white skunk stripe down her center part.

I busied myself behind the counter, so as not to appear startled by their invasion. "It's Ivey."

Like Medusa, she fixed her gaze directly on me—ice crept through my veins. "What's that?" Hattie snapped.

I looked her square in the eyes. "My name, it's Ivey, not Ida."

Hattie waved her hand dismissively. "Oh, yeah. Whatever. This is Piper, Stace, and Teegan."

The trio looked at me with vapid expressions, tilted their heads, but said nothing.

I snorted. "Uh, hi—do they talk?" I made a talking gesture with my right hand.

The one (I later learned) called Stace rolled her bright blue eyes, her mouth agape. "God, what a—"

Hattie laughed. "Girls, why don't you be polite and say 'hi' to the shopgirl?"

The four girls cackled after their leader. I shivered. Yikes! Shades of *The Craft*, a fave movie of mine, but not one I'd like to experience IRL.

Piper sported extra-long braids piled on her head, with two framing her long face. "This place reminds me of my grandmother's house! Who wants all this sunflower crap?"

I stayed behind the sales counter so I wouldn't be tempted to scratch the witches' eyes out. "Well, according to our sales today, I'd say about thirty-five hundred dollars' worth of people."

"Humph," muttered Teegan, who was a little frumpier than the other three girls but attractive, nonetheless. "Who'd want sunflowers anyway? I prefer roses."

Hattie's eyes darted around the booth. "Not that Ronald's ever gotten you any flowers. Roses or not."

I winced. Being Hattie's friend must be a real joy.

I slapped my hands on the counter enthusiastically. "Well," I made my tone perky. "Did you know that sunflowers are native to North America? Not only are they beautiful, but they are used for medicine, clothing dye, food, and oil." I knew these girls didn't care, but I liked the idea of tweaking them with nerdy facts. "And Peter the Great loved the sunflowers he saw in the Netherlands so much, he brought them back, and now they grow in Russia!"

The girls looked at me like I'd just peeled off my face.

"Ew." Teegan squished up her round face and glanced at Hattie. "Why does she think we want to hear about that?"

I smiled as wide as I could. "Because I love fun facts! Is there something I can help you find?" I addressed Piper. "Maybe for your grandmother?"

Hattie whispered something to her cadre. They all stared at me, stuck their noses in the air, then walked out of the store without a word. Hattie adjusted her brightly colored, silky tank top, fashionably half-tucked into her skinny jeans. She looked ready for battle. She prowled around the counter and sidled up uncomfortably close to me—a fixed expression on her flawless face. "I don't know what you think you're doing, Ivey, but you are messing with the wrong girl."

At least she got my name right.

I backed up as far as I could in the tight space behind the counter. "I don't know what you're talking about." My confident demeanor started to waver as she closed in on me.

Hattie's frozen face softened slightly. I'm sure, not from mercy, but from her successful attempt to intimidate me.

She sneered. "There's something not right about you and your family—and I'm going to find out what."

Her comment snapped me out of my cowered position. I squared my shoulders and stood my ground.

"What are you even talking about? You don't know anything about me or my family. Is this about me working with your ex-boyfriend? Are you jealous?"

Hattie scoffed at the suggestion, "Please. I could snap my fingers and Rafe would come running." Her eyes raked me up and down. "You are the furthest thing from his type."

Wow, she was terrifyingly sure of herself.

I trembled inside my prickled skin, but my initial intimidation had turned to righteous anger. I stepped forward, now crowding her. "I may be new around here, but my grandparents lived in Walloon for years, so just back off." I pointed a shaky finger at her face.

She flinched and stepped back but kept talking. "My father is the District Attorney, and I can find out anything I want about anyone."

I balanced myself against the counter and wall behind me. "There's nothing to find out, so do your worst." My face had grown hot.

A bizarrely serene smile spread across her porcelain skin. "Oh, I will, little Miss Summer Girl," she sputtered. "Oh, and Rafe might be my ex for now, but we have history. I know him—way down deep." She crooked her perfectly coiffed eyebrow. "Has he mentioned Antonio?"

"As a matter of fact—" I started to reply.

"You watch out because I see you!" Hattie turned on her heel, then flounced out of the Sunnyside, leaving a trail of sickeningly sweet-smelling perfume in her wake.

Chapter 20
Ivey

I was on remote control tidying up the store while I replayed the deeply disturbing convo with Rafe's ex. When I heard him and Lauren approach the storefront, I straightened my shoulders and shook my head hoping to eject Hattie's comments right out and onto the storeroom floor. What was she up to? And why? I was irate at how shaken I still was.

Rafe hobbled in carrying a bulky plastic container stuffed with sunflowers.

I grabbed one side of the container. "Wow." I huffed. "This is much heavier than it looks!" I braced my legs as I clutched it.

Rafe grunted. "Uh-huh, let's drop it over there."

We made our way across the storeroom and set the flowers down. I dropped to the floor and mindlessly started sorting them.

Lauren had joined us in the storeroom. She held a watering can. "Whoa, girl. It's been a long day, so let's allow the stems to soak up some water. We'll sort them in the morning."

Dang! Seeing Lauren brought my family back to mind, frustrated tears welled up. But wait a minute. Why was I giving Hattie's comments any credence? She was a jealous, mean-spirited be-yotch. I mean, who cared if she thought she knew something about my family? We didn't have any secrets that anyone would possibly care about. My brain hazed over, and my pits dampened. Sweat dripped down my back.

Did we?

I needed to get out of there and call my girls—get some perspective.

I must have looked insane because Lauren bent and touched my shoulder. "Are you okay? You look like you've seen a ghost."

I fanned my face and stammered. "Oh, no, I'm fine. You're right, it's been a long day. Do you mind if I go on home?"

Lauren stepped back; the corners of her eyes crinkled with concern. "Not at all, Rafe and I can handle closing— right, bud?"

Rafe's concerned gaze settled on me. "Absolutely. You do look a little pale. Do you need some water?"

I tried to sound light and breezy as I used my palms to push off the floor. "Probably low blood sugar," I said, heading for the curtain. "Great first day! See you guys later."

Lame exit strategy, but I felt like I had no choice.

Chapter 21

Ivey

It was Clara's day off from Maylene's, so we Facetimed. She looked fantastic as usual, her sable hair spiraled like a halo as she clutched a sage-green pillow in one hand and shakily held her phone aloft with the other. Clara was pissed. "Who the hell does that bitch think she is, talking about you or your family?"

I knew my girl would support me with the perfect amount of shared indignation.

"I know!" I'd stretched my legs on the bed, my laptop on my thighs. I'd been surfing the net for information on Hattie before Clara called—not that I had any idea what I'd find.

Clara fiddled with a hoop earring. "I'm sure she's BS-ing 'cause she's jealous about you and Rafe working together."

I pushed the sweaty hair out of my eyes and rubbed the middle of my forehead. "I hope so; it's all kinda a blur."

Clara pushed up on one elbow. "Anything juicy on social media?"

I caught a glimpse of her bedroom in the screen's background. Honestly, Clara needed to be an interior decorator—she had an eye for color and texture. Her current obsession was plaid; she had incorporated it into her room, her clothing, even her backpack and notebooks. Nothing matched, but it flowed effortlessly.

I shifted the Facetime screen to the left, minimized, then clicked on the Charlevoix County District Attorney's webpage, and, voila, there was Hattie's father, Scott P. Foster. "I'm on her dad's work website." He'd been in office for three years.

"Ives! Focus!" urged Clara. "Before you go down that rabbit hole, do you have any idea what she could possibly be hinting at?"

I shook my head, but something niggled at my stomach. Was it dread?

I maximized Clara on my screen hoping her face might help me focus. "Okay." I closed my eyes and scrolled through my brain. When I got into this type of stress mode, my mind scattered all over the place like a deck of cards flung up in the air. My thoughts jumbled and diffused all over—totally out of order. "Hattie and her pal patrol came into the store, mean-girled me for a while, then they left, and Hattie got in my face. She said her dad was the DA and that I was *messing* with the wrong girl.'"

I clicked back to the DA page and found a photo of Hattie's parents at some fancy party with the mayor or governor. Her dad was handsome, in that suited-up, lawyer way, but with unsettling eyes—a piercing black that made the pupils hard to discern. Hattie's eyes were different, possibly because she took after her mom (also, gorgeous) whose eyes were blue to the point of lavender. There really wasn't anything on Hattie's social media other than the typical selfies and group shots, until—

My spine deflated into the bed. "Oh no!" I groaned.

"What? What?" Clara's cheeks flushed.

I, silently, scrolled through dozens and dozens of photos of Hattie and Rafe—

hugging and

kissing

and hugging while kissing.

"Just pics of Hattie and Rafe when they were going out."

Clara propped her phone, then grabbed her laptop and clicked to Hattie's Instagram. "Eew."

The corner of my mouth curled up. "I agree!"

Clara tapped her chin. "Have you googled your family? If there's anything to find out, maybe it'll pop up online?"

I snickered. "Talk about eew. How invasive is that—googling my own fam?"

Clara shrugged and laid back on her pillows. "I find your lack of faith disturbing."

We both laughed at the Star Wars reference.

Clara's expression turned solemn, piercing. "Seriously, you're an intuitive person—you honestly don't have any clue about anything hinky going on in your family?" She brought the phone screen up close to her face, which made the hairs on my neck prickle. Clara was a true crime buff, so she used words like "hinky" all the time.

My spine tingled. "God, no, you're freakin' me out!"

Clara pulled her laptop away from her face. "Well, if you don't want to google anyone, I guess you have no choice, but to talk to your aunt or your parents. You can do all the research you want, but they are the only people who really know—" She stopped abruptly.

"What?"

Her lips flattened, but her eyes shined. "Could this possibly have anything to do with your parents' paranoia about your Uncle Michal?"

I shivered. "Hmm." My mind flew to the framed photos of Lauren and Michal around the house, how odd I thought it was for Lauren to be comfortable enough to have them around when my parents refused to even acknowledge him as family. Could it be my mother's overinflated sense of loyalty? Or my aunt being the tenderhearted person I've always known?

I scratched my forehead. "You know, you bring up a good point."

Clara grinned.

I heard Lauren's Jeep pull up outside. "I will think about it, for sure. Hey, gotta go, my aunt's home. I love you, Clarebear!" I waved at my laptop screen.

Clara waved back. "Love you, too. Keep me posted!"

I closed my laptop, set it aside, then curled into a ball, my thoughts bouncing from neuron to neuron.

Lauren knocked on the bedroom door even though I'd left it open. "Hey," she said gently, coming over and sitting on the bed's edge. "How are you doing? Do you feel okay?" She patted my leg.

I wanted to unburden myself and tell Lauren what happened with Hattie, but I chickened out. "Yeah, just tired. I think I'll take a quick nap, if that's okay."

Lauren nodded. "I'll do a few things around the house; then we can see about dinner—sound cool?"

I grunted in the affirmative. After another reassuring pat on my leg, Lauren got up, then left the room, shutting the door quietly behind her. I hugged the pillow to my chest and closed my eyes.

Chapter 22

Ivey

When I woke up, the room was thick with darkness, and my hungry stomach ached. I guessed Lauren had decided to forgo making dinner, but I needed food—even just a cracker, so I crawled off the bed and left the room feeling along the walls with my fingertips. Maybe falling asleep so early in the evening had jumbled my head, but the hall seemed ominously extended. The kitchen light beckoned, so I inched forward when I heard muffled voices—some of which were male.

Huh? Does Lauren have someone over? Does she have a boyfriend? She hasn't mentioned anyone…

The kitchen light was on, and a group murmured in the dimly lit den—Lauren, Mom, Dad, my sisters, and some guy lying on top of the coffee table. The man's face was blurry, like how the news pixelates people's faces when they wanted to be anonymous.

My family abruptly stopped and fixed their eyes on me.

My mother beckoned. "Ivey, dear, come sit!" She had a horror movie smile plastered on her face. In fact, everyone in the room had the same smile, except the guy on the table who was asleep, or was he dead? Icy shards of terror crashed over me.

My voice came out all craggy. "Mom? What are you doing here? You're in Arizona—"

She reached out to me, her fingers bizarrely long. "Come in, come in, sleepyhead!" "We're here with Pops and Nan." With that, my grandparents materialized. Had they been there the whole time? My head felt dizzy and light. I dutifully greeted my grandparents when they flashed that same creepy grin.

Nan's lips curdled further up her cheeks. "Ivey, why won't you help your auntie?"

"I—" Before I could ask Nan what she was talking about, we transported to a sunflower field (presumably Corbett Farm), but I couldn't make out the night sky above us. It was like we, and the field, existed in a lightless void. Everyone was seated as they had been, but the man on the coffee table hadn't made the journey.

I heard a faint voice. "Ivey! Help me!" yelled Lauren. She was out in the field, far away.

"Aunt Lauren!" I called, my panic building. "Where are you?" I frantically pushed through the dense towering flower stalks, but she didn't sound any closer despite how far I delved into the field.

Her voice was high-pitched and clearly terrified. "Help me! Why won't you help me?"

My heart thumped way up into my ears. "I'm coming! I'm coming!" I moved deeper into the flowers. "Are you hurt—"

Then, poof! It was me lying on the coffee table with my family staring down. In unison, Daisy and Rose taunted me, chanting, "Why, why, why?"

I tried to sit up, to say something, to defend myself, but I couldn't move. I heard Lauren's far away voice start to overtake my sisters'.

"Are you asleep? Ivey?"

I struggled to answer.

Lauren's voice sounded closer, clearer. "Ivey? Wake up! Ivey?"

I opened my eyes, blinked at the diffused light coming in the window, and saw Lauren standing next to the bed, her face pinched with worry. I sat up and wiped my damp forehead. "I had the craziest dream."

Lauren's eyes downturned. "You were thrashing around. Come tell me about it at dinner. I made chicken salad."

"Okay, just give me sec." I crawled off the bed, took a deep breath, smoothed my hair, then followed my aunt into the kitchen.

Chapter 23

Ivey

The next day, Lauren and I went for an evening walk around the lake. I'd decided I had to do it—I had to ask about Uncle Michal despite my parents' warnings. I couldn't get that crazy dream out of my head. I usually don't subscribe to dream interpretation, but I knew in my heart that my subconscious was cluing me into something vital.

Lauren and I walked by the Square. I noted how tranquil it was when the shops had closed for the evening. It wouldn't be fully dark until 9:30—it was still twilight. The pavement gave way to crunchy gravel, then sandy pebbles as we approached the first row of houses lining the lakeshore. We silently headed toward Nan and Pops' old house which wasn't directly on the shore but close enough to access the lake by a footpath.

As we strolled along, I thought back to when I first met Uncle Michal. He had been incredibly tall in my mind's eye. Of course, I was little when he and Lauren got together. I don't recall being at the wedding, which would make sense; I couldn't imagine my parents footing the bill for us to go to a destination wedding in Michigan. But I clearly remembered seeing him at my grandparents' house. I recalled that his resting face was stern, but so was my Dad's, so I wasn't afraid of him. He had leaned down on one knee, extended his hand formally, and said, "Nice to meet you, little Ivey." It was sweet, this large guy making himself smaller to shake hands with me. I felt a rush of warmth thinking of my mysterious uncle, but then sorrow for Lauren.

She cut the silence and elbowed me. "I thought the first week went well, despite the little boy gang activity on Opening Day."

I was distracted by the potential crap storm I was about to cause. "Yeah, pretty good, considering." I muttered.

Lauren kept her face forward, but she must have noticed my pensiveness because she asked, "Is everything okay? Your mood took a nosedive at the end of the day."

It helped not to look directly at her, so I blurted out, "Rafe's ex-girlfriend came by while you two were at the farm." It came out more dramatic than I'd intended.

"I see." Lauren's expression didn't change. "What happened?"

Our feet crunched along the path while I filled Lauren in. The tree line thickened as we walked onto Merritt Road. Most of the houses were set back from the street, so you had to search for peeks of color through the trees to find the buildings. Some homes were snuggled deeply into the vegetation, so that all you saw was a mailbox by a driveway entrance.

Lauren listened intently, then halted, turned to me, and cocked her head. "Hattie's last name is Foster, right?"

I nodded. "She mentioned that her father is the District Attorney. It's like she thinks we're criminals or something."

Lauren's face fell, then turned ashen. She looked disoriented, her eyes filled with tears.

"Oh my God, Aunt Lauren!" I grasped her hand then looked around frantically for a bench or rock or fence to sit or lean on. I spotted a split-rail fence next to a rusty mailbox, so I led her over to it. "Here, drink my water." I handed her the Aquafina bottle I'd been toting.

She took a big gulp of water, then handed the bottle back to me. "Thanks." She hiccupped. "I'm fine. Ivey, how much do you know about your Uncle Michal?"

Chapter 24

Ivey

"I don't remember much," I told Lauren. "He was nice to me when I was little. Mom and Dad told us that you divorced, and not to bring it up to you."

Lauren wiped at a fallen tear. "That sounds like Carrie and Frank. Not that I'm criticizing!" She looked panicky—flushed and sweaty.

I put up my hands, motioning to calm her concern. "No, I understand. Mom was obviously upset for you, and I think Dad didn't want any of us to start crying," I paused. "Not that crying is the worst thing in the world."

Lauren put her arm around me. "There certainly is nothing wrong with crying. Our situation was painful—neither of us handled it well. How could I expect anyone else to deal with it any better?" She dropped her arm, then pulled away from the fence. "Let's keep walking, and I'll fill you in the best I can."

She took a deep breath in, gazed wistfully up at the trees, and began. "Michal and I met while I was finishing my master's at Michigan State. My old Toyota was on its last legs, and Pops recommended a garage where Michal worked." Lauren rubbed her shoulders, warming a chill. "You wouldn't believe how handsome he was! Long, wavy hair pulled back in a ponytail. I'm a sucker for a guy with long hair." She elbowed me and grinned.

I couldn't help but smile back. I could tell she still loved him very much. I wondered if that love tortured or sustained her.

"When we met, he'd only been in the U.S. for a few months, so his English was horrible. That didn't matter, though. I loved teaching him English and learning about his culture and language. Michal didn't talk about his family very often, though, and I never got to meet any of them. He loved his mother country, but he had no interest in ever going back." Lauren hesitated, looking down at her feet. "I should have encouraged him to tell me about his life in former Czechoslovakia, but—" She shook her head. "He got so overwrought when I brought it up that I, frankly, feared what he'd tell me. I was so stupid, but I could only plead youth, and being head over heels in love."

I bumped up against her, trying to lighten the mood. "There's nothing wrong with loving someone and not wanting to force him to talk about stressful stuff," I said, hoping my comments were encouraging.

Lauren bumped me back. "You're so sweet, but I'd do so many things differently…"

I bounced on my heels, impatient to know more. "How long did you go out before you got married? I don't remember attending a ceremony."

Lauren wrang her hands. "No, you wouldn't. We eloped—Pops and Nanny didn't approve."

My jaw dropped. "Why not?" My grandparents seemed like the most compassionate and accepting people in the world.

Lauren's eyes misted up. "I know. It wasn't about Michal being an immigrant or anything like that. Maybe they foresaw our troubles." We had stopped outside the Market Square. "At the time, I thought they carried a torch for my high school boyfriend, but that was silly." She fanned herself. "Let's talk about this at home, I need a glass of wine to finish this up."

Chapter 25

Ivey

I knew not to push my aunt to divulge her memories to suit my timetable, but I was about to jump out of my skin. We walked silently toward the house. Once inside, I settled on the sofa while Lauren poured herself a glass of wine.

She called from the kitchen. "Can I get you anything?"

"Another water'd be great."

She fetched a bottle from the fridge, then, with a drink in each hand, joined me in the den.

Lauren nestled on the sofa alongside me, pulling a throw over her knees. "Thanks for giving me a few minutes to collect my thoughts," she said, then snuggled further down.

"Of course!" I tried not to look too eager, but I've never been great at hiding my emotions. "You said that you guys eloped?"

Lauren's somber expression brightened. "Oh, yes! We went to a Justice of the Peace in Ann Arbor after I graduated. Super low-key, but I thought it was so romantic." She chuckled as she swirled her wine, seemingly lost in thought. "I remember after the ceremony; he took me to a cute brunch place where we had eggs benedict and mimosas. Michal would have preferred a beer, but he was a good sport."

I pulled my knees up onto the couch. "Did you move back to Walloon, then?"

She sniffed then dabbed at her nose with a tissue concealed in her hand. "No, no. Michal worked at the garage for another year or so, and I got a job at a floral distribution center. That's where I learned how profitable the sunflower industry could be. I shared the idea with Pops, and he agreed to finance Corbett Farm. Michal and I bought this house. We'd hoped to start a family here."

I felt the grief radiate from her. "I'm sorry I'm bringing all this up. If you don't want to talk anymore—"

Lauren raised the hand with the tissue and shook her head. "I want to tell you, Ivey. I understand why Carrie and Frank didn't explain the details to you girls, but there's no shame in admitting that my marriage didn't work out. Some things are out of our control."

I scowled. "Well, you're nicer than me." I practically spit out the words. "I'm pissed that Mom and Dad didn't think that we could empathize with you. It's exhausting pretending to be happy and perfect all the time."

Lauren squirmed. I could tell that I'd made her uncomfortable by criticizing my parents.

"Anyway, Pops warmed to Michal and gave him a job, right?" I said.

She smoothed the blanket across her lap, then took a healthy swig of wine. "He did, indeed. And it worked out nicely for a while. Michal's automotive experience filled a need at the hardware store. I thought we were happy then—busy, but happy." She glanced at the framed photo across the room. "But Michal had a tough time adjusting to life here: he paced around the house in the evenings, when he sat down to eat or watch TV, Michal tapped his foot or drummed his fingernails. I tried to understand, but his restlessness stressed me out. I was putting a ton of energy into Corbett Farm and had hoped he would support me by finding a hobby or making some friends."

Lauren set her glass on the coffee table, then turned to blow her nose. "But that wasn't the real problem." Her body tensed. "We had suffered two miscarriages by that point."

My tears welled up as her words penetrated "I'm so sorry."

Lauren looked minuscule buried on the sofa, covered in that blanket. "Oh, thank you, honey. Having children meant the world to Michal. His face lit up when we talked about it; we dreamed together about names and their little personalities. His whole demeanor changed when I was pregnant. He became optimistic."

I wiped at a tear. "Mom never said anything about you being pregnant or miscarrying. Did she know?"

"She did know, and she was a real support system. Try not to judge her too harshly. We didn't grow up sharing much personal stuff. You smile and move on, y'know?"

I nodded for Lauren's benefit. "I know." My mother's lack of transparency fixed itself at the front of my mind.

"Anyhow, I'm taking too long to get this out," Lauren rubbed her forehead. "After my third miscarriage, the doctor sensed our stress and recommended we take a break from IVF. Michal was devastated. He started hanging out at the Walloon Saloon—drinking and shooting pool. Initially, I was glad that he was relaxing and meeting some people, but he started staying out all night or coming home drunk. We fought all the time. Then Pops' store got robbed."

"Oh no!" I gasped, my palms on my cheeks. "Don't tell me! Uncle Michal?"

Lauren hung her head. "Yeah. Pops fired him. Michal swore up and down that he didn't steal anything, but then he moved out. He stayed at the Econo Lodge for a couple of months, and we tried to work things out, but the police informed me that Michal had skipped out on his hotel bill and appeared to have left town." She sniffed. "I never heard from my husband again."

We sat there on the sofa, silent for a couple of excruciating minutes, each of us retreating into our respective beverages.

I was flummoxed. "So, he simply vanished?"

"Yes," Lauren whispered.

"What else did the police say?" My thoughts were muddled. How does a person just disappear? Could this be what Hattie alluded to?

"Pops asked them not to investigate any further. I was terrified that something else might come up, and he'd end up in jail or deported." Tears streamed down her face. "Plus, I was devastated and embarrassed. I couldn't believe that Michal had abandoned me."

"Wow, that is really sad." It was all I could think of to say.

Lauren started to stand, then she nudged the throw off her knees and onto the floor. "I don't know about you, but I'm worn out. Can we pick this up tomorrow?"

I retrieved the furry throw from the floor and pulled it around myself. "I really appreciate you telling me your story. I can't believe you went through all that."

We hugged, and Lauren went off toward her bedroom, depositing her wineglass in the kitchen first. I sat there for another thirty minutes thinking about all that Lauren had said about her short and tragic marriage. There's *got* to be more to Michal Lyska's disappearance than marriage problems. I know lots of kids who have divorced parents, and they still have contact—even if that contact is contentious.

I scanned the den, wondering why my family thought hiding the issue was productive in any way. I got up and rambled about the room looking at framed photos of Lauren and Michal. I picked up a photo that may well have been taken around the time of their wedding. Lauren had a sprig of baby's breath tucked behind her ear while her messy blond curls blended with Michal's loose deep brown locks. Their cheeks were pressed together so they fit in the selfie; Lauren's smile was toothy and bright. Michal's look was understated, but his eyes told the story—he was in love, and happy. I turned my attention to a smaller wood-framed photo of Michal alone. He stood outside this house with the lake view behind him about to get into a jacked-up GMC truck. He wasn't smiling in this one; he looked rather intense or even a bit bothered.

What if I disappeared? Or Dee or Rose? Would Mom and Dad just ignore it? Of course, not—that's silly. Was it that Michal wasn't a blood relation? Was that why Mom and Dad erased him from the collective consciousness?

And what information could Hattie's father have on my uncle? The store robbery, of course, but was my uncle involved with other criminal activity? Am I jumping to far-fetched conclusions? Maybe it truly is that my aunt wants to put the whole painful episode behind her.

I looked at my phone—10:39 pm. I started back to my bedroom, but as I passed by Lauren's closed door, I heard her crying. The sound was soft like the mewling of a kitten curled up in a blanket or pillow. I felt horribly selfish for making Lauren re-live the pain of her marriage and the strange circumstances around it.

Was I making too much out of all this? Was I seeing a mystery where there wasn't anything but fallible people navigating a painful situation?

Chapter 26
Hattie

People assumed that Hattie Foster was a typical "Daddy's girl," but it wasn't true. Maybe at one time when she was quite little, but not after what she saw and heard before her brother was born.

Just because her father was revered in the Walloon Lake community, and she shared half his chromosomes didn't mean she was like him at all. In fact, Hattie didn't know how her pathetic father managed to get elected as District Attorney, and she was utterly perplexed that he kept such a "tough but fair guy" public image.

Every time Hattie came down the sweeping front stairwell, she remembered being nine years old and lurking on the third step from the top on a long ago Christmas Eve. It had been the first holiday since they'd moved into the big house, and she couldn't believe how beautiful the foyer was. The memory was so vivid—it was as clear as wearing a VR headset.

She had been wearing her favorite green and red striped flannel nightgown, her hair in soft curlers for church the next morning. Hattie breathed heavily with unbridled excitement; she was expecting an American girl doll that year. Never had she wanted a toy as much as that doll. If she didn't get it; she was sure she would die.

Hattie'd been sitting on the slippery step for what seemed like an hour when her parents approached the cavernous hallway from the kitchen to her dad's office. Their voices were tense, and their conversation clipped. Hattie felt a pit form in her tummy—she hated when her parents fought, which happened more often since moving into the new house. She started to get up from the step to return to her bedroom when her father yelled.

"I want a divorce! There's nothing else to talk about!" She heard a slam and crash from the office below her, then a scream and her mother crying.

"Scott, why are you doing this? We're a family—we have a business together!" she said through her sobs.

Hattie's father groaned loudly. "Aliyah, you know why. Don't make me say it!"

Why would her father have wanted a divorce? He wasn't happy with their family? Did she, Hattie, do something wrong? What would happen to her?

Hattie was dizzy. She forgot about the American Girl doll she'd been obsessing about for months. A hot ball of hate formed in her heart, directed straight at her cruel father. The heat inside her body made her skin grow chill bumps. Hattie hugged the flannel nightgown closer, rose, and tip-toed to her bedroom.

As she crawled under her comfy feather duvet, Hattie had vowed to hate her father for the rest of her life.

Her parents ended up staying together and having her brother, Adam, who lit up Hattie's life. Her father fooled a lot of people at the District Attorney's office. They had no idea what a loser he truly was—a terrible husband and disinterested father. The only positive aspect to her father's neglect was that Hattie had tons of time to successfully snoop through his things when needed, like now.

Meeting Ivey Des Jardins at the Walloon Market a few days ago was a true pain in her butt. Hattie had heard that Rafe took a job at that weirdo flower place from Morgan when she and Hank had dinner at Mariachi's. Unbeknownst to Hank, Hattie had requested to dine there so she could "run into" Rafe. (While she and Rafe were dating, he'd mentioned wanting to work at Mariachi's this summer.) Hattie refused to believe that Rafe could have any interest in that prissy, mousy girl.

After first meeting Ivey, Hattie had gone straight home, snuck into her father's home office, opened the second drawer of his shiny black, oversized desk and found his current password. Seriously, how dense was he? Her fingers click-clacked over the computer's keyboard. Hattie had vaguely heard of Lauren Corbett, but she couldn't remember the circumstances, so she'd first searched for "Ivy Corbett" on social media. If she didn't have to use her father's access to Charlevoix County records to find dirt on this girl, all the better.

She'd found nothing after a few minutes of trying all sorts of spellings of "Ivy" and "Corbett."

"Damn it," she sputtered. Hattie considered for a moment, drumming her fingertips on the desk. "Ahh!" She went to Lauren's Facebook, perhaps her niece was listed as a friend.

Bingo! *Ivey Des Jardins.* "Isn't that so fancy spelling her name with an 'e'? Hattie said to herself. "And 'Des Jardins'? How affected is that." She scrolled through Ivey's news feed while chewing on her thumbnail, then she jumped to Ivey's Instagram. Nothing threat worthy jumped out at her—no overly sexy bikini photos, drinking, smoking, or profanity.

Hometown: Brandon, Florida. Rising Junior, Brandon High School.

Photos of Ivey with two friends named Clara Casperson and Kelli Winter.

Parents—Carrie and Frank Des Jardins, and sisters—Daisy and Rose.

Oh Lord, Debate Team? So lame. Art Club, ugh? Who cares? Hattie tapped her foot.

This line of investigation wasn't getting Hattie anywhere, and she wasn't going to have the house to herself for much longer. She checked her cell phone for the time and decided to risk using her Dad's access to County records—probably no point since Ivey didn't live here full time, but she knew Ivey's grandparents had been Walloon natives.

Hattie went onto the employee section of the Charlevoix County District Attorney's Office and carefully typed in her father's latest password—*whew! Success!* Where to start? She shrugged and started with Ivey Des Jardins.

No hits.

Of course not, Ivey hasn't been here long enough, and honestly, Hattie didn't expect to see a list of crimes.

She tried Lauren Corbett.

Bingo.

It looked like she was married to a Michal Lyska, who had an expired green card. Lauren held business licenses for Corbett Farm and the Sunnyside. The farm had been cosigned by Paul Corbett, who had a past license for Walloon Ace Hardware. The hardware store had a list of shoplifting cases that were either convicted or settled before the business had been sold.

One incident caught her eye—Michal Lyska had been arrested for the theft of $1,247.00, but Paul Corbett hadn't pressed charges. A few months later, a warrant had been issued for Michal Lyska due to an unpaid hotel bill. His whereabouts were listed as unknown.

Hattie smiled contemptuously.

Now she had real ammunition.

Chapter 27
Hattie

But today's hinting at these discoveries didn't turn out as Hattie had hoped. It had been patently obvious that Ivey had had no idea about her uncle's troubles with the law, which was beyond irritating. She replayed their two encounters in her head as she plunged a Swiss Army knife into an over-stuffed throw pillow in her bedroom. Hattie slashed at the pillow, grunting quietly so as not to alarm Liza, the family's live-in housekeeper, who was downstairs preparing a fantastic smelling dinner.

"That stupid, ugly, stupid bitch!" Hattie snarled, her eyes fixed, focused and blazing. "I'm Ivey and I'm just a moronic freak!" She made her voice squeaky and baby-like.

Once the pillow achieved a satisfactory level of destruction, Hattie exhaled and felt the anger dissipate like sand running through one's fingers. She rose from the floor where she'd laid out a 2 x 2 cardboard piece cut from an Amazon box so that her pillow-murdering habit wouldn't mark the whitewashed floors. Hattie closed the purse-sized knife that she had kept after she found it in one of her mother's old suitcases. Placing it in a silk jewelry bag with a drawstring closure, she pocketed the bag and then lifted the piece of cardboard to inspect whether she needed to replace it for next time. She decided that the cardboard would suffice for one more use. Hattie slid open the left door of her walk-in closet and hid it behind a stack of boot boxes. Now, to dispose of the pillow without her parents or Liza finding it.

She snickered. Neither of her parents would inspect a garbage can if their lives depended on it—but Liza was another story. She'd been with the Fosters since Hattie was four years old. Aliyah Foster (Hattie's mother) hired Liza Vilkis after Hattie's brother, Adam, was born.

Liza, always thrifty, chided everyone in the family about throwing away things that could be recycled or upcycled. Hattie loved Liza dearly, and she'd learned quite a few cool ways to use plastic containers, old scrunchies, and even those wire ties on produce bags for ingenious things, but Hattie could not or would not be able to explain a shredded velvet throw pillow tossed into the trash bin.

The pillow mutilating habit had come about after Hattie's therapist suggested punching a pillow when her anger bubbled up.

That worked for about a week. Two years ago.

Hattie had added the Swiss Army knife to the routine and found that raging out on pillows was an effective way to vent. She'd been good at hiding it, too. The only downside to the operation was the hiding and replacing the pillows. Luckily, Hattie had unlimited access to her parent's credit cards, so she bought replacement pillows when she could. It was stupid, childish, and wasteful, but it kept her from killing people.

Metaphorically, she told herself. Metaphorically killing people.

Hattie shoved the tattered pillow into an opaque plastic bag and was about to creep down the back staircase to dispose of it in the trash can behind the garage when she heard the click-click of her mother's Louboutin's coming down the hall—right toward her room.

"Shit!" Hattie spat. She tossed the bag into the closet and dragged the door closed.

"Honey! Knock, knock," her mom announced in a sing-song voice.

Hattie yelled, "Mom, what? I'm busy!" She pulled the silk bag with the knife out of her jeans pocket and stuffed it in her desk drawer, plopped down on the furry pink office chair she received last Christmas, and tried to look busy on her laptop.

The door cracked open, and her mother's face peered around it. "What could you possibly be busy with? It's summer!" Her head hung halfway up the doorjamb like Jack Nicholson's in *The Shining*.

Hattie swung around in her chair. "Um, I was just checking on my college apps," she lied. What parent could question that?

Her mother pushed the door open, then walked into the room still carrying her Louis Vuitton laptop tote. She'd come home early from the law firm that Hattie's father left when he became the District Attorney. Hattie wished her mother would stay home with Adam as she had with her. Six-year-old Adam needed their mom more than Hattie *ever* did. He was on the autism spectrum, and Hattie worried that her parents pretended that he didn't need their extra attention. She knew differently.

Her mother sat daintily on the bed and tucked the tote to her side. "Any news?"

"Not yet. What's up?"

"I wanted to remind you that dad and I are going to that gala in Petoskey tonight, and you'd promised to bring Adam to his basketball game."

Hattie palmed her forehead. She had forgotten, and it was Liza's bunko night, so, she had no backup.

"Oh, yeah." She was going to have Hank come over, even though he was getting annoying lately. All he wanted to do was make out or talk about football. "What time's the game?"

Her mother looked relieved, her porcelain skin, slender nose, and silky dark blunt cut echoed Hattie's. "The game is at six, but Coach wants the boys there at five-thirty, suited up and ready to play."

Hattie's mom gathered her tote, preparing to leave the room. "We appreciate it. Take the Volvo." As she made it to the hallway, she added. "And make sure Adam gets a bath after, okay?"

"Yeah, sure." Hattie knew that Adam would most probably throw a fit about the bath, but she had a few tricks up her sleeve to coax him, including his favorite video game or a gluten-free cake donut. Maybe, once her brother fell asleep, she could do some more research on Ivey Des Jardins' family.

Chapter 28

Hattie

Hattie gathered the Star Wars comforter up under her brother's armpits. "Shhh, now, Addie, let's show Mommy and Daddy that you can get yourself to sleep without a fuss."

"But I'm not sleepy," Adam whined, despite his droopy eyelids.

Hank Purcell leaned his bulky body against the doorframe. "Hey, kid, go to sleep, huh?" He picked at an incisor. "How do you expect to grow big and strong without a good night's sleep? Ya wanna stunt your growth?"

Hattie sighed and gave Hank a death glare. "Will you shut—go downstairs, please? You are not helping!"

Why did I invite him over here?

Adam paled. "What does 'stunt' mean? Will I get sick? Will I die?" He tried to wiggle out of Hattie's tucking, but she proved faster than her brother.

"Of course not, darling. Hank doesn't know anything about anything!" Hattie leaned closer and whispered in Adam's ear. "I don't think he's any smarter than a bunny rabbit. I'll turn on your music, and you'll fall right to sleep, okay?"

He yawned, satisfied with his sister's answer. "Okay, I'll try." He let out a big sigh and turned toward the wall.

Hattie tip-toed to his dresser and turned gentle rain sounds on a Pokémon shaped speaker. "Night, night, Addie."

Downstairs, Hank had sprawled himself across the leather sectional in the family's media room. As Hattie approached, she balled up a fist and punched her boyfriend on his beefy bicep.

Hank flinched. "Hey!" He rubbed his upper arm. "For a little person, you sure can punch!"

Hattie planted herself in front of the sofa, not really blocking the television, but making it hard for Hank to see. Her hands were firmly placed on her tiny hips. "You almost ruined Adam's bedtime routine. I told you not to come upstairs. He has specific steps he needs to do to calm down."

Not much bothered Hank Purcell, and Hattie knew it. "Aw, I just wanted to be alone with you, baby." He reached out and pulled her onto the couch. Hattie let him envelope her in a massive bear hug. He started nibbling on her neck. "Come on, I just want to be with my girl."

"Oh, all right," she said through Hank's convincing kisses.

Ten sweaty, breathless minutes later, Hattie put a stop to their making-out. Her parents would be home soon, and even though they wouldn't mind Hank being at the house, they would mind if the two of them looked disheveled and pink-faced. "Hank, stop. My parents will be here any minute."

Hank took a big breath in and let Hattie move off him. "Damn, girl. You got me all worked up." He ran his hands through his damp blond hair, making it stick straight up.

Hattie smoothed his spiky hair back to make him look presentable. "Why don't you find something to watch while I check on Adam? He must be asleep, or he'd be down here by now."

Hank grabbed the remote control off the coffee table, and he started flipping through the channels. Hattie climbed the stairs slowly on her way to check on her brother. The hallway leading to Adam's bedroom was lined with built-in bookshelves, tastefully decorated with collectibles and leather-bound books.

Hattie's thoughts went back to her encounter with that irritating Ivey. She wondered why annoying people seem to flock to her. Hattie wasn't sure that she even wanted to get back together with Rafe. He could be such a goodie-good, but he sure was sexy. She loved kissing him. Hank was okay—handsome and muscley, but (*God*) was he stupid. He followed her around like a puppy, which at first, she'd enjoyed. Perhaps, she needed someone who challenged her—someone she could talk to about things.

She and Rafe had had great talks that usually devolved into arguments, but even the arguments were sort of exciting. Hattie peeked into Adam's room and saw her brother sound asleep. He'd kicked all the covers off, one little foot hanging over the edge of the mattress. She smiled. Adam was the only male she loved unconditionally. The only one who truly deserved her love.

She started back down the hallway toward the media room when she spotted a row of yearbooks tucked amongst her father's old law school textbooks. Hattie used to look through her parents' high school and college yearbooks when she was a little girl, fascinated with the odd fashions. She slid her father's senior high school book out and flipped to the index.

Hattie shifted from her left foot to her right, then back again. Her mouth dropped open, and her breath quickened.

Hattie dropped the book on the floor, but it stayed open to page 114. "Son of a damn bitch!" The couple highlighted on the page mockingly smiled up at her.

Chapter 29

Ivey

We'd worked non-stop since Opening Day, so I was relieved when Lauren decided to close the Sunnyside early. I hadn't seen or heard from Hattie since her cryptic accusations, and my talk with Lauren had brought up more questions than it answered. I shifted myself on the rocking chair with my laptop on my thighs. I should have brought a pillow to pad my boney behind.

I shook my head to clear out my wayward thoughts. If Hattie had discovered things about my family, I should be able to find that same info, right? District Attorney's offices surely have databases that aren't available to the public. Her father must have a password or encryption. Did Hattie get his password?

I wondered if Rafe knew anything about Hattie's access to her father's work. I hadn't asked him anything more about their relationship. I realized that I didn't truly know either one of them. So far, Rafe was semi-perfect, and Hattie was a complete wench. Hattie's comment about knowing Rafe down deep reverberated in my head. What an odd choice of words. Of course, Rafe's handsomeness had clouded my judgment—somewhat. I was still poised to discover that he could be a cleverly disguised slimeball. But, having been present when Hattie bothered Rafe despite his wishes, I could somewhat understand his stormy behavior back on that first day outside this same porch.

I had technically not been allowed to date when I first met Oliver Trammell. He'd transferred to Brandon High from a private school in Virginia when his father was stationed at MacDill AFB. We met when Mrs. Dougherty, the school counselor, asked me to show Oliver around the campus. He was the quintessential tall, dark, and handsome—so much like Rafe.

Oliver had wormed his way into my friend group, managing to charm both Kelli and Clara. Not much of a surprise with super friendly Kelli, but Clara could be a tough nut. That's why his descent into jerkdom shocked me. I could always count on Clara's intuition about people. I was still working on trusting my own.

We went out in groups, which was the only way my parents had allowed me to date last year. Oliver started "negging" me in fits and starts. For example, he'd say how much he liked my "natural" look, but a few minutes later complain that my same hair looked stringy and unwashed. He'd only say these things when my girlfriends couldn't hear, so I didn't have any proof of his personality shift. Oliver started to make "suggestions" about what I wore, where I went, and the people I hung with. He wanted Clara out of my friend group, which was not gonna happen.

We'd only been together out for a couple of months when his increasingly manipulative behavior came to a head. I'd met him at a school basketball game where we joined up with the girls and their boyfriends, Travis (Kelli's) and Sanjay (Clara's). Several members of the debate team joined us, and we had a fun time cheering on Brandon High. I was especially charged up: yelling, cheering, and generally being loud. Oliver pestered me to lower my voice and stop making a fool out of myself. That hurt my feelings and embarrassed me, but having my friends there, I ignored his remarks and continued to cheer.

We all stood on the far-right edge of the bleachers, about fifteen feet above the hard gym floor. Oliver grabbed me around the waist and pulled me close to him. Crazily, I thought he was being gallant, keeping me from falling off the bleacher's edge.

He whispered in my ear. "I don't appreciate you ignoring me, Ivey. You'd better stop making such a scene, or you might just accidentally slip off these bleachers." His voice was cold, and the hairs on the back of my neck prickled. He loosened his grip a bit, then shifted toward the edge of the bleacher causing me to lose my balance— the only thing keeping me from falling was his arm around me.

I screamed. "Oli—" My arms flailed as I tried to find my balance.

He plastered a concerned look on his face and dramatically pulled me into an embrace, so that everyone around us could see. He wrapped his wretched arms around me and kissed my head. "Oh, baby!" he gasped, sounding panicked. "That was a close one!" He looked around, making sure everyone got a bird's eye view of his heroism." Then he chuckled. "You better stay close to me, or you'll get hurt!"

That was it for me. I wriggled out of his arms, climbed down the bleachers, and ran to the girl's bathroom—only keeping my composure until I was safely inside a stall where I burst into tears.

Just thinking of the last time, I had spoken to Oliver made me get goose-pimply, so I willfully pushed it out of my mind. Rafe wasn't like that. He'd been nothing but polite over the past few weeks. Even Clara'd said I needed to loosen up and give Rafe a chance.

So, I looked over at the line of busy docks where the sparkling aqua-blue water of Lake Walloon shone through. The fresh air wafted over my skin.

I turned my attention back to my computer and googled "Michigan lakes'" and "water color." I learned that storms and intense winds stir up the quartz sediments in the lakebeds. When the sun shines on the swirling quartz, it makes the shimmering blue tones reminiscent of the Caribbean.

Along with regular families like mine, a bunch of extremely wealthy people lived on Walloon Lake. Across from Lauren's house were massive boats—all gleaming chrome and pearl-white paint.

Some docks were old-fashioned wood, but most were that greyish all-weather stuff. When I looked to the left, the Hotel Walloon took up most of the scenery. Each hotel room had a cute little balcony giving the building a European flair. Bright white Adirondack chairs faced the lake at the hotel's private beach. Stacked boulders dotted the shore between the hotel and the town square shopping area.

The docks bustled with people either loading up or disembarking from boats: kids laughed and ran around, adults toted Lands' End or Vineyard Vines' bags full of towels, snacks, and floaties of varying sizes. It was an inspired view—full of energy, sunshine, and smiles. People looked either pleasantly exhausted from their boat ride or aching to get onto the water.

Rafe and I had been talking about fun things we did when we were kids, as I mindlessly sorted sunflower stems earlier in the day. He was particularly nostalgic about a campsite that he and his brother had discovered.

"It's been a long time since we've been there together. Tonio makes himself scarce now…" Rafe's voice trailed off. He looked down at his feet, then raised his eyes back to me, blinking through his thick lashes.

I arranged and rearranged the flower stems. "Is he at college?"

Rafe stopped stacking sunflower seed bags, then rubbed the back of his neck. "Nah, he was accepted at a couple of places but… never went." He indicated the plant remnants next to me. "I'll take any trash."

Dried flowers shed something awful, so I'd collected scrap pieces into a pile. "Oh, thanks." I pursed my lips. "I hope I'm not being too nosy."

Rafe waved his hand. "No, no, not at all. Tonio's been, uh, trying to find himself for a while. It's been tough on my parents." It looked to me like Tonio's problems were hard on Rafe as well—his face was pinched, his eyes sorrowful. "He's a good guy and smart too. I wish he'd give himself a break."

I wished we could get back on a peppier subject. "I'm sorry your family has had to deal with that." Rafe's face shadowed over, and despite how sexy that dark look was,

I wanted to bring back the light. "I wonder what that campsite looks like now." I spoke without thinking. "We could rent some jet skis and go—"

Did I just basically ask him out? What was I doing?

I brushed the plant scraps into the bag Rafe held next to the counter.

He grinned.

All the oxygen flew out of my lungs.

"I'll do one better. My family has a two-seater. How about later today?"

The blood rushed to the surface of my skin, making me warm all over. God! Say something. "Yeah, sounds terrific! There's a dock across from Lauren's."

Rafe hefted the bag over his shoulder. "Oh yeah, I know that one. I can be there around four. Does that work?"

Hellz, yeah. I nodded like a crazy person. I couldn't believe I'd just asked a guy out, and the earth didn't swallow me whole. He said yes, and I hadn't burst into flames.

So, while I rocked in my chair, looking at my phone, thinking about Rafe, Hattie, Hattie's dad, and my uncle, Lauren came around the corner dragging what looked like a bunch of two-by-four wood planks.

She stopped, adjusted the planks, and then dropped several in the gravel. "Shh-oot!" she yelled, after spotting me on the porch.

I flung myself off the rocker to help her. "What on earth do you have here?"

Lauren blew the hair out of her face. "Since your watercolor lessons with Stassi start next week, I figured every artist has to have an easel, right?" She dropped another plank.

I stooped to pick up the wayward pieces. "Really? How cool! You are way too good to me." Now that I held the wooden parts, I could see they fit together with metal brackets, nuts, and bolts. Lauren and I gathered all the pieces and then hauled them up the porch.

"I thought we'd set the easel out here," Lauren said. "You and I need figure out how to put this thing together. Where is that hardware baggie?" We piled the wood on the left side of the porch, she started patting down every pocket in her cargo capris. "Ah-ha!" She held up the bag like it was a pot of gold. She was so cute.

My voice cracked. "Um, you don't know how much it means to me that you did this, but—"

"Oh no." Lauren's face fell. "I overstepped." The baggie dangled pitifully from her hand.

I gave her a reassuring hug. "I love it, but Rafe and I are going on a jet ski this afternoon!"

Lauren dropped the baggie, put her hands up to her face, and screamed into her palms. "Ivey! That's so great! I knew you and Rafe would hit it off. Oh my, let's see. Do you have a bathing suit? You're much taller than me." She scratched her forehead thoughtfully. "That's ok. You can wear shorts and a tank top—"

Lauren paced the porch. I could practically hear her brain going a mile a minute.

I grabbed her wrists. "Aunt Lauren, I'm good." I met her eyes. "I brought a couple of bathing suits. I'm already freaking out about the whole thing, though. Can we do the easel tomorrow?"

She grinned. "Of course, of course! Go! Get ready!"

I pulled my phone out to check the time. 3:20. I needed to get moving. Hopefully, he wouldn't be early.

Chapter 30

Rafe

Rafe checked the hitch joining his truck and the trailer carrying the two-person jet-ski.

Man, I hope I don't get there embarrassingly early.

He climbed into the driver's seat, cranked the ignition, and noted the time on the dashboard clock—3:40 pm. Rafe shook his head and turned off the engine. He decided to play with his phone for a few minutes to make sure he'd arrive fashionably on time. Was that a thing?

Rafe was surprised that his work conversation with Ivey had turned into a casual date, but he was pleased. He had no idea why he'd shared Tonio's issues with her. She was easy to talk to, possibly because she wasn't a hometown girl that he'd known forever. Realizing he didn't have to say anything made him want to talk more.

Rafe checked the weather app—clear all night. He hoped he'd remember how to find Brother Isle. An incredibly dumb name, but they'd been kids, and the name had stuck.

Rafe remembered the first time they had come upon the wildly overgrown little piece of land. Antonio was thirteen and Rafe, nine. The boys had floated out in a battered, old canoe on some holiday weekend. Was it Labor Day? Memorial Day? He couldn't remember which, but it didn't matter. The lake had teemed with families, noisy, crowded boats, and dangerously zig-zagging jet skis. They didn't have the two-seater Yamaha yet, so the only choice was Ole Mabel (another noncreative name). No one remembered how or when the beat-up canoe came into their lives, but it had been there when the boys wanted a lake adventure.

Brother Isle was elusive—mainly because it wasn't an island at all. Technically, it was an isthmus, jutting into the State Park territory at the northeast end of Walloon Lake. A lake tributary bisected the parkland, and when the boys had come ashore that first time, maybe it had been the sweltering day or pure exhaustion that led them to believe the area was, in fact, an island. The trees were sparse off the tributary, mostly scrubby pine trees and firs. The swampiness accounted for minimal shrubbery, so there'd been room for a modest camp area. The boys thought they had discovered a secret paradise. After they'd returned home, they embarked on planning the perfect campsite. The next morning, after loading up Ole Mabel with chopped wood for a fire, a few bags of collected rocks, and an old Army surplus tent—they were ready to conquer their new "world."

Rafe smiled as he recalled how excited Tonio had been. In nine-year-old Rafe's mind, Tonio was the bravest, most imaginative big brother anyone could have.

Tonio had used a sketch pad from mom's teaching supplies to make a list of vital camp items. He drew a blueprint that showed where to set up the tent, so it wouldn't get soggy in the rain, plus the best place for the fire pit to avoid the wind. He'd been a Boy Scout, so Tonio knew his stuff. Rafe hadn't been interested in scouting, he much preferred baseball, but the allure of being his brother's trusted companion on this adventure had filled him with delight.

Dad had helped pile all the camp items into Ole Mabel, then loaded her and the boys in his old truck, taking them to the exact dock where—

Oh, man!

Rafe snapped out of reminiscing just in time. The dash clock said 3:52, and now, he was sure he'd be late.

Chapter 31
Ivey

Back in my room, I'm disgusted with my choices, so I threw each bathing suit on the shag carpet. I stood, naked, in front of the mirrored closet doors, exasperated, trying to calm the raging acid in my belly.

Does everyone get this nervous? God! I wish I could just calm down and think.

I took a few breaths. In, 2, 3, 4. Out, 2, 3, 4.

Time to be pragmatic, as Clara would say. These were the only suits I had.

I retrieved the pale pink and white striped two-piece suit from the floor and held the top to my chest. It was the sportiest of the three suits. If we did do any swimming, I wouldn't have any wardrobe malfunctions.

(Deep breath in…) It'll have to do.

I wrestled with the stretchy material, pulled it over my breasts, and settled the "girls" in the lightly constructed cups. The retro suit bottoms came up over my belly button—the style made my legs look okay. I grabbed the blue tank top I'd worn to work and some denim cut-offs. I slipped on my flip-flops but changed into Converse low tops instead. I freshened my ponytail.

"Wow! That's a sick jet-ski!" I exclaimed after Rafe backed his truck into the dockside boat launch. He grinned and made his way to the trailer hitch. "Thanks! I'm glad you suggested we do this. Haven't had the old jet ski out yet this summer."

I fidgeted with my bathing suit strap. "Can I help with anything?"

"Yeah." He handed me two black plastic plugs. "Do you know where the drain holes are?"

I nodded. "My grandparents had Yamahas too." I walked around the back of the jet ski and found the drain holes.

Rafe attached a bright blue lashing strip to the craft, then climbed in the truck to back the trailer into the lake. I positioned myself in the shallows to help guide the jet ski, keeping it from floating away or banging into the other docks or boats. Once the craft started to float, Rafe pulled his truck forward, then parked in a nearby space. I looped the lashing strip around a post and met Rafe by his truck.

He playfully punched me on the arm. "Hey, we're a good team."

I smiled. "I agree."

Before I knew it, we had jetted away from the busy lakefront, Rafe driving and me holding on to his waist for dear life. The air blew bracingly across my face and whistled in my ears. It'd been a while since I'd ridden a jet ski, and wow, did I miss it. There was nothing like flying across the water—every stressful, scary, or annoying thought blew away. My body tingled as the water pelted my legs and feet. I pulled my limbs into my core, so I stayed fixed on the back seat. Rafe pointed out some cool spots around the lake, screaming over the wind. I couldn't make out anything he said, but I appreciated his efforts.

Despite the lake's chill, I was warm, like, inside my skin—I felt safe. It's hard to explain. I guess everyone has their way of sussing people out. I got warm or cold right beneath my skin. Sure, there were times my "radar" didn't work; case in point—Oliver, but I was usually accurate. I was little when I first experienced the telltale icy sting.

It had been Daisy and Rose's eighth birthday, and we had the party in our San Antonio backyard. I remember it had been hot as Hades, the air humid like a soggy rag over everything that July morning. My mother had come up with a creative theme for the twins' celebration. We each decorated a halved paper plate with colorful crepe or construction paper, sequins, or glitter to achieve the likeness of our namesake plants (Daisy made her plate/mask look like a daisy; Rose made hers look like a rose). I had been super pumped to decorate my mask with leaves and green pipe cleaners to look like English ivy. I was six years old.

The party had started, and the guests had arrived. Mom spread craft materials over a picnic table along with colorful plastic bins full of markers, bright crayons, and glue sticks so everyone could make masks. We all had a fantastic time coming up with ideas. Sheldon Pugh crafted clamshells out of peach-colored construction paper, complete with plastic "pearls." Chloe Ramirez liked my ivy so much that she covered her mask with sequined clovers. Mom and Dad had even organized an impromptu parade, so we pranced around, shouting and squealing, showing off our masterpieces.

After more games and cake with pink icing, the party had moved inside to watch a Disney movie while the moms chatted and cleaned up. My mother presided over the outdoor clean-up as two others rinsed and stacked plates in the kitchen. In their defense, the moms didn't know I had snuggled up under the breakfast bar directly in front of them. Despite the heat, I was covered in chill bumps.

Mean Mom 1: Daisy and Rose are gorgeous girls, aren't they?

Mean Mom 2: Oh yeah, I've tried to get Carrie to put them in the Supreme Darling Miss pageant, but she won't do it.

Mean Mom 1: (lowering her voice to a whisper) Well, she probably doesn't want to hurt the little one's feelings. The poor thing doesn't compare to her sisters in the looks department.

Mean Mom 2: Shhh. Oh, my word! That is some stinkin' thinkin'. Ivey's got to grow into her nose and do something with that hair. I'm sure she'll "pretty up" soon enough.

Mean Mom 1: I hope so. It'll be tough growing up with sisters like that. Let's hope Ivey has a brain cell or two.

Mean Mom 2: Yeah, bless her heart.

Only being six, I didn't grasp everything the ladies had said. I mean, the tone and intent were lost on my little brain. Obviously, the ladies never wanted me to hear their conversation or insult me. My memory's pretty sharp, though. After I heard those hurtful words, I gathered up my *Tangled* bedspread, then skulked to my bedroom. In general, I'm not a big crier, and when my feelings got hurt, I tended to get quiet, so that's what I did. I also couldn't seem to get warm.

My mom had kissed my forehead as she checked on me later that evening. "Did you have fun at the party, sweetie?"

I picked at my comforter's tag, not looking at her. "I guess."

"You didn't have a good time at the party that I worked all day preparing?" My mom sighed dramatically, placing her hand, palm out, on her forehead. I knew she was trying to lighten my mood.

I grimaced. "Someone said something that made me cold all over. I feel bad."

Mom appreciated it when we named our feelings. "Oh, no! Honey, what happened?"

"A couple of the moms, I don't know them, said my nose and hair aren't as pretty as Dee and Rose."

Mom's eyes went wide, and she scooted closer to me. "When was this?" Her voice, now, high pitched and shaky.

"While we were watching *Beauty and the Beast.*"

Mom pondered for a moment. "They said this in front of you?"

I worried that I might cry after all. "No, I was in my spot. They were washing dishes."

Mom didn't look at me, she stared into space. "Ah, Sarah Levitt and Cheryl Frasier. I asked them to do the dishes…" Her voice had trailed off, and she had a funny, scrunchy look on her face.

"Mom?" I'd whispered. "It's okay." Even though it wasn't okay, I'd just wanted to go to sleep.

Mom's face had flushed when she turned her attention back to me. Her breathing had quickened. "Birdie, I can only imagine words like that hurt. Sometimes grown-ups don't realize that they're being unkind, but that's no excuse." She wiped at her eyes. "You are just as beautiful and special as your sisters. Dad and I love you so much— we might burst with love!" Her face had softened as her words soothed me. She gently stroked the hair off my forehead, then hugged me close, and told me everything a good mother would say to reassure a hurting child.

The next day Rose told me that Mom had called both moms and told them off. Believe me, Mom's defending me was cool, but when I went to school the following Monday, I got teased mercilessly for not only being a baby who tattled, but an ugly baby at that. I'd wished I hadn't said a thing.

Along with my regret about tattling, the ladies' disparaging words tunneled like termites into my brain. I know it sounds silly all these years later, but it's like, I had to work extra hard to bring myself up to an acceptable level, up to my sisters' starting point of awesomeness. It was exhausting.

So, long story short, I trusted my skin-chilling sensation, so I didn't have to rely on anyone to defend me. I knew it was not a superpower or anything, but I felt as if I had some control over crap that happened.

Chapter 32

Ivey

Brother Isle

The jet ski slowed as we approached the shoreline. Rafe stood up and scanned the area.

He pointed to the left of scraggly firs. "There's where Tonio and I usually landed."

I gave him a thumbs-up, as he resettled himself in the driver's seat, and maneuvered around to a pine lined harbor. "It does look like an island!" I yelled.

Rafe nodded. "Sure does. Man, the approach here looks practically the same!"

He pulled the jet ski as close to the shore as possible. We both jumped into the water, then dragged the craft onto the bank. Rafe unfurled the lashing strip and tied it around a stout tree trunk just in case water encroached.

I scanned the area. "This is epic!"

Rafe grinned. My excitement seemed to please him. "Our old campsite's through here." He pushed through the foliage while I followed close behind. About a hundred yards in, the trees thinned out, and we found the clearing with a crude fire pit marked with rocks. I could imagine the fun having a secret campsite would be for two kids.

Rafe gestured toward the fire pit. "Pull up a comfy rock."

I saluted. "Yes, sir!"

He planted his hands on his hips and looked out over the space. "I am the captain, now!"

So cute I could cry. (I loved that he quoted the movie *Captain Phillips.*)

"Terrible Somali accent, Rafe."

He shrugged. "Hey, I tried. Wanna start a fire?"

We hunted around for dry twigs and piled them in the pit. After building a decent stack of wood, Rafe dug in his pocket and pulled out a disposable lighter. He knelt and lit several branches near the bottom of the pile. As the fire sparked and smoked, I breathed in its comforting scent.

Rafe sat down next to me, and our knees grazed. "So, here we are, Brother Isle! What do you think?" He spread out his arms with pride.

I looked around, taking in the whole scene. "I think it's fantastic. Really! Did you guys clear this area?"

"Yeah, it's weird thinking how long ago that was." He hesitated for a moment, lost in thought. Then he shook his head slightly and let out a quick laugh. "Tonio was so bossy. I remember picking up and piling rocks over there." He pointed to a small group of stones scattered along the tree line. "He kept thinking of reasons to go back to the boat instead of helping me."

I laughed with him. "I think older brothers and sisters must have a special knack for that."

"I bet that's it, for sure." He picked up a nearby branch. "You haven't talked much about your sisters—what's their deal?"

"Hmm, how to say this nicely?" I drummed my fingers on my chin.

"Don't hold back on my account." Rafe poked at the fire with the branch, then turned and gave me his full attention.

"Well, I love my sisters." I started, and I looked directly into Rafe's eyes, which was super weird and a little uncomfortable, at first. Rafe nodded encouragingly. "But I don't have much in common with them."

He leaned in. "How so?"

"Dee and Rose have each other—through everything. They look alike, and they think alike. I don't know, we got along fine when we were little. My friend Clara says, 'Three's a crowd' and that it's natural for two to pair off."

Rafe rubbed the back of his neck, thoughtfully. "Sure, I get that. Tonio and I have developed different interests too."

"It's not their fault that everyone worships my sisters. They are attractive, intelligent, and talented," I added.

"So far, it sounds like you fit in with them."

I playfully punched his arm. "Okay, you are my best friend now." My Grinch heart grew two sizes. "So, what's going on with your brother?"

Rafe put his hands up like a surrendering criminal. "No, no! We're talking about *you*."

I chuckled at his adorableness but turned serious. "Am I off base thinking that you worry a lot about him?"

He nodded warily. "Yeah, yeah I do." He threw a few more sticks on the fire. "My parents are messed up about it which rubs off on me, I guess. They try to put on brave faces, but their concern for Tonio comes out like anger— especially my Dad."

"I hear ya; my dad can be the same."

Rafe straightened up and breathed heavily.

I sensed that he wanted to change the subject, so I decided to fill him in on my 'investigation' in a roundabout way. "So, how did you and Hattie get together? I do *not* see it."

"I wondered how long that would take," he responded, with a smirk. "Hattie's got a big personality—"

I choked a little bit. "That's an understatement."

Rafe raised an eyebrow. "Did you guys have a run-in?"

"A run-in?" I cleared my throat, then pursed my lips. "That's a benign way to describe it."

"So, what happened?" He flashed that I'm-completely-listening gaze which melted my heart and made my stomach flutter.

"First," I wasn't going to let him off the hook. "How did you two get together?"

Rafe squirmed on his rock perch, then stirred some glowing hot embers back and forth with his branch. "We've known each other since we were kids." He elbowed me playfully. "I always thought she was annoying, by the way. She used to chase me around and try to kiss me in elementary school. What can I say? Hattie's gorgeous, and I *am* a guy after all." He blinked his eyes enhancing his angelic expression.

I wiggled my finger in his face. "Oh no! You aren't getting any sympathy."

"It all happened so fast, my head was spinning, and I found myself asking her to a football game." He shrugged. "Believe it or not, she *can* be charming when she wants to."

I sighed and made a "tch" sound with my tongue. "So far, I haven't been on the receiving end of her charming side."

"Anyhow, I snapped out of it fairly quickly, but I thought she really liked me, and it was nice having a girlfriend—most of the time. She must have gotten bored though 'cause she broke up with me and immediately started going with Hank." Rafe gazed up at the sky. "So, that's my sordid story. Now you!"

I took a deep breath in and exhaled slowly. "Well, Hattie came into the Sunnyside on Opening Day after you and Lauren went to Corbett Farm." I rubbed the space between my eyebrows. "She had three snotty girls with her."

He gave me a knowing look. "I'm not surprised. They're joined at the hip, and Hattie's timing tends to be spot on."

"Yeah, well, I can handle mean girls, but Hattie's on another level. She basically threatened me with vague gossip about my family."

Rafe recoiled and his eyes went wide. "What on earth—?"

I squared myself with him, so our knees practically touched. "Did you know Lauren was married?" I decided to start at the beginning.

"Yeah, I remember Dad mentioning that Lauren had some relationship challenges, but Dad hates gossip. He's never mentioned anything else, though."

Another good reason to like Rafe and his family.

I nodded as my body clenched. I had so much to say, and it felt like it might burst out. "Lauren told me all about her marriage to my Uncle Michal, and it was super sad. My grandfather had to fire him because he stole some money from the hardware store, then my uncle up and disappeared." I lowered my shoulders, relieved that I got all that info out.

As Rafe listened, the corners of his mouth turned down. "Wow, that is mysterious and sad. Lauren's always seemed so, hm, sunny, for lack of a better word."

"You're so right! I saw her sorrowful side as she talked about Uncle Michal, though. She loved him. I'm sure she still does." I rubbed my hands on my thighs. "Hattie told me about her dad being the District Attorney, and she threatened to spread gossip about my family."

Rafe pensively stroked his chin. He didn't seem surprised by Hattie's threats. "Hm, it's true that her dad's the DA. But what would Mr. Foster know—oh, I get it. The stolen money."

I raised my eyebrows and tilted my head in a whattaya-gonna-do kind of way.

"Hattie's definitely got a gift for picking at people's vulnerabilities."

We sat there quietly for a few minutes, Rafe poking the fire and me wondering if I was making way too much out of everything. I mean, Hattie was just a run of the mill mean girl, right?

Rafe broke our silence. "What did your parents say about all this?"

"Well." I dragged out the "l" sheepishly.

"Ivey, really? You haven't asked them what they know about your uncle disappearing?" His voice raised several octaves.

I winced. "Hey! Don't be so judgey! I have my reasons."

"Okay, okay. Can I ask why?"

I looked down at the sandy ground, then dug my toe into it. When I looked back up at him, Rafe smiled sweetly.

He scooted closer to me, so our knees rubbed together. A comforting warmth spread through me. "Tell me," he said quietly.

I thought back to my dream, momentarily about to tell him, but it seemed so freaky that I dismissed the idea. "Lauren didn't specifically ask me not to talk to my parents, but I got the feeling that she's embarrassed about the whole thing. I thought back to when Mom told us about them splitting up, it was so, I don't know, abrupt, and nonspecific." My face felt hot and sweat dripped down my back. "Then my Dad—"

"Yeah?" He encouraged me.

I sighed. "He basically shut down all discussion."

"Got it." Rafe nodded. "The ole let's-keep-family-stuff-in-the-family, right?'"

"Exactly!" It was cool to have someone understand. "I'd like to find out about my uncle without stressing Lauren out, especially whether Hattie really knows anything about it." I thought about Lauren crying in her room, and my voice trailed off. Something else nagged at me, but I wasn't sure how to put it into words.

What if my bringing up Uncle Michal and this whole drama lead Mom and Dad to freak out, and make me go home? Wait! Isn't that what I would have jumped at when I first got to Walloon Lake?

I looked at my phone—5:37 pm. I didn't have anything to get back to, but Brother Isle felt stifling. The scrubby foliage sat ominously, and the fire now felt too warm for the still evening.

Rafe glanced at his phone reflexively. "We should probably get back. I'm sorry Hattie said all that nonsense. Do you want me to talk to her? I'm not sure how successful I'll be but—"

I shot up from my rock seat. "No! No, please don't! It'll make it worse." My God, what if she blabbed to Lauren directly?

"Okay, I won't." His face fell.

I touched his hand lightly. "Thank you so much for offering, but I'm pretty sure that's exactly what she wants."

Rafe kicked sand onto the fire, extinguishing it with a hiss. "You're probably right. Would you mind if I helped you investigate? Two heads and all that?" The adventurous boy within him shined through.

I needed some help, and Rafe was the only person besides Lauren who I knew well enough to trust in Walloon. "I'd love that."

Chapter 33

Ivey

I liked Rafe's cozy bedroom despite the underlying scent of unwashed athletic socks. The smell reminded me of my dad's gym at home, so it was comforting in a bizarre way. I looked over at the corner laundry basket; there were more clothes around it than in it. Mom got all over my dad about that same thing. Funny.

"Oh, man, I'm sorry." Rafe dashed over to gather the scattered clothing. The walls were painted a light brown with dark, stained trim around the windows and door. He had a packed bookshelf across from his double bed. I had checked out some of the titles, and I was impressed. *Moby Dick*, *The Fountainhead*, *Catch 22*, and tons of sci-fi fan fiction. It made me smile.

I swiveled on the wooden stool that Rafe had set up next to his laptop. "Please, no problem. It's your room! I'm the invader."

He laughed. "You are not an invader. I should have cleaned up better."

I'd ridden home with Rafe after work since we'd decided to search online for any info about the theft at Pops' store or anything about my uncle. We'd already looked through several news stations' websites.

Nothing.

"When is Morgan coming by?" I'd agreed to let Morgan in on the situation because, according to Rafe, he was a research maniac who hoped to work in intelligence someday. One sure can't judge a book by its cover because Morgan looked more like a skater boy than an aspiring spy.

As if he'd heard my question, Morgan popped up in Rafe's doorway, out of breath and still wearing his Mariachi's polo shirt. The faint odor of Mexican food followed him in.

He plopped onto the bed and opened the laptop he'd brought with him. "Hey guys! I had to go by my house to get my computer. One of the waiters had a Nintendo Switch stolen out of his car, so I didn't have it with me."

Rafe had finished picking up his laundry and was now in a beat-up gaming chair. "No problem, thanks for coming over."

I nodded at Morgan and smiled. "Rafe told me about your mad research skills."

Morgan cackled; his face lit up. "I hope he didn't oversell me! Let's see now. Which network should I use?"

Rafe told him. "Torres2, and the password is Pistons4128, capital 'P', no spaces."

Morgan tapped the last key with a dramatic flourish. "Got it! But first, Ivey, fill me in on everything." His eyes then fixed on me, boring into my skull.

Now I'd gotten another non-family member involved. "Well," I sputtered.

I squared my shoulders, lifted my chin, then told Morgan about my two encounters with Hattie and my talk with Lauren.

Chapter 34
Hattie

Hattie liked one thing about her home life—family dinner. Of course, she didn't care *at all* about hanging with her parents, but Adam usually had calmer evenings when they were all together. He'd babble away about his day: school, basketball, occupational therapy, or counseling.

That evening, Adam had requested the family gather around the kitchen island rather than the dining room. The kitchen was bright and sunny since the recent renovation swept away the dark wood cabinets and chunky butcher block table for creamy sage-painted cabinetry and a quartz-topped island with six linen-covered barstools. Mom and Dad were surprisingly engaged with her and Adam, so Hattie ventured a harmless line of questioning.

"So, I met someone interesting at the summer market a few days ago." She shoveled some Caesar salad into her mouth.

Her father was fresh from City Hall, still wearing his dark gray pinstripe suit and dress shoes. "Oh, really?" He looked uncomfortably balanced on the barstool, one foot on the floor.

"I heard the shops are doing great this summer," said her mother. "I haven't had a chance to get down there yet." She gestured with her fork. "Addie, let's go this weekend! Would you like that?"

Adam nodded enthusiastically as he chewed a mouthful of Liza's chicken pot pie.

Hattie sniffed at her mother's hijacking the question directed at her father. "Her name is Ivey," she started again, looking directly at her dad. "She works at the sunflower place."

Her dad looked up from his dinner distractedly. "Mm-hm," he grunted.

"She said that her aunt owns the place—"

That comment got the reaction Hattie had hoped. Her father choked on a bit of lettuce. "What?"

Hattie's mom looked worriedly at her husband, then patted him on the back. "Are you alright, dear? Say something!"

Hattie scrutinized her father as he shrugged off his wife's help, then gained his composure. He cleared his throat and brought a napkin to his lips. "Sorry, ahem, went down the wrong pipe." His voice was ragged. "Now, what were you saying?" His DA face was back on.

Hattie played coy. "Lauren Corbett, she's Ivey's aunt. Her name's familiar, isn't it?"

"Oh," said Hattie's mother. "She owns Corbett Farm, right, Scott?"

Hattie's father remained emotionless, but she knew better. He was rattled. "Yeah, yeah. Miss Corbett's family were long-time residents. They had a place off Merritt Road."

Hattie pushed her salad around with her fork. "Ivey's super nice, I may invite her over for dinner sometime," she lied.

Her mother's face lit up. "Oh, I love that idea! Please do invite her."

Hattie frowned at her mom, her eyebrows knitted together, and lips pursed. "Try not to jump out of your skin, Ma. You've made it perfectly clear you don't like my friends."

"That is not true." Her mother placed a hand on her chest defensively. "I think it's easy to get stuck in a rut with friends in a small town. Expand your horizons, right, Scott?

Holy hell, with the "right, Scott," thought Hattie. *Always looking for his approval. Pathetic.*

Hattie's father cleared his throat again and slid off the barstool. He left his plate for Liza to clean up. "Yeah, yeah, sure, whatever." He continued out of the kitchen, loosening his tie and mumbling to himself all the way to his home office.

Chapter 35
Ivey

Rafe and I leaned attentively into Morgan's computer screen.

"Guys, I can't see the screen!" He gestured for us to move back.

"Sorry!" we said simultaneously, then scooted back a bit. Morgan scanned the US Immigration and Naturalization database he'd accessed. "It looks like your uncle did apply for naturalization, but he never followed through with the paperwork. So, I guess it's possible that he returned to the Czech Republic. I've plugged his name into every criminal database I can access, and I don't see anything after the arrest at your grandfather's store. Like your aunt said, Paul Corbett never pressed charges, and Charlevoix PD didn't bring charges either, which is kinda irregular."

"Why?" I scootched farther from Morgan, so we weren't right on top of each other as we talked.

Morgan took his fingers off the keyboard. "Usually, when a crime's committed, and the police have a suspect who's caught red-handed, as they say, the county will bring charges even if the victim—in this case, your grandfather—doesn't want to. Hmm, that's intriguing."

I leaned back in toward the computer. "Now what?"

"The Assistant DA was Scott Foster, Hattie's dad."

Rafe and I locked eyes from either side of Morgan. "Ives, do you think your grandfather could have asked Hattie's dad not to bring charges?" Morgan asked.

I shook my head. "Hmm." I swiped a non-existent stray hair off my forehead. "I can only imagine that Pops may have wanted to give Michal a chance to redeem himself. Lauren did mention that she feared Michal being deported."

"Well, there's only one way to find out," Morgan added, in a teacher-y voice.

"Yeah." I reluctantly agreed. "I need to talk with Pops."

After a few more clicks, Morgan asked, "Did your aunt divorce your uncle? I'm not finding a divorce decree."

I thought about my discussion with Lauren. "I don't know about that. My parents certainly think she filed for divorce, but I didn't ask about that in particular."

Rafe leaned in again, focusing on the screen. "Mahoney, Blake & Foster Attorneys? That's Hattie's parents' firm. Why're you on this site?"

Morgan glanced at Rafe, then back at the computer. "According to Michigan law, in order to obtain a divorce from a missing person, you have to jump through a lot of hoops. This is the closest law firm to us with info on the process. Coincidence, huh?"

"Yeah," I said, ruefully. "Quite the coincidence."

"Let's see." Morgan's eyes tracked back and forth as he read down the page. "Federal law requires seven years to declare a missing person dead, but with sufficient evidence of an accident or foul play—"

"Wait!" My voice cracked. "No one said anything about my uncle being dead!"

Morgan stopped scrolling, "I didn't mean anything by that; I'm just looking through some of the things your aunt could have done if she had wanted to divorce. Most likely, she'd have to do this 'divorce by publication.' "

My breathing quickened, my apprehension building. "Go on."

"Hm, she'd have to place an ad in the local papers announcing the intent to divorce after a 'good faith' search. If she did, I might be able to find the ad online."

"Let's check." Rafe said.

I rubbed my forehead. We were going down a weird and frightening path.

Morgan took his fingers off the keys and somberly looked at Rafe. "Dude, calm down. All the big newspapers require a subscription now, and I'm not made of money. I've already run Michal's name through the free databases and found nothing. Ivey, could Lauren possibly have a death certificate for your uncle?"

I shivered. "Ew, I don't know. How would a person get one without a body?" I can't believe I said that.

Morgan thought for a minute. "You'd have to have friends in strategic places or deep roots in the community."

"Another reason to hit up my grandfather," I mumbled more to myself than the guys.

Chapter 36

Ivey

Back at Lauren's the next day, I prepared myself to ask Pops about his version of the fateful events. I figured since Mom was in Sedona visiting them, I had a good excuse to call. I usually didn't call Pops or Nan just to chat. I wondered for a second whether that was normal. Do most grandkids chat up their grandparents on a regular basis? Maybe, if they live in the same town. Kelli's grandmother lives with her, so they're physically and emotionally close. Daisy, Rose, and I talked to extended family on holidays and such. I shook my head, realizing that I was procrastinating.

I'd figured out a way to slide into the convo with Pops—I'd tell him about the little boys' caper on Opening Day. Then I'd segue into asking about his store without making a giant production out of it. Hopefully.

I sat on my bed scrolling through social media when texts from Rafe and Morgan popped up, urging me to get on with my phone call. I felt a flash of indignation at the guys' impatience. I mean, this was my family! Neither of them had to have to live with the consequences when I stirred up bad memories, so I texted back some frowny faces.

I decided to make the call outside, so I started over to the Adirondack chairs at the back of the Hotel Walloon. The chairs were there for the hotel guests, but no one cared if the locals occasionally used them. I headed to the furthest chair from the dock where Rafe and I had jet-skied out the other day.

As I crunched across the gravel, I worried about Lauren. She'd been quiet since our talk, not rude or unfriendly, just not as, well, verbal. Despite that change in her demeanor, the store was doing great, with no major issues. We had fallen into a predictable routine: working ten to two, restocking for the next day, doing our own thing in the afternoon, then dinner together.

Nestled in the Adirondack chair, I texted my mother.

Good time to call?

Three seconds later, my grandparents' landline number showed up on my screen. I swiped to answer, tapping the speaker. "Hey!"

"Ivey, I'm so happy to hear from you. How are things going there?" chirped my mother.

I squirmed, anxious to get to the point. "Things are great. The weather's fantastic. How're Nan and Pops?"

Mom sighed. "Nanny's still weak from her fall, but she's working hard at physical therapy. She's getting some sleep now. Pops is rambling around here as usual."

"Good, good. Is he close by?" I hoped I sounded carefree. "I'd love to say 'hello.'"

"Uh, sure." Mom sounded a bit put out with my suggestion. No big shock, though. "Dad? It's Ivey. She'd like to talk with you."

I heard my grandfather yell, "What? Oh." I heard scuffling, the phone dropping to the floor, then Pops' booming voice through the speaker.

"Ivey, dear!"

I rubbed a clammy palm on my jeans. "Hey, Pops. You sound so good. Mom says Nan's getting stronger. What have you been up to?"

Pops coughed in that gagging way older people do. "Well, you know, it's more about getting Nan up and about right now, but I've been doing some woodworking. They've got a workshop here on our old fart's compound."

"Pops! You're certainly not an old fart." I giggled. Pops had referred to himself like that as far back as I could remember.

"How's Lauren doing? The store? I saw something about some summer storms coming through in a few days." Classic Pops. He was a Weather Channel junkie.

"I'll have to check about the weather, but the store's busy and Lauren seems pleased. We had a crazy thing happen on Opening Day though."

I told Pops about the little boys and their botched shoplifting adventure.

He acknowledged that kids pulled stuff like that at the hardware store more often than people would think. "We had to keep an extra close eye on the candy around the register—it was a prime target." He chuckled, then wheezed.

We chatted about other funny and not-so-funny things that happened during the forty-some years that he owned the hardware store. I decided to take the plunge.

I tried to keep my tone lighthearted as I approached my true line of questions. "Did anything ever happen where you had to call the police?"

Pops didn't seem bothered by my shift. "Oh, of course, all merchants deal with the police every now and then. It's an unfortunate part of the business."

I poised myself, taking in a deep breath, "Lauren mentioned a sticky situation with Uncle Michal."

Silence—like I chucked a stone down a bottomless pit.

Sweat broke out on my upper lip. "Pops?" I squeaked.

"Lauren brought up Michal?" His voice had transformed, grim and agitated.

Damn.

I pinched between my eyebrows again, my skin itched. "Um, yeah, not a big deal. I hadn't remembered much about him, so Lauren and I talked about their breakup, and she'd mentioned you had to fire him. That must have been uncomfortable." Kind of like this conversation.

I had never heard my grandfather sound so offended. "It was beyond uncomfortable, and possibly, the hardest thing I've ever had to do." His voice was hollow, devoid of his usual self-deprecating humor or grandfatherly wisdom. "Is Lauren talking about Michal often?"

The sweat spread down my body: my chest, my back, and the bottoms of my feet. "No, Pops, not a lot." I fibbed. "I'm curious that Uncle Michal up and disappeared. Mom made it sound like they divorced. It sounds more mysterious than that."

My grandfather once again fell silent. I'd most certainly screwed up.

"It's been nice talking with you, dear. Here's your mom." He sounded like a robot.

I heard my mother barking questions as she took the phone. "Dad, are you alright? You're white as a sheet. Sit down." And to me, "Ivey, what the hell did you say?"

I stood up from the chair, took the phone off the speaker, and held it to my ear. "I—I don't," I stammered, trying to keep my voice calm. "I asked about the hardware store and … Uncle Michal."

Mom went ultrasonic. "Why did you bring up Michal? I specifically told you not to! What's wrong with you?"

Prickles shot up my back and my neck throbbed. "Nothing's wrong with me!" I shouted, full of indignation. "I'm simply trying to understand my own family."

Mom menacingly whispered. "Your grandfather has been through quite enough without reliving that mess. For God's sake, now I must deal with this."

She disconnected.

I stared at my phone for several seconds, stunned at my mother's intense reaction. I shuffled back to Lauren's house, praying I hadn't given my grandfather a heart attack.

Chapter 37
Ivey

I was relieved that my aunt wasn't back home from Corbett Farm when I dragged myself across the street. I texted Lauren to assess whether my mother had contacted her— not yet. I leaned against the breakfast bar, then filled Rafe and Morgan in on my disastrous discussion with Pops.

Rafe: I'm so sorry it went badly—that sucks

Morgan: U aren't serious that ur pops might have had a heart attack, right?

Ivey: jk talk 2morrow.

I silenced my phone and rubbed my aching forehead. I worried the guys were offended by my curt reply, but I had all these soul-sucking emotions. I needed a quiet minute. Lauren would be back in thirty, so I paced around the den and kitchen area.

What will I say to Lauren when Mom fills her in? Will she be angry at me for upsetting Pops? Will she want me to leave Walloon?

I rubbed my stomach, as if that would help calm the churning, then grabbed a diet coke from the fridge, popped the top, and took a long drink. It was probably my imagination, but I felt the caffeine blessedly flow into my bloodstream. Lauren had mentioned Stouffer's Lasagna for dinner, so I checked the freezer, removed the box, and then turned the oven to 375 degrees.

While waiting for the oven to heat up, I returned to the den and looked through the bookcases, chuck full of paperbacks interspersed with the occasional hardback. I was thinking that I'd find a book to take my mind off my current predicament when a group of four faux leather volumes caught my eye. My mother had similar ones.

Her high school yearbooks.

I slid Lauren's senior yearbook off the shelf and brought it back to the bar. I flipped through the shiny pages. First, I found Lauren's individual senior photo, the one where the girls wear that black shawl-like thing. She looked so young! Her hair was much blonder, and it cascaded over her shoulders. I read the caption under the photo that listed her activities and honors.

French Club 1,2- JV Cheer 1, 2- Varsity Cheer 3, 4- Social Com 1-4, National Honor Society 3,4, Homecoming Court 1-3, Homecoming Queen 4, JV Soccer 1,2 Varsity Soccer 3,4 Student-Athlete Award 3,4

I didn't realize Lauren was so popular or accomplished. She was featured on every other page, scarily like my sisters. I crash landed on page 114. There was Lauren—Homecoming Queen Class of 2001. She was standing next to the Homecoming King, and according to the caption, her boyfriend—Scott Foster.

Chapter 38

Ivey

Seriously? Lauren had the perfect opportunity to clue me in about Hattie's father being her high school boyfriend— but she big fat didn't. Why? I burrowed into the couch, holding my head in my hands. Why do people keep lying? I started to tear up. *Wait.* Lauren had mentioned something about Nan and Pops loving her high school boyfriend. That passing comment roared into my brain.

I rocked back and forth, hugging myself and wiping at my watering eyes. Lauren would be back any minute. I needed to calm down. I fanned my face. There must be a good (or awful) reason she kept that info nugget from me. Scott Foster must either mean a great deal to Lauren or extraordinarily little.

Ten minutes later, she breezed in the front door, lugging a giant tote bag full of paperwork. "Whew! It's starting to get windy out there. Something smells good." Lauren dropped the bag right inside the door.

I turned from the *New Girl* episode I wasn't watching. "The lasagna has about twenty more minutes." I informed her flatly.

She strode toward her bedroom. "Oh, thanks, honey! I appreciate you getting it started. I'll jump in the shower, then toss us a salad. Remember your lesson with Stassi tomorrow."

I was only half-listening when I heard Stassi's name. My mood brightened. I looked forward to doing something new and creative, away from this family stuff.

My aunt reminisced about her and my mother's childhood as we ate our lasagna in the den with plates on our laps. I couldn't help but think of Brother Isle and Rafe's adventures growing up at Walloon Lake.

Should I tell her about my talk with Pops? Or wait until my mom tells her?

Lauren cracked herself up with one memory. She and Mom had set up a tent, determined to "rough it" in the backyard. Mom was nine; Lauren was six. Pops had helped them set up the tent and brought Coleman lanterns as an alternative to a firepit. However, Mom and Lauren were undaunted in their desire for a true camping experience.

Mom had known that Uncle Paul, who was already a teenager, had a secret pack of cigarettes in his room.

And with those cigarettes was a Bic lighter.

So, Mom and Lauren had humored Pops into thinking they'd gone to sleep, all snuggled into way-too-warm sleeping bags, surrounded by all their stuffed animals. But heck no! Don't expect the Corbett girls to give up on a plan. Uncle Paul was at a friend's house, so once it got dark, and my grandparents were watching tv, the girls had sneaked back into the house, up to Uncle Paul's room, and found the lighter in a shoebox under his bed. Much to my grandparents' surprise, when they checked on the girls, they'd found them sitting around a successfully constructed fire pit, complete with bricks around the edges, roasting marshmallows.

Lauren slapped her knee when she finished her story, her smile wide. "Your mom and I were a sneaky team."

I rose to deposit my dinner plate in the sink. "Sounds like it!" An understatement, for sure.

Now tell me about your high school boyfriend who may or may not have covered up your ex-husband's disappearance.

Down girl. My thoughts were tacky, but I couldn't take even one more secret.

Chapter 39
Rafe

It was after midnight when Rafe had finally drifted off. A tap at the window startled him awake. Friends had summoned him that way in the past, but they normally texted ahead. He had no idea who this could be. Buried under the covers, he peered from under the blanket, hoping that if it was a serial killer, maybe he'd go away.

The tapping continued, so Rafe decided to face the would-be killer. He threw the covers off, jumped up, and made for the baseball bat propped against the wall. Rafe raised the bat over his head when he recognized the stricken face of his brother, Antonio, standing pitifully in the drizzle.

Rafe set down the bat, then cranked the window open. "Jesus, what the hell are you doing? Why don't you use the door like a normal person?"

Tonio looked side to side as if he expected someone to jump out of the overgrown hedges. "Meet me by the shed," he whispered. He turned, and slunk toward the backyard, not waiting for an answer.

Rafe stood for a minute, rubbed his neck back and forth, thinking he should ignore his brother's drama and go back to sleep. *He must be high, or he'd have texted me instead of acting like a shady-as-hell stalker.* Despite his trepidations, Rafe knew he had to find out what Tonio needed—even in the wind and rain.

Rafe pulled on the jeans he'd worn earlier, grabbed a tee shirt from his top drawer, slipped on an old pair of Crocs, then opened his bedroom door as quietly as possible. The last thing he needed would be for his father to find Tonio on the premises. Thinking about their last blowout made Rafe quake in his plastic shoes. He crossed through the den into the kitchen, feeling along the darkened hallway. When he got to the back door, Rafe saw his brother hunched over in the moonlight, cradling his left arm, bringing a cigarette to his lips.

He opened the sliding glass door just far enough to fit through sideways, slid it closed, then crossed the soggy few yards to the back of the Torres property.

He reached for his brother, but Tonio flinched away. "Okay, what's going on?" Rafe asked.

Tonio clutched his left arm again and winced. "I need your help, bro."

Rafe noticed Tonio's hoodie and jeans were ragged and dirty, like he'd been wearing them for days. "I figured that. What?"

Tonio looked down, took a drag of his cigarette then threw it on the muddy ground. "Let's talk in my car, come on." He started toward the side of the house.

Rafe looked up into the rainy sky, said a silent prayer, then followed.

Tonio had parked two streets down. The brothers walked together silently. It was windier than usual, but between gusts, the neighborhood was deathly still. They approached a beat-up primer coated El Camino that Rafe didn't recognize. *Oh, well,* Rafe thought. *The car is the least of my worries.* Then, *but what if it's stolen?*

Once in the car, Tonio tried to start the engine when Rafe grabbed his arm.

"Whoa, Tonio, look at me!" Rafe's brow wrinkled. "We're not going anywhere 'til you tell me what's going on."

Tonio took his hand off the ignition, his shoulders slumped. "Okay. I owe money to this guy, and I've been doin' some jobs to work it off—"

Rafe sighed. "God, man, did he do that to you?" He gestured at Tonio's arm.

"Do ya want me to tell you this, or not?" Tonio barked, turning to Rafe, his eyes now wide and his body rigid.

Rafe nodded. "Go on, go on."

Tonio crooked his thumb toward the rear of the car. "Anyhow, I have this thing in the back that he wants me to, uh, move, but I had to dig it up first, and I effed up my arm. I didn't know who else to ask." He hung his head. "I'm sorry to bug ya."

Rafe hoped he didn't sound as disappointed and terrified as he was. "What is it? Drugs? Money?"

Tonio gazed out the windshield. "I don't know, and I don't want to." Rafe looked in the same direction. "But it's heavy, and with this arm, I barely got it in the back."

Rafe rubbed his sweating palms on his thighs. "You've got some major self-control when you want to."

Tonio whipped his head toward Rafe. "What's that supposed to mean?" His eyes flashed, full of panic.

Rafe flinched back toward the car door. "I meant I'd want to check out what it is, chill!"

Tonio composed himself and took a deep breath in. "Well, if you knew this guy, you wouldn't want to know." Tonio cranked the ignition, then put the car in drive. "This is a bad idea. I'll drop you back at the house and figure something else out."

Rafe reached for his brother's shoulder. "Tonio, listen, come to the house with me. We'll tell Mom and Dad, and—"

Tonio stomped on the brakes. "Absolutely not!"

"I thought I'd give it a try," Rafe muttered. "But I'll help you, of course." He tugged on Tonio's good arm. "But you have to promise me that this is the last time you'll do anything to help whoever this is."

Tonio punched a string of navigation coordinates into his phone, set it on the dash, then gunned the engine. "Unfortunately, that's completely up to him."

Chapter 40
Rafe

The Torres brothers didn't talk as they followed the navigation-led twists and turns through the increasingly rainy night. The only other sound was the thump, thump of the windshield wipers.

"Approaching the destination," said Siri's soothing tone. "Caution! The coordinates lie outside the navigation area,"

"Yeah, no shit," remarked Tonio as the El Camino sloshed through muddy pools on the sparsely paved road. The thick vegetation formed a cavern of sorts as the car's headlights sliced through the darkness only a few feet ahead. "I hope we don't get stuck." The car hit a rut and threw the brothers forward and then back into their seats.

Rafe exhaled loudly. *My God, what will we do if we get stuck out here with whatever's in the back?* He reminded himself to take one catastrophe at a time, then said a quick prayer to be on the safe side.

"I guess we'll have to bury it as close as we can to the coordinates," Tonio said. He leaned toward the dash and squinted into the blackness. "I don't see any property markers or anything."

Rafe surveyed the area outside the car. "I wonder why they gave you coordinates instead of an address. Feels like a Jason Bourne movie."

"I've got no clue. Let's stop here and get on with it." Tonio pulled the car off the muddy road, shut off the engine, and squished his way to the tarp-covered bed at the back of the vehicle.

Rafe joined his brother, and they yanked the water-soaked cover to the ground. Inside the El Camino's open bed sat a cheap-looking mock treasure chest, like a prop for a pirate-themed party. It was made of plastic-coated particleboard rather than real wood, but it had an authentic-looking padlock attached.

Tonio glanced at Rafe as they pulled the trunk to the edge of the bed. "Another reason why I didn't look inside," he said, tugging at the lock.

Rafe nodded. "Okay, let me try it by myself, mind your arm." He clutched the trunk's metal handles.

"I don't think that's gonna—" Tonio protested, as he stepped out of the way.

Rafe had the pirate trunk halfway off the bed when he paused to balance it on his knees. Suddenly, his Crocs betrayed him, and his feet slipped under the back bumper of the car. Rafe landed on his posterior, stuck in the muck. "Damn!" He pushed the trunk back up onto the bed from his position on the ground, then scrambled to his feet. Tonio suppressed a grin, then helped Rafe with his good arm. Together, they lowered the trunk to the sopping ground. "I guess Crocs weren't the best choice." Rafe fruitlessly wiped at his jeans.

"There's a couple of shovels; grab 'em, will ya?" Tonio stayed focused as he slowly dragged the trunk further away from the car with his one good arm.

Rafe crawled halfway into the bed and fetched the shovels. Once he got them, he chucked one to his brother. "Well, the rain's made the ground softer—that's a plus!" he said with a crooked smile.

Tonio raised his eyebrows, jabbed the ground with his shovel, and they both began to dig.

Chapter 41

Rafe

Rafe was positive he'd never been so drenched and so muddy—not even when he was a kid. A quick look at his phone showed the time as 3:17 am. He clutched the crucifix around his neck. His stomach growled hungrily. He and Tonio had successfully buried the mystery trunk, and they were on their way back home. The gravity of the situation bore down on them as they drove in silence.

Tonio spoke first. "I'll never forget this, bro. Thanks. For doing most of the work." He glanced at his little brother. "Man, is there an inch of you not covered in mud?"

"You don't look much better." Rafe stifled a yawn. "You know, I'd do anything for you. To be honest, though, I'm scared shitless, and I'm sure we just broke about three hundred laws."

Tonio maintained his stoic veneer. "Probably not that many."

"I feel *so* much better," Rafe muttered. "So, you'll be square now? With this guy you owe?"

"If I'm lucky," Tonio said, flatly.

Rafe stretched forward, head down, elbows on his knees, then massaged his neck with both hands. "What do you mean if you're lucky? You told me once you did this job that you'd be out."

Tonio's shoulders sank. "I know."

"Did you lie to me just to get my help?" Rafe's voice reached a screechy pitch.

Tonio grunted and veered the car to the curb. Once parked, he rested his head on the steering wheel. "I know that Dad's painted this picture of me—"

Rafe couldn't keep the indignance out of his voice. "Dad's terrified for you."

Tonio lifted his head from the wheel and looked his brother in the eye. "I'm not as bad as Dad says. I've had some trouble, yeah. After high school I made stupid decisions, but I'm clean now, and I am trying to get myself out of this hole." His eyes were tired and teary.

Rafe relaxed his shoulders. "So, when will you know if this favor squares your debt?"

Tonio lifted his phone. "I already texted that it's done." He shook his head. "No reply yet, but that's not unusual."

Rafe wiped a smudge of dirt off his cheek. "I love you, Tonio. I want you to be okay."

Antonio smiled broadly for the first time that night. "That means a lot." He started the car again, looked back over his shoulder, then eased onto the asphalt.

Rafe glanced down at his filthy hands. "I'm not sure I can sneak back into the house without making a mess. Where are you staying?"

"I'm at a campground outside town."

A wave of unease washed over Rafe. "You're not in a tent, are you?"

Tonio kept his eyes fixed on the road as the rain pounded the windshield. "I rented the cheapest trailer in the park—it works for now."

They drove silently when Rafe thought about his day date with Ivey. "I went to Brother Isle last week."

Tonio's head jerked back. "Oh man, I haven't thought of that place in forever!"

Rafe ran a hand through his hair, then remembered all the mud. "It looks practically the same." He grinned. "It was cool to check it out—those were good times."

"Yeah, very good times," Tonio tapped the steering wheel. He smiled again. "What made you think to go there?"

Rafe wiped his hands on his shirt. "Y'know, I'm working at Lauren Corbett's store, and the girl I met—"

Tonio chuckled. "Ah, a girl, huh? Wait! I thought you were going with that smokin' hot Hattie something."

Rafe couldn't help but be surprised that Tonio knew anything about his life over the past year. "Yeah, she broke up with me a couple of months ago, but it's okay. She was, uh, challenging, and not in a good way."

"So, who's the girl from work?"

"Her name's Ivey, she's Lauren's niece." Rafe wasn't sure how deep he wanted to get into about Ivey, but he found talking to his brother about something other than, well, anything they'd talked about in the past few hours, surprisingly soothing.

Tonio raised his eyebrows. "Cute name, you like her?"

"Yeah, I do. She's super cool and chill, but she's only here for the summer so, who knows?"

The brothers cruised along for another ten minutes until Tonio flicked the right blinker on, and a broken-down pawnshop came into view. Rafe's eyebrows crinkled, concerned at this new development. "What're you doing?" His voice shrill. *Now what?*

Tonio pulled into the neighboring gas station parking lot, pulled around to the building's rear, and pointed at a rusty water faucet. "Let's rinse off before I take you home."

Tonio had towels in the back seat, so once they rinsed off as much mud as possible, they dried their faces and arms and spread the towels on the car seats. The somewhat drier seats made the rest of the drive more comfortable. Once they were back in Walloon, Tonio parked the car where they'd started earlier. The brothers exchanged a quick embrace, and Tonio thanked Rafe again for his help. Once Rafe exited the vehicle and started the walk home, Tonio leaned across the front seat and rolled down the passenger window.

"Rafe! Hey!"

Rafe returned and squatted at the driver's side door. "What?"

"I know I don't have to say this but, I do have to say this." Tonio's expression was grim. "Don't tell anyone about tonight. Especially not that new girlfriend."

Rafe clicked his tongue. "Of course, I won't. I'm not a moron."

Tonio clenched his jaw. "I'm dead serious." He drove away, leaving his brother standing on the sidewalk, shivering and sweating at the same time.

Chapter 42

Ivey

I didn't think it would be possible for Rafe to look terrible, but he proved me wrong. His shiny black hair looked dull and stringy; his skin was blotchy with dark circles under his usually bright eyes. He skulked slowly into the Sunnyside storeroom the next morning, rather than with his confident swagger. I stifled a gasp.

"Hey." Rafe spoke without making eye contact.

"Hey," I said, looking him up and down. Whatever happened to him last night probably explained why he didn't respond to my texts. I wanted to get his opinion about Lauren and Scott Foster. When he didn't text back, I figured he was asleep. "Are you okay? You look—not yourself."

Rafe sat down on one of the crates we'd used as "breakroom" chairs. "I didn't sleep well last night." His voice was low, somewhat guarded, as if it physically hurt to speak.

I sidled up to him. "You should go home; I can handle things for a few hours."

"I just need some coffee, didn't have time to make any this morning." He put his head in his hands.

I don't know if it was instinct or what, but I knelt and placed my hand on Rafe's sweaty forehead, brushing aside the lanky lock covering it. "You're burning up."

He clasped my hand and brought my palm to his lips. "Gracias, mija," Then he closed his eyes, settled his head on my shoulder, and fell asleep.

Lauren found us a few minutes later, right as my knees were aching to move. I'd wrapped Rafe up in my arms and let him snooze. I enjoyed his warmth, even if it was from a fever.

"Oh, my God, are you guys all right?" She, too, knelt, and placed her palm on Rafe's forehead.

He moved at the sound of Lauren's voice, so I pulled away slightly, still supporting his head. "He's definitely got a fever, but he dragged himself to work," I whispered.

"Let's get him to the house. Poor thing!"

We each took an arm and guided a barely cogent Rafe out to Lauren's Jeep.

Once we got to the house, I stood with Rafe slouched against me while Lauren readied the sofa with a sheet, pillow, and blankets. I scooted Rafe over to the sofa and tucked him in. He burrowed into the back of the couch with a sigh.

Lauren and I stood looking at him, our heads tilted sympathetically. "You don't think he's hungover, do you?" Lauren asked.

I winced. "I don't think so. I feel like I'd have smelled it on him."

Lauren nodded. "True, but—"

"But what?" I glared at my aunt. "You think he's on drugs?" I couldn't believe she would think such a thing. Rafe had been nothing but dependable and responsible while working with Lauren, and he genuinely cared for her.

She reached for me. "Of course not, I'm sure he's got a seasonal bug. I don't want to worry his parents, but I will let them know he's resting here." She pulled her cell from her back pocket. "I can't help thinking about his brother's problems, though."

Righteous indignation flooded my system. "Rafe is not like his brother!" I barked.

Lauren shushed me. "Let's go talk on the porch. Let him be." She went to the front door, but I hung back momentarily to watch Rafe lying there, snoring quietly. Obviously, my first impulse was to defend him against any assumptions, but, what if? No! I pushed the thought out of my brain, then joined my aunt outside.

She was on her phone, presumably with one of Rafe's parents. "Okay, no problem. I'll let him rest here. I assume he has his phone, but I'm not sure." Lauren held up a finger and glanced at the rocking chair next to me. I took a seat. Lauren checked her watch. "Ivey or I'll check on him at noon. Okay. See you at the Farm around two. Thanks, Marc."

She disconnected and set her sights on me. "I'm sorry I implied anything derogatory about Rafe. I guess my mind goes to the worst sometimes."

My indignance had waned. "I understand. I know you trust Rafe and want the best."

"I do. Plus, I have so much respect for Marc and Gabby. They've been through the mill with Antonio." Lauren paused. She fiddled with a strand of hair. "But that's not my place to discuss."

I arched a brow. "Well, you've brought it up two times in the last fifteen minutes." Wow, that came out a lot snarkier than I intended.

Lauren's lips tightened into a line. "Yes, I guess you're right. Has Rafe discussed his brother with you?"

I flashed to when Hattie Foster asked me the same thing. It seems that Antonio is Rafe's "scarlet letter." My tenth-grade lit teacher would be proud.

"He's mentioned that Antonio has had some hard times," I grudgingly admitted, wringing my hands on my lap.

Lauren pondered my words while gazing at the lake. "According to Marc, Antonio's been arrested twice for possession. He's been given suspended sentences both times due to prison overcrowding." Her face was grave. "Marc and Gabby asked him to move out about two months ago. It's been an agonizing process. I can only imagine it's been stressful for Rafe."

"Yeah," was all I could think of to say. Daisy and Rose were true pains in my ass but in the opposite way. The only involvement they've ever had with the police was when the Brandon High JV Cheerleaders held a Fraternal Order of Police fundraiser. Everyone thought it was super cute when dressed in their cheer uniforms, they presented a giant check to the Chief of Police. Barf!

Lauren rubbed her palms together. "I probably shouldn't have told you the Torres' business, but since you and Rafe are seeing one another—"

I stood up, feeling overly fidgety. "I don't know if I'd say we're seeing one another."

My aunt chuckled and patted my arm. "Okay, whatever you call it! Hanging out?"

I smiled despite myself. "Yeah, hanging out. I'd say that's it."

"Will you go open the store?" she asked me. "I'll leave Rafe a note to call us when he wakes up."

I nodded, then started down the path to the Square, wishing I could stay with Rafe.

Despite the earlier drama, the day continued about as boringly as a day could. Rafe texted both of us around 11:45, saying he felt better and could come back to work. Lauren texted back, telling him to sleep more and drink water. She insisted on driving him home on her way to Corbett Farm. Since the text chain included my aunt, I sent Rafe a thumbs-up and smiley emojis, but he sent me a heart.

Chapter 43
Ivey

Stassi Sumter had giggled when she saw Lauren and I sitting amongst the pile of wood and scattered nuts and bolts—looking forlorn and feeling out of our depth with the easel project.

Stassi had floated out of her 4Runner, wearing a magenta tunic, deep blue leggings and chunky black boots. "Oh, dearies! Let me help. I'm a whiz at construction." She'd climbed the porch stairs, dropped an Ikea bag full of supplies next to me, then had breezed back to her truck to extract a toolbox from the backseat.

Lauren and I had looked at each other with astonishment. We'd been working with an Allen wrench and a rusty Phillips head screwdriver possibly made in the 1940s.

An hour later, Stassi commented, "I think watercolor could be your medium," as she examined my first attempt.

I studied the sunflower filled vase she'd set up for this introductory lesson. "You think so?" My heartbeat faster at the compliment. I placed a foot on the porch to balance the stool we'd set up in front of my successfully assembled easel.

Stassi smiled at my question. "I definitely think you're a natural." She pointed at the paper tacked on the easel. "Now, remember, watercolor is all about layering. That's how we achieve depth. What do you think would add depth to the petals?"

Her hair smelled like coconut and moved forward as she leaned in. I hoped I didn't smell like sweat and rancid dry shampoo. "Um, let's see." I bit my lower lip." I glanced at the colors next to me. "Use a darker green to add shadow?" I tentatively dipped my brush in the olive paint.

Stassi stood up. "Yes! Wonderful!" She settled into a nearby rocking chair and fanned her face. "Keep goin', whew, its warm today."

I nodded as I studied my work. "Yep."

Lauren came through the front door with a tray of lemonades.

"You must have ESP." Stassi laughed. "Ivey and I are parched."

Lauren grinned, setting the tray on a side table. "So, how's our girl doing?" She glanced at my painting, her hands on her hips. "Oh, Ivey! It's just lovely."

I beamed and sat a little straighter. "Thanks." I could get used to all this praise.

Lauren pulled her car keys out of her purse and clicked the key fob. "You girls have fun; I need to pick up a few things at the grocery store. Ives, do you need anything?"

I told her that I didn't, and off she went.

Stassi and I chatted about my painting, technique, and her experience in the art world. "Well, I'm small-time—for now," she said with a confident wink. "But, in October, I'll have a few pieces at a Detroit gallery."

I turned to her. "That's amazing! Congrats."

She grinned. "Thank you. I'm psyched about it. I'm a member of an artist collective in Petosky. It's all artists under thirty who've grown up in the area."

"That's so cool to have a group to coordinate with," I replied, wondering how a collective functioned.

Stassi changed the subject before I had a chance to ask more. "So, how are things going this summer? Things good staying here with your aunt?"

"Yeah, it's been interesting." I tapped some color off my brush, then delicately added a few more strokes to the paper.

Stassi leaned forward, her bracelet laden wrists clicking as she set her chin on her hands. "Your answer is interesting. You seem a bit stressed, though. Let's take the paper off and let it dry flat."

I unclasped the clothes pins holding the watercolor paper and laid it gently next to the lemonade tray. I took a glass, sipped, then returned to my seat. I sighed. "Being here with Lauren is great."

Stassi rolled a finger. "Go on."

What should I tell Stassi? I don't know her. Come to think of it, I was saying that a lot lately. Who did I even truly know around here?

I waved my hand. "It's nothing. Family stuff."

Stassi looked at me with understanding eyes. "Ah, family stuff." She slowly nodded. "Families are challenging."

We sat in silence for what felt like minutes but was probably a few seconds. We sipped our drinks, waiting for my painting to dry—which didn't take long in the heat.

"You didn't know Lauren before she asked you about my art lessons? Right?"

Stassi set her glass down. "No, I didn't know her personally, of course, everyone around here knew your grandfather's store. I recognized her last name when she called me."

"Well, this summer is the longest period of time that I've spent in Walloon," I started. "And some of the things I've grown up thinking about my family—my grandparents, Lauren, may not be—" I felt my eyes go crazy wide. "Accurate."

She pondered my statement, grabbing her hair and twisting it behind her head. "What do mean 'accurate'?"

Now I'd done it.

I cleared my throat. "For example, my parents told me that Lauren and her husband divorced years ago. I mean, I literally remember my mother setting us down and telling us about it."

"Okay." Stassi sat patiently.

"Since I've been here, I found out that he basically, vanished, like poof!" I opened my fists like flashes. "So they didn't divorce, as I've always thought."

"That is intriguing." Stassi brought her hands behind her head and fiddled with her hair. "Is it possible that your parents honestly thought they'd divorced? That Lauren told them that?"

I chewed my bottom lip. "I don't think so. Lauren told me that my parents were fully aware that Uncle Michal disappeared."

Stassi nodded. "Hm. I wonder if it was in the news."

I shook my head. "Rafe and a friend of his googled it with me."

Lauren's Jeep crunched up to the house, back from her grocery run. Stassi and I waved. Conversation over.

Lauren brought the groceries in while I helped Stassi gather her supplies. We walked to her 4Runner where she left me with a nugget of wisdom. "In my experience, Ivey, truth will out, whether it's good or bad. You—" she pointed a finger at my heart "—you need to ready yourself for either outcome. My best piece of advice, if you want it?" She placed the supply bag in the backseat and slammed the car door shut.

"Yes! I do, very much." I clasped and unclasped my hands, impatiently.

Stassi climbed into the driver's side of the 4Runner, pulling her tunic in and stuffing it under her thigh. "I lessen stress by imagining the worst possible outcome, then making a plan to handle it."

I exhaled; a bit disappointed. "Oh." Why would I want to imagine the worst?

Stassi rubbed my arm. "I know, that sounds hideous, doesn't it? Just try it with something small. Once you have a plan to handle the worst outcome, you'll feel a sense of confidence. Then," she spread her arms as wide as the open door allowed. "When the worst doesn't happen, whatever does happen won't be that scary."

I raised my eyebrows. "That really works?"

Stassi pulled the door closed, but the window was open. "It sure does! See ya next week." She was off with a wave.

Chapter 44

Ivey

"I'm not kidding, you were adorable!" My cheeks hurt from grinning about Rafe's having fallen asleep the day before. "You kept mumbling in Spanish."

He palmed his forehead. "So embarrassing." He inhaled half the McGriddle we'd picked up for breakfast, before the Sunnyside opened this morning. Rafe licked his lips. "You weren't kidding about this—it's frickin' delicious!"

I smiled. "It's only got about three thousand calories, so enjoy!" I set my McGriddle down. "So why were you so exhausted yesterday? We were worried."

Rafe blushed and shifted in his seat. "Um, I'd stayed up late playing a horror game, so I was too jazzed to sleep. I guess."

"Well, my advice is to lay off the horror games." I raised my left eyebrow.

Rafe laughed. "You've got a brilliant grasp of the obvious, don't you?" He playfully rolled his eyes, but still, I sensed there was more behind his late night than he cared to explain.

"Ahh, sarcasm. The lowest form of comedy." I happily played along.

"You know you love it." His eyes twinkled.

I wadded up my McGriddle wrapper. "I do, for sure."

"Here, let me throw that away for ya." Rafe rose from his chair.

I handed him the wrapper and stood up as well.

"Oh," he whispered as we made our way to the storeroom. "Morgan asked us to meet up at Mariachi's later. He has a break around three thirty."

"I'm down," I whispered back.

Chapter 45

Ivey

I snuggled myself into the front seat of Rafe's truck, on our way to meet up with Morgan. "I'm excited to see the famous Mariachi's."

Rafe smiled. "It's a cool place to hang out. The stuffed poblanos rock." He shifted his eyes my way. "They're even better than my mom's."

"That's high praise, I'm sure." I looked down at my lap. "I have a confession to make." I made my voice sound flat and sorrowful. "I've never had a stuffed poblano."

We had stopped at a light, so Rafe turned to look at me, all sweet dark eyes, the corners of his mouth turned down. "That's the worst thing I've ever heard—we better get there quickly to correct this problem." When the light changed to green, he gunned the accelerator, and I grasped the door handle to steady myself.

"You're crazy!" I felt light as air as we cruised along.

I suppose I expected a hole-in-the-wall restaurant, nestled in a strip mall, with red, green, and white decorations—like our fave Mexican place at home, but Mariachi's turned out to be more upscale. When we pulled into the parking lot, I took in the stand-alone structure: windows all around, a pale-yellow exterior, and a vast covered outdoor dining area. Chunky terracotta pots in assorted sizes and colors dotted the entryway bursting with fragrant blooms and creeping succulents.

We entered, and the hostess took us to a well-worn leather booth which looked out onto the porch. In the center of the restaurant was a gleaming bar, surrounded by chrome-plated bar stools. The music was soft, and there weren't many people eating, but there were a few day drinkers.

Rafe caught me checking out the patio. "Do you want to sit outside?"

"Oh, no! I like it here. The AC feels great." That was one thing about the store—despite being Michigan, it got hella hot and stuffy in the open-air Market.

Morgan appeared and slid into the booth next to me. "Hey, guys! Thanks for comin' over!" He gave us a goofy, toothy grin. He and Rafe bumped fists.

"Thanks for inviting us!" I piped up. My stomach growled.

Morgan set his laptop on the table. "I only have about a thirty minute break. Do you want to see what I found out or eat something first?"

We looked at each other, then Rafe insisted, "Food, please!"

Morgan took our order—stuffed poblano plates for Rafe and me, then he went into the kitchen and fetched us chips and salsa. Another waiter, Kyle, brought us a pitcher of Coke and glasses.

Once we were all back in the booth, Morgan opened the laptop he had fetched when he'd ordered our food. "Okay, I recalled when Ivey mentioned Michal hanging out at a local bar. I couldn't remember the name only that it rhymed."

"The Walloon Saloon," I reminded him.

"Right! There aren't that many bars with rhyming names, so it was fairly easy, but!" Morgan said with a wave of his hand. "The place changed its name to The Wheelhouse." He turned the computer screen so Rafe and I could see the photo. Despite the new name, everything else about the bar looked worn down.

Rafe pulled the computer closer, his brows knit together as he scanned it. "It's strange that I've never heard of this place. It's only a few miles away."

Morgan slid the laptop back in front of himself. "For good reason; it's not really a family place. My research told me that the police spend a lot of time there—and *not* drinking after their shifts." He clicked a key with flourish. "That was a big part of the name change—an effort to clean up their image. I spoke with the owner, Peter Habibi, and, wait for it, he remembers your uncle."

Excitement zipped through my veins. I felt like I was glowing. Someone outside the family knew Uncle Michal. "That's amazing! Can we talk to him?" I practically levitated out of the booth.

"Great job, man. I knew you'd find something helpful." Rafe took a salsa-laden chip and loudly munched on it.

Morgan grinned, obviously proud of his discovery, "Thanks. How about we go tomorrow afternoon?"

Rafe and I nodded in agreement just as Kyle materialized with our food and carefully placed the hot plates on the table. The poblanos smelled heavenly! Spicy and fragrant. "Hot plates." Kyle reminded us.

Between bites, we discussed the yearbook photo connecting Lauren with Hattie's father. I mentioned how confused I'd been that she hadn't divulged that relationship when we'd talked about Uncle Michal.

"Your aunt's so nice, Ivey," Morgan said. "Maybe she truly doesn't think her dating Hattie's dad was any big deal."

I dabbed at my mouth with my napkin. "You may have a point." I shrugged. "I mean, she specifically asked me to confirm that Hattie's last name was Foster, but then—"

My contrary brain chided me. Nothing good would come from sticking my nose in things that weren't my concern. I mean, we all have things that we don't want to discuss, right? Was I betraying my aunt by snooping into her past? Probably. On the other hand, I'm a part of this family too! What's wrong with wanting to know the truth? An unpleasant warmth enveloped me, my face flushed, and my stomach churned up. Oh my God, am I having an allergic reaction to the poblano? I sipped my soda, which settled my stomach somewhat. I started to calm down. Just a garden-variety anxiety attack. Having such a physical response to the conversation felt like the dumbest thing, but I fought through it successfully.

Morgan drummed his fingers on the table, looking into space. "Maybe your aunt had a horrible breakup with Mr. Foster? That's why she didn't mention it?"

Rafe set his fork on his plate. "Or was it so inconsequential that she didn't think it worth mentioning?"

We all went silent, pondering. I wrang my hands under the table, still battling the aftermath of my anxiety.

"All breakups have drama, right?" Morgan dipped a chip in the salsa. "Although, I have zero personal experience in that arena." He poked out his bottom lip which lightened the mood.

Rafe snorted. "Yes, they do have drama."

I flashed on my breakup with Oliver and then swallowed some rice. "I guess it's a rite of passage. Still…"

"Speaking of Hattie." Rafe clicked his tongue. "Not that we were. I wonder if she knows about her dad and Lauren?"

I pointed my fork at him. "I'm one hundred percent sure she would have mentioned it when she ambushed me the other day."

Morgan took a couple big mouthfuls of food, closed his laptop, then slid out of the booth. "I've got to get back to it, but I'll come to check on you guys." He tucked the computer under his arm with a grin, took the empty pitcher, and hurried back to the kitchen.

I turned my attention to Rafe, who had consumed his entire poblano, while I'd only eaten three bites.

He could probably eat two more peppers and not gain one ounce. Totally off topic, but I wondered if guys think about their weight as much as girls. It's perhaps like Kelli jokes—God's most likely a man. Of course, I know God's not a man or a woman. Well, I don't know for sure, that's what I think, what I've always believed. He's like an entity—

"You, okay?" Rafe's voice pulled me out of my head. "You look far away." He laced his fingers together over his empty plate.

"I was thinking about God being a man." I decided to disengage my "talking to guys" filter for the moment. It's kind of like the family holiday filter—nothing heavy at the table.

Cute little wrinkles formed around Rafe's eyes. He settled back and draped his arms across the back of the booth. "Now, I didn't expect you to say that!"

I half-smiled. "I know I'm random."

"Not at all, tell me more." He laser focused on me.

I was thrilled his eyes hadn't gone all blank. I told him about Kelli's theory and how my mind had wandered to the God issue after my initial thoughts about weight.

Rafe nodded. "Guys worry about their weight, too—for sure. But we don't talk about it much. I've always been skinny, though. I got teased about it. Here look at this." He pulled his phone out and furiously swiped until he found what he wanted.

I pushed my plate aside and leaned forward to check out the photo. A smaller and slenderer Rafe was on the screen, standing next to a pleasantly plump older gentleman seated in a lounger. I had to cover my mouth to keep from screaming at the cuteness.

"Is that your grandpa?" I grabbed the phone without asking. "Oh, sorry!"

Rafe laughed. "Please go ahead and look. There are a few more pics if you swipe. They were from Christmas when I was seven or eight. Anyhow, you can see my Tito put on a few pounds over the years. Maybe I will too!"

I handed back the phone. "You are both adorable. And handsome. Thank you for showing me. You had some major front teeth action."

He gritted his gorgeous white teeth together, so I got a good look. "I did, didn't I? I hope I've grown into them."

I can't believe he doesn't know how hot he is. "Erm, yeah, you definitely have grown into them."

Rafe pocketed his phone. "I know girls worry about their weight all the time. My mom talks about it, and Hattie went on and on about it—she needed me to assure her that I didn't think she was fat, completely annoying." He scratched his forehead. "Wait, do I sound like an asshole?"

I squirmed, hearing Hattie's name again. Seriously, I needed to get over Rafe having dated her. "No, you don't. Weight's a touchy issue. I've known girls with eating disorders, and it's terrible. Luckily, my sisters and I tend toward being thin. But it's always in the back of my mind. I don't like to eat too much in front of people. I don't know. I guess that's warped, huh?

Rafe's face scrunched up; his voice lowered an octave. "That sucks. I don't think *anyone* should feel self-conscious about eating—it's a basic human function!"

"It's just the way it is, I guess." I shrugged.

Rafe rearranged the utensils on his plate. "Back to the God thing." He folded his napkin and tucked it next to the plate. "It's a fascinating subject. I know He's not a man per se, but I picture Him as an old guy with white hair and a long beard." He chuckled. "Probably from the illustrations in my kid's Bible. Does your family go to church?"

I mimicked his napkin folding then pushed my plate toward the table's edge. "We haven't gone very often since we moved to Florida, but we went to a Methodist church in San Antonio. Your family's pretty devout?" I popped a chip in my mouth.

Rafe pulled a silver cross on a leather cord from his collar. "We're Catholic, so we go to St. Francis every Sunday. The Church has gone through some serious stuff, and I wonder how things will shake out, but it's important to my parents that I go with them, especially since Tonio left the house." He got a faraway look on his face when he mentioned his brother's name.

I readjusted my crossbody bag, so I could access my wallet. "My dad grew up Catholic, but he drifted away from organized religion after his time in Afghanistan. Mom's family was Methodist, so she wanted us to attend some type of worship when we were little."

Rafe's eyes shined. "Wow! I knew your dad was in the military, but he served in Afghanistan. That's sick!"

I half-smiled because my dad's achievements aren't mine to take credit for. "Thanks—we're proud of him, for sure." I sighed. "He doesn't talk about it, which is kinda disappointing. It's got to be one of the most intense things a person can do—fight in a war."

"I completely agree. I'm both fascinated and scared when I think about serving in the military," Rafe replied.

Morgan appeared and gave us our bill. Rafe offered to pay, which was another example of his gentlemen-ness, but I insisted on paying for my own meal. We discussed meeting Morgan after work tomorrow to visit The Wheelhouse together.

I wondered what I would learn about my mysterious uncle. I hoped that Mr. Habibi had good things to say, but in my heart, I doubted it.

Chapter 46
Ivey

We drove back to the house after we'd settled our bill, both of us chatting excitedly about getting potential deets about my uncle. Unexpectedly, Rafe stomped on the brake so hard that the seatbelt gouged my shoulder.

"What the—?" I gasped, grasping my chest while glaring at Rafe. His face turned sickly pale, his eyes bulged, and his body shook as he stared out the windshield. He didn't verbally respond, as he jammed the truck in reverse, glanced over his shoulder, and skidded away from Lauren's house. But we'd both seen the police car parked next to Lauren's Jeep.

"Wait! We need to check on Lauren!" I screamed as he maniacally maneuvered the vehicle onto Main Street and gunned the engine. "Rafe! Slow down!" I pulled on his arm.

He yanked his arm away from me. "Shut up!" His voice was terrifying, and his beautiful white teeth were clenched. "You don't get it."

I flashed on two disturbing memories simultaneously: the first time I saw Rafe and the last time I spoke to Oliver. My mouth went dry, and I clutched my arms protectively around myself. "Rafe, please," I said, with the calmest tone I could muster, despite my racing heartbeat. I couldn't believe Rafe's transformation. Do all guys have this petrifying side?

His head swiveled but he looked past me. Sweat dripped from his forehead; his mouth was a hard line.

My instinct told me to jump out of the truck and sprint back to Lauren's, but good sense took over. I tentatively reached for Rafe's arm again. My whole body quivered, like my bones had turned to noodles. "Rafe, pull over. It's okay." I held my breath, hoping he'd listen.

He finally took his foot off the gas, and the truck decelerated. I pointed to an upcoming gravelly patch, and he steered the truck toward it. Rafe turned off the engine, and we sat there, both of us hyperventilating.

Rafe's whole demeanor softened. His shoulders dropped as his breathing evened out. His fathomless brown eyes teared up. "I'm so sorry." His voice cracked as if speaking was painful. "I don't know. I don't. Seeing the police—" He grasped wildly at my hands.

Despite my own raging concern for Lauren, I disengaged my seat belt, scooted as close as the seats would allow, and then placed my palm on his cheek. "It's okay. We're okay. Just catch your breath." Why is he freaking out so badly? It's not like he's done anything wrong.

Rafe muttered "sorry" a few more times before he eventually got his terror under control. "I'm good. I'm good." He rubbed his palms together, then on his jeans. "I don't know why I freaked like that. I'll take you back." He wiped his forehead with the back of his hand.

He'd put on a forced smile, but I didn't buy it. "Look, I don't like seeing the police either. It makes me want to pee myself if I see one while I'm driving."

Rafe snorted, then inhaled deeply. "Thanks."

I retook his hand—it was sweaty and shaky. "We can't let Lauren deal with the police alone. Who knows? Maybe there was a break-in at the store or trouble at the Farm? Don't you want to make sure everyone's good?"

Rafe sniffed, then nodded. "Of course, of course. I hadn't even thought of that." He tried to start the engine, but I stopped him.

"Wait a minute." The blood rushed to my head. I hoped he didn't get angry again. "Rafe, I can't have you telling me to shut up, no matter how freaked out you are." The words hung in the air between us as I waited for his response.

Rafe brought his hands to his face. "Oh, Ivey, I'm so incredibly sorry." His hands went to his lap. He gazed at me, his lips trembling. "I didn't even realize I said that. I'm such a shit."

My heart turned to mush as I clasped his hands again, bringing them to my chest. "No, you're not."

He leaned over and softly placed his lips on mine. My heartbeat skyrocketed and my skin caught fire—this time with excitement, not terror. Rafe's lips were firm and intoxicating, lingering on mine as the moment's passion flooded through me. I leaned forward, laced my arms around his neck and pull him closer. His mouth was soft and tangy from sweat and salsa. Time stood still as we clung together. My mind blurred as I breathed him in, forgetting my aunt, my uncle, and anything else except that exact moment.

When we pulled away, he tilted his head and studied me, blinking those long dark lashes. "I've wanted to do that for a while." A flicker of concern came over him. "I hope that's okay."

I sat back, my lips still tingling. I sighed dreamily then pulled the seat belt across my chest. "I'm glad you did."

We drove back to the house, and Rafe pulled his truck alongside the police car. "Do you mind if I take a minute to get myself together?" He looked pale again, but not angry.

I nodded. "Of course. You don't have to come in if you don't want to." Please come in with me. I'm not sure I can handle all this by myself. "I'll understand." My eyes welled up, so I blinked to keep from tearing up.

Rafe smiled and pecked my cheek. "I'm coming in, don't worry."

"Only if you want to." I flipped the mirrored visor down, smoothed my hair as well as I could, then climbed out of the truck. I dashed in the screen door where I found my aunt slumped over, softly weeping into a tissue. The Sheriff, a fit man around fifty, rose from the couch next to Lauren and extended his hand.

"You must be Ivey. I'm Edgar Preston, Charlevoix County Sheriff." His demeanor was professional, and his expression solemn.

Lauren lifted her head and waved me over next to her.

I shook the sheriff's hand. "Yes, I'm Ivey Des Jardins, Lauren's niece. What's going on?"

"Ivey, honey! Please sit," Lauren beckoned, blubbering.

I ground my teeth and my stomach churned as I sank onto the couch next to Lauren and put my arm around her back. "What's going on?" I repeated, directing the question to my aunt this time. Rafe had followed me into the house, but he stayed at the door. It was clear that the Sheriff had told Lauren something much worse than shoplifting.

Lauren sobbed out, "They've found Michal's body!"

My breath caught in my throat. "What?"

"Lauren, may I fill Ivey in?" The Sheriff calmly asked.

She nodded, then fell against my shoulder.

I glanced at Rafe, who nodded for me to go on. "Please."

Sheriff Preston seated himself on the adjacent loveseat and focused his clear blue eyes on me. "We received an anonymous tip on our crime hotline that led us to decomposed remains. We believe the remains to be Mr. Lyska and that he may have been murdered."

Lauren flinched, then descended into sobs. I squeezed her, so she knew I was fully here for her. "I don't know what to say," I whispered through her messy curls. "Should we call Mom? Nan and Pops?" She didn't answer, only moaned, and sobbed. I pulled her closer, feeling her quivering shape reverberate against me.

The Sheriff pulled a notebook-sized photo from a folder and handed it to me. "I've asked Lauren to keep this information to herself for the time being. I'm here because I needed her to identify a piece of jewelry we found among the remains."

My hand shook as I grasped at the photo. A gold ring. The photo showed a close-up of an interior inscription:

LC & ML All my love

The sheriff folded his hands and set them on his lap. "Lauren has confirmed that she gave this ring to Mr. Lyska on their wedding day." He tilted his head in a comforting way.

Tears sprang from my eyes, which made the room blur. I heard Rafe speak up.

His voice sounded edgy, sharp and a bit rude. "How do you know someone didn't plant that ring?"

The Sheriff swiveled. "And you are?" He sounded annoyed by the interruption.

Rafe stepped forward and offered his hand to the Sheriff. "I'm Rafe Torres. My father manages Corbett Farm."

Sheriff Preston rose halfway and took Rafe's hand. "Oh, yes, You're Marc's younger boy. You make a good point, Rafe. Asking Lauren to identify the ring is just one step.

Rafe nodded; his shoulders seemed to relax.

The Sheriff collected the ring photo from me, then turned back to Rafe. "I hope I can count on your discretion, son."

Rafe rocked back on his heels, then placed his palm on the wall, steadying himself. I could see and feel how agitated Rafe still was. He rubbed his neck, which I had come to know as a habit. Our eyes briefly met, and my thoughts went back to our kiss just minutes ago. My emotions had fluctuated wildly in the past ten minutes. The angry and menacing Rafe had peeked through when he spoke with the sheriff.

Lauren was barely coherent, so I asked, "Other than the ring, how do you know the, uh," I couldn't bring myself to say the word *body*, "that it's my uncle?"

The sheriff turned from Rafe back to me and Lauren. "We've preliminarily identified the remains through dental records. We contacted Dr. Patrick Elias when the ME notified us about the ring. Michal Lyska is the only outstanding missing person in the County, so thankfully, our preliminary identification proceeded quickly."

Rafe had inched away from the front door but remained separate from the vortex of emotion in the den. He ran his fingers through his hair. The air in the room hung heavy and humid.

Sheriff Preston continued, "Our crime scene investigators still have a few reports to complete, plus the DNA confirmation will take another two weeks, hopefully, less." He removed several business cards out of his breast pocket and set them on the coffee table. "Please reach out to me with any questions over the next few days. I've also added Grace Rictor's card. She's an excellent counselor, and she's helped guide families through situations like this."

The Sheriff took Lauren's hand as he knelt in front of her. "I'm so sorry, again. You can count on me to find out what happened to your husband."

Lauren grasped his hand with both of hers. "Thank you, Ed."

The Sheriff turned to me. "I know it may be challenging to keep this quiet until we complete our investigation. Please reach out to me or Grace with any questions or concerns." Sheriff Preston deftly rose from the floor and hitched up his pants. I caught a glimpse of his holstered weapon which only solidified the gravity of this situation in my head and heart. Seeing a gun so close made me shiver.

The sheriff whispered something to Rafe as he approached the front door.

I turned my attention to Lauren. "Let's get you to your room." I'd planned to tuck her in, bring her a drink, and encourage her to rest, but I found moving Lauren off the couch proved challenging. She was like a stone buried deeply in the earth. I wasn't sure she even registered what I'd said.

Rafe closed door behind the sheriff. I asked him to help me move my aunt, so we each took an arm and gently eased her off the sofa. Lauren's head hung sorrowfully, as she continued to sob. "Oh, Ivey, Michal's dead—how could this happen? This must be a mistake, right?"

"I don't know, Aunt Lauren." I looked pleadingly at Rafe, hoping he might have something to add. "All we can do is wait for the police to finish their investigation."

I couldn't believe this was happening.

"Everything'll be clearer after you get some sleep. Ivey's right," Rafe finally said, backing me up.

I beamed at him. Lauren allowed us to guide her into her bedroom, where Rafe propped her up as I pulled back the duvet and top sheet. We eased her down onto the mattress, removed her Nikes, then tucked her legs under the covers. I assured her that I'd be right back. We tiptoed out of the room and closed the door.

Back in the den, I fell into Rafe's arms and burst into tears.

He pulled me close and set his cheek on my head. "It's okay, everything's gonna be okay." His voice was soft and soothing, his chest warm and solid.

"Do you really think so?" I whined into his shirt. Waves of fear and panic crashed through me.

He hesitated a beat too long. "Of course, it will." I looked up at his beautiful face, genuinely serious and concerned. "What can I do to help?"

I reluctantly pulled away from his comforting embrace. "Could you pick up some Tylenol PM to help Lauren sleep?" I wiped at my stuffy nose.

"I sure will. Is there anything else you need?"

I walked over to the fridge to check. "Maybe some bottled water?"

Rafe followed me into the kitchen, then kissed my cheek, sending pleasant shards of electricity zinging up and down my spine. "You'll be all right?" He rubbed my arm.

I nodded. "I will. I don't know what I would have done if you hadn't been here. What did the Sheriff say to you before he left?" I hesitated. "Only if you want to tell me."

Darkness flickered over Rafe's face, but it dissolved just as quickly. "He offered to talk to my dad about your uncle's discovery. Apparently, Lauren agreed to it before you and I showed up."

"Oh yeah, right." Lauren had two businesses. I chewed the side of my thumbnail while I thought about what this news could mean for Corbett Farm and the Sunnyside. "Your dad certainly has the farm covered, but the Sunnyside…"

Rafe squeezed my hand and then made for the front door. "Let me run out, and we'll talk when I get back."

It occurred to me that Rafe had stayed with Lauren and I despite his intense desire to flee from the cops. "Hey, are you okay?"

He nodded. "I'm fine." But his voice was weary, exhausted. He closed the front door gently.

I stood there, in the cheerful kitchen, sunflowers everywhere, absorbing the weight of the day's events. My uncle was dead and, possibly had been for years. Morgan's suppositions about his whereabouts suddenly weren't so far-fetched. My mind was on full tilt. On the one hand, the mystery of my uncle's whereabouts seemed solved. But why was he killed? And who could have done it? The Sheriff told us that an "anonymous" tip led the police to his remains.

I couldn't help but wonder who had tipped the police off. Why now, after all these years? Could Hattie's digging into my family have anything to do with it? Oh my God, how could I possibly ask Lauren anything about her relationship with Hattie's father now?

Chapter 47

Rafe

Rafe had to purposefully move his feet forward after he left Lauren's house. His head felt heavy. The weight of realizing how utterly naive he'd been, thinking the other night's events would fade into the past.

How could he have been so stupid? Why did he help Tonio bury that damn trunk? He couldn't speak to Tonio's state of mind, but Rafe had had to suspend his good judgment through the whole thing. The breath caught in his chest. He steadied himself by the truck, both hands pushing against the driver's side door, willing himself to stay upright, not retreat to the fetal position his body craved. The sheriff's whispered comments played through his brain on repeat—the parts Rafe hadn't disclosed to Ivey.

"Now that I see you up close, Rafe, the resemblance between you and Antonio is remarkable. I hope *you're* staying out of trouble." The sheriff had continued about alerting his father while Rafe's body had slowly turned to ice. Now that he was outside, breathing fresh air, Rafe asked himself a million questions. The police discovery was just coincidental, right? The Sheriff didn't get into where the remains were even found. But, he couldn't help wondering if he or Tonio had left fingerprints. No, they'd worn those yellow kitchen gloves, and Tonio took them away. Rafe wondered if his brother had disposed of the gloves. Hopefully, Tonio wasn't driving around with them in that El Camino.

The El Camino. Was it Tonio's? Could the cops trace the tire tracks? It had rained so hard that night; the mud had slopped all over, and the tires had spun several times. No, there weren't tracks. He was sure of it.

Not that he had any connection to the car Tonio drove that night, except—his fingerprints would be on the car's interior.

Calm down, breathe. Don't be such an idiot.

Rafe climbed into his truck, backed out, and onto Main Street. He figured the best thing to do was to behave as normally as possible. He'd go to the CVS, pick up the Tylenol and water, bring them back to Ivey, then make an excuse to get home.

He could do this.

Rafe switched on the satellite radio and listened to an MLB channel as he drove the three miles to CVS. Despite it being summer, when Walloon Lake was the most populated, Rafe felt isolated, like the only person in town. The drug store's parking lot was empty, so he eased into a front space, exited the vehicle, and pressed the key fob to lock it. Rafe stood looking at the small, black device when he thought to pick up a prepaid phone.

A burner would be the safest way to contact Tonio from now on.

Back in his truck, Rafe had to use a buck knife to get the phone out of the package. "Hey, it's me."

"Are you okay?" Tonio's voice sounded jagged and gaspy.

After bringing Ivey the CVS items, Rafe had parked down a dead-end road outside Walloon Lake. "No, I'm not. What we did the other—" His words shot out.

"Don't talk about it, " Antonio warned.

"I need to talk to you, if not now, asap." Acid rose in Rafe's throat, threatening to choke him. The truck's cab stifled him, so Rafe cracked his window and inhaled deeply.

Antonio groaned. "Alright, be vague."

Rafe took the phone from his ear and looked at it, frowning. *How am I supposed to be vague?* "Tonio, the cops got a tip and found some human remains. I'm pretty sure they found what we buried the other night. I hope I'm wrong."

"No!" Antonio shouted, then lowered his volume abruptly. "How do you know all this?"

Just thinking back to earlier in the evening made Rafe's body tense. "The Sheriff was at Lauren Corbett's. He thinks the remains are her ex-husband," Rafe continued. "Did you have any idea about any of that?"

Antonio didn't answer right away.

His brother's silence bore into Rafe's bones. "Tonio?"

"I told you that night—I didn't ask," Antonio finally said. "This is bad. Let me think. Where are you?"

Rafe heard his brother's rapid breathing. "I'm parked at the end of Sanders Industrial. I didn't say anything, y'know, to the Sheriff."

"Obviously, we'd both be screwed," Antonio deadpanned.

Rafe gazed out the windshield at the star-filled sky. "Yeah." On any other night, he'd love this part of living in Walloon. It was far enough from a big city to see the stars on a clear night like this. Especially in the summer, when the days were long, it was almost like the stars knew they didn't have as many hours to shine, so they tried harder to put on a fantastic show.

Rafe heard the tv channels flipping in the background on his brother's side of the phone.

"I'm checking the news, and I don't see anything." said Antonio.

"The sheriff told us to keep quiet until the DNA results come in, like two weeks."

"Okay, how'd they know who's body it was then?" Antonio's voice cracked.

Rafe hung his head. "That part's super sad. They found his wedding ring. This is unbelievable." Tears pooled in his eyes.

Tonio cleared his throat. "Keep this phone on you, man. You were smart to buy it. Go home—get some sleep. I'll figure out what to do,"

That did it. A curtain of teardrops rained down from Rafe's eyes. The kindness in his brother's voice undid him. "Okay," was all he could say.

"Hey, bro. None of this will come back on you. I promise—no matter what," Antonio assured him. "I love you."

"Love you, too." Rafe rubbed ferociously at the tears on his cheeks.

Chapter 48
Hattie

Hattie knew it was wrong to revel in her father's discomfort, but it felt so satisfying. "You seem agitated this morning, Dad. Anything up at work?" Her mother and Adam had left earlier, so she and her father sat at the breakfast bar. Hattie had wanted to sleep in, but her bedroom abutted her parents, so she roused herself when she heard her father get up.

Liza topped up Hattie's father's coffee. "I'm sure Mr. Foster has everything under control, Miss Hattie. How would you both like your eggs?"

"Poached, please, on an English muffin?" Hattie replied. "You're the best, Liza!"

Hattie's father looked up from his phone and grunted, "Same."

Hattie poked her father's arm. "Dad, you're being rude. It's so embarrassing!"

Liza tutted, shrugged her shoulders, then turned to the six-burner gas stove behind her and cracked an egg.

Hattie's father finished sweetening his freshly poured coffee and sipped hastily. "For God's sake, Hattie, Liza knows how much I appreciate her. Right, Liza?"

Liza turned and flashed her long-time employer a sincere smile. "Of course, Mr. Foster." She returned to the eggs.

Hattie's father continued, "As a matter of fact, things at work are just fine, but thanks for asking."

"Good, that's great, Dad. I worry that you work too hard." Hattie remarked, sweet as saccharine.

Her father burst into laughter. "You've got to be kidding me? Since when?"

Hattie was surprised at her father's mirthful and frank reply. "You don't think I care about your health? What kind of a daughter do you think I am?" She placed her hand at her neckline, feigning a shocked expression.

Scott's face slightly softened. "I think you are a brilliant daughter, and the best sister Adam could ever have." He patted her knee.

She dutifully smiled at her father but remained suspicious of his unusually straightforward response. "Thanks, I think."

"Poached eggs on muffins," Liza announced, with a lilt in her voice. She set a plate in front of each Foster. "I'm going to do some laundry now. Do you need anything else?"

"I'm good, Liza, thank you!" Hattie's father pronounced, his eyes firmly on his daughter.

She met her father's stare with a self-satisfied squaring of her shoulders. "I'm good too. I'll put the plates in the dishwasher for you."

"Thank you, darling!" Liza shouted on her way to the terrace-level laundry room.

Just as her father took a big bite of his egg sandwich, Hattie poked the metaphorical bear. "So, Dad, I looked through your high school yearbook the other day."

Her father's barstool squeaked as he slowly turned, pointedly chewing his food. Heat built in Hattie's belly. Her father's calm demeanor now felt threatening.

"And?" His sharply prominent Adam's apple rose and sunk as he swallowed.

Hattie struggled to maintain her wits, but her voice remained confident and steady. "I was surprised to see a photo of you as Homecoming King. You never mentioned that before, even when I was on the Court last year."

"It was a long time ago."

"I know, but—"

Her father now faced her, their knees almost touching. "I get the feeling you want to ask me something else." His black eyes drilled into her lilac tinted ones. "What is it?"

Hattie went all in. "You dated Lauren Corbett—why did you lie about knowing her?"

Her father's face didn't move, granite-like. His expression unreadable. Was he angry? Frightened? Annoyed? His eyes flashed while he inhaled. "I didn't lie, Hattie. I don't know Lauren Corbett anymore. I knew her for a brief period when we were kids."

Hattie tilted her head and looked at him warily. "Dad, please don't 'lawyer' me. You flat-out lied, and you know it!" She slammed her tiny fist, so her multiple bangles clanked on the marble counter. "Walloon's a small town, but the only time I've ever heard the name Corbett has been concerning the hardware store." She wriggled off the barstool. "It's like you've pointedly treated her whole family like ghosts."

Her father winced at the word "ghosts" and flattened his lips. "Okay, you are being ridiculously dramatic—"

Hattie stamped her foot like a toddler in a toy store. "Dad!"

He put up his hands, signaling for calm. "I'll tell you the boring story behind Lauren Corbett and myself. Sit down and finish your breakfast, for God's sake."

Hattie clicked her tongue, sighed disgustedly, then climbed back on the barstool. "Finally."

"Lauren and I dated junior and senior year. She went off to Michigan State, and I went to Northwestern, and our romance faded—that's that. I met your mom, and Lauren met her husband. When we returned to Walloon, we had nothing in common." He took a quick sip of coffee. "It's not like Lauren sought me out either. Satisfied?"

Hattie chewed her lip. "Who broke up with who?"

He glanced at his Tag Heuer watch. "I don't remember. I think it was mutual."

Hattie looked down at her plate and shook her head. "I don't believe you."

Her father's countenance relaxed somewhat when his cell phone vibrated. He pushed his plate away, then rose from his seat staring at the phone with some bewilderment. "Well, you have a right to your opinion, honey." He kissed the top of her head and strode out of the kitchen.

Hattie sat there, feeling admonished and patronized. She knew there had to be more to him and Lauren's connection than her dad was letting on. He had built his whole career by making, cultivating, and keeping relationships. He needed to have the public behind him. Why would he keep a decades-long silence with a family of local business owners? Unless there was bad blood. Very bad blood.

She finished her breakfast, then gathered their plates and brought them to the porcelain farm sink. Instead of simply rinsing the dishes and putting them in the dishwasher, Hattie decided to wash them herself. She pulled on a pair of kitchen gloves and turned the faucet all the way hot. As she stood there waiting for the water to warm, Hattie reviewed their conversation. Dad had *seemed* sincere when answering her questions. She knew that he was not only a trial attorney, but a politician.

Was she inventing a drama where there was none just 'cause Ivey bugged the hell out of her? Dad was cool as a tray of ice cubes this morning, but he had definitely reacted (in his low-key way) when she brought up Lauren Corbett.

She finished the plates, swished soapy water in the coffee mugs, and set everything on a nearby dish towel to dry. Hattie switched off the faucet and yanked the gloves off just as a startling crash came from the front of the house. She dropped the gloves and sprinted down the hallway toward the front living and dining rooms, her bright pink Sketchers split splatting along.

"What happened?" Hattie cried, as she came upon her father standing in the arched ceiling entryway next to a pile of crystal shards—the remnants of her mother's favorite Murano vase.

Her father didn't take his eyes off his phone. "It's nothing. I bumped the table. Would you get Liza to clean this up? Mom and Adam will be back soon—gotta go." He strode out of the front door, slamming it in his wake.

Hattie stood there looking from the floor to the door and back again. Her mother was going to lose her mind when she saw this destruction. Her father was such a jerk. He left the shattered vase all over the floor and his breakfast plate for Liza (or herself) to clean. As she contemplated her father's character or lack thereof, Hattie noticed the other items on the cherrywood table where the vase normally sat. Two crystal candlesticks and an 8 x 10 framed family photo sat upright, as usual.

Her father hadn't bumped into the table—he'd picked up the vase and, purposely, smashed it.

Chapter 49

Ivey

I soon realized we'd need something stronger than Tylenol PM to help Lauren sleep through the night. She woke up every few hours, remembered about Michal, then broke down into hiccupy sobs. I'd never considered myself especially adept at comforting others, but Lauren relaxed when I snuggled close and slept next to her.

I couldn't sleep, though. It must be like having a newborn—I worried my aunt might cry herself to death. We finally both fell into a deep sleep around four thirty. At 7:43 am, I received a most unwelcome text message from my sister, Daisy:

Daisy: WTF did you say to Pops?

Ivey: hello to you too

Daisy: not kidding

I should have known that Mom would complain to my sisters about my convo with Pops. As if either of them could *do* anything. I decided to play dumb since they thought I was anyway.

Ivey: idk

Daisy: something about Uncle Michal?

Ivey: I'm the one here in MI—you don't know anything

Daisy: rude

Ivey: ur rude!!! Lauren talked to me about her marriage, so I asked some q's—chill!!! There's a lot more important stuff going on

My stomach gurgled and grumbled, partly because I was starving, but mostly from stress and worry. How am I going to keep the police investigation quiet? It's only been half a day and it's eating me up. I watched the three tiny dots blink, blink, blink.

Daisy: u know that crap bothers Mom so stop, I don't need her bitching.

I glanced at Lauren, snoring softly, burrowed down deep in her duvet. Why was my family so weird? Remember to say as little as possible, Ives.

> *Ivey:*   Fine

> *Daisy:*   ru ok?

Now, that was unexpected. One of my sisters was concerned about me. Damn, here come the tears. I wiped at my weepy face.

> *Ivey:*   I'm ok. Lauren's very diff from Mom is all. She's got a lot on her plate

> *Daisy:*   I guess, just don't rile up the parents?

> *Ivey:*   k

There weren't any more blinking dots, so I tossed my phone aside, leaned across Lauren, and retrieved her phone from the nightstand. She'd given me her passcode yesterday, so I scrolled through her contacts looking for a doctor who could prescribe more potent sleeping pills. I gazed up at the ceiling and realized that would bring questions. The less people involved, the better.

I shook off my sister's text because I needed to figure out what to do about the Sunnyside. Before the crap hit the fan yesterday, Rafe and I had set up the store for today with fresh sunflowers and baked goods. Some things could last until tomorrow, but Lauren wouldn't be in any shape to help by then either.

Lauren stirred as I thought through options. Her eyes fluttered open, and she stretched languorously like a cat.

A cat! Peppercorn. I was glad that I hadn't left the house without feeding her.

"Hey." Lauren's voice was gruff from sleep. Her eyes were barely open, and she didn't lift her body from her prone position. She cleared her throat. "What time is it?"

"It's a bit before eight. How are you feeling?"

She covered a yawn. "My body's numb, but it hurts too."

I moved closer, so she didn't strain her voice. "I'm so sorry. Can I get you something to eat? Toast? Coffee?"

She pulled the covers up to her neck. "No. But thank you. I need more sleep."

"Lauren, I need to—" but she'd already fallen back to sleep. I scooted off the bed, then went to the kitchen for a morning diet coke when I got a text from Rafe.

Rafe: How is she?

Ivey: still asleep, long nite

Rafe: I bet—did she say anything about work?

Ivey: No, didn't get a chance to ask

Rafe: what should we do?

I stood there, leaning against the kitchen sink when it hit me—I could do this. I could run the store; I knew where everything was and how to restock. Especially with Rafe's help, we could keep the store open while Lauren got herself together. I knocked my soda can off the counter with my excitement.

Ivey: meet me @ the store at reg time

Rafe: u got it!

I did an exaggerated fist pump, picked up the soda can, took a shower, then pulled on light pink shorts, a white tank top, and my flip-flops. I rifled through my tote bag and found a pen and paper, then scribbled a note for Lauren telling her where I was. Back in the kitchen, I poured a cup of orange juice, unwrapped a scone, ripped off a paper towel, brought everything back into Lauren's bedroom, and placed it on her nightstand with the note.

By 9:15 am, I was out the door and ready to start the day. I breathed in the sweet, warm air, letting it fill my lungs. A spark of worry niggled at me while I walked, but the sun's rays penetrated my cheeks, burning away the negative self-talk.

I can do this.

My uncle's fate truly broke my heart. Yet, I felt empowered, certainly by the situation, but empowered, nonetheless. If I hadn't come to visit Lauren, who would have been here to help her? Rafe's dad, for sure, but managing Corbett Farm was his job. Mom could have come, but Nan and Pops needed her in Arizona.

I smiled, thinking about my last-minute idea to bring Peppercorn into Lauren's room before I left. The kitty had kneaded the covers next to Lauren and plopped down right beside her, gently purring. I hoped Peppercorn's little warm body would give Lauren comfort and help her rest. I was kinda proud of myself for thinking to do it.

I approached the Walloon Market. A spark of sunshine started at my toes, traveled up, and came bursting from my chest when I saw Rafe unlocking the wooden shutter panels, ready to open the Sunnyside. He turned and flashed me a warm smile. I was sure Rafe had no idea how much our newfound friendship meant to me. For the first time, I felt like I could handle stuff without deferring to my parents or my sisters.

Rafe walked toward me. "Hey there." He looked rested and calm.

I grabbed his hand and squeezed, then kissed him on the cheek "Hey."

He chuckled. "What's that for?"

"I appreciate you so much, Rafe." I looked up into his sweet eyes.

He took my hand in his, then pulled me close. "I appreciate you, too."

I knew where this was leading, and even though I was down for a kissing sesh, we had things to do. "I have a proposition for you."

Rafe stepped back, let go of my hands, and slid his into his pockets. I loved the way he did that. He looked like a little boy—in a non-creepy, cute way.

"And what would that be?" He raised his eyebrows up and down.

"Not that!" I joked. "Yet…"

He blushed a bit. "Well, damn."

I laughed and squeezed his arm playfully. "Would you be willing to help me run the Sunnyside while Lauren's grieving? Like, just us two?

Rafe tilted his head, his eyes widened. "Of course, I will. I assumed we'd handle the store 'til she's feeling better."

I leaned in and fish-kissed his face.

"Whoa!" He chuckled and clutched me close. "I thought this wasn't the plan yet!"

"You're right." I pulled away, my face hot. "I guess I thought you'd run for the hills. Lauren's situation is intense stuff, and in the wide scheme of things, the store isn't so important."

A few other merchants had started opening their shops, so Rafe and I retreated to the storefront and settled at the bistro table.

Rafe cradled my hands in his. "I'm your man, Ives. You can count on my help for sure."

"Awesome!" I squeezed his fingers. "Oh! We'll need your dad's help since Lauren usually gets the flowers."

A shadow crossed Rafe's face; his shoulders rounded. He withdrew his hands. I hadn't known him for long, but I hadn't expected this heavy a reaction when his father came up in the conversation. "The Sheriff talked to my parents last night. They were freaked out but eventually calmed down. I told them how great you were with Lauren." He rubbed his neck. "They care about her a lot—not just 'cause of Dad's job, but 'cause she's been a good friend."

I didn't know what to do with my hands when Rafe pulled away, so I fussed with my hair. "Your family means the world to her as well." I laced my fingers together and propped my chin. "Changing the subject, I think we should still go talk to that guy at The Wheelhouse after work today. I think it's even more important that we find out what he knows. Oh God—Morgan! The Sheriff didn't want us to tell anyone about my uncle's—" I lowered my voice and looked around the market area.

"Don't worry," Rafe assured me. "Morgan's a stand-up guy. If we ask him to keep this to himself, he most certainly will."

"Good, good." I had so many thoughts bouncing around my brain: Lauren's health, the store, my grandfather, my parents, the enormity of a murder investigation, Hattie's comments. My surge of confidence earlier dimmed, seeming stupid and naive.

I inhaled deeply, then released it slowly. "Okay, I'll go check on Lauren around noon. Can you text Morgan about meeting us later?"

Rafe pulled out his phone with a flourish, his thumbs flying over the keyboard. He looked up momentarily, shook his head, then chuckled. "Done. Okay, boss, what's our next move?"

I stood and gestured to the stockroom. "Let's get those sunflowers and sell our butts off!"

Chapter 50
Hattie

Hattie cleaned up the shattered vase as quickly as she could, glad that Liza hadn't heard the crash. It would have started a whole scene. She stood, momentarily holding the shards in a dustpan, about to go to the kitchen to dump it when she had a lightbulb moment. She smiled and walked to her father's office to dump the shards into his unlined waste bin that was only for show or the occasional tissue.

She set the dustpan on the edge of her dad's desk, then pulled her vibrating phone from her pocket. It was Stace.

Stace: Come swim!

Stace's family had a gorgeous lagoon-style saltwater pool. Hattie sighed. That pool was the reason she'd befriended Stace in the seventh grade. Hattie was about to respond when she noticed the still-open screen on her dad's desktop computer. She dropped her phone on the desk— it clanked and echoed through the bookcase-lined study.

Hattie pulled out the office chair, settled in, and grabbed the computer mouse. "Oh, my God." She couldn't remember a time when her father left his computer screen on, and she was going to take advantage of it. *Well, well, well.* The file on the screen detailed a missing person report filed by none other than Lauren Corbett. *So, Dad still has some interest in Ms. Corbett's life.*

Hattie's finger hovered over the mouse; her heart sped up. She felt surprisingly conflicted—at first. Hattie wanted to find something to hold over Ivey's head, but a missing person? That was more sad than sinister. Hattie wasn't a freaking monster after all.

Her phone vibrated again, and she shot it a scornful look. Amazingly, the phone quieted. She raised her brows. *I wish it were that easy to shut everyone up.* Hattie turned her attention back to the missing person's report.

Michal Lyska. DOB. Czechoslovakia. green card. Spouse, Lauren Corbett. Last seen. court orders/arrests.

"Yes!" She clicked on the "Arrests" link.

Ivey's uncle had been arrested about four months before he went missing—felony theft from Corbett Ace

Hardware, but Paul Corbett had not pressed charges, so Lyska had been released.

Hmmm.

Then, there had been an unpaid hotel bill that had been escalated to theft but was eventually paid by Lauren Corbett. The hotel's receptionist had been the last person to see Mr. Lyska.

Well, Hattie thought, looking around at the dark wood paneling lined with her parents' various framed degrees. At first glance, it looks like Ivey's uncle up and left—not surprising considering he may have stolen money from his father-in-law. *Wait a minute!*

Hattie backed away from the computer, suddenly, her hands shook. She stared at her quaking fingers, taking in the added information. She grabbed the mouse again and returned to the missing person's page. Her father was the Assistant DA on the case. She reviewed the Ace Hardware arrest, likewise. Her father had gone to his office immediately after their kitchen conversation and had searched for this report.

He flat out lied to my face, thought Hattie, her face hard. *This happened five years ago. Being a kid, I might not have been aware of something like a missing person, but Dad knew Lauren from high school—dated her. Why didn't he mention it at the time?*

Even to say, "Isn't it so sad?" Now he destroys Mom's vase after looking at these files.

Her father had given her mom the vase after the divorce talk Hattie had heard as a child—a peace offering, perhaps. Her mother treasured it. A symbol of their reconciliation.

Hattie felt somewhat nauseated, but also intrigued, as she clicked back to the original webpage, then picked up her phone to text Stace. She wondered if her mother knew anything about Lauren or her husband, but that'd be tricky. Her mother would blab, and her father would shut the whole subject down. Hattie heard Mom and Adam come in the kitchen door. She tapped her phone screen.

Hattie: I'll be right over

Chapter 51

Ivey

I shook Lauren gently, but she didn't wake. It was an odd feeling—I was happy she was resting, but worried that she'd been asleep for such a long time. I glanced at the untouched scone and juice on the side table.

"Aunt Lauren," I urged, pushing on her shoulder. "Please wake up, please."

She rolled over, covering her eyes from the meager sunshine peeking through the still-closed blinds. "What? Oh, Ivey, what time is it?" Her voice was still hoarse from sleep and crying.

I looked at the bedside clock. "It's a little after twelve." I tried to sound cheerful, but not *too* cheerful.

Lauren continued to lie flat, placing her hand on her forehead. "I don't have any energy."

"I know." I picked up the glass. "At least sip some juice. I brought a scone, too. You'll never want to get up if you don't eat."

The beginnings of a smile started at the corner of her mouth. "You sound like your mom when I was sick as a little girl."

I handed her the glass. "Good! Now drink up!"

Lauren sat up, fluffing the pillow behind her back. She took a microscopic sip, so I set the scone (with a napkin) on her lap. "Now a bite of this," I urged.

She complied—somewhat. "Thank you for taking care of me; I know I'm being completely pitiful."

I cocked my head and encouragingly patted her hand. "You're grieving. Take the time to do it."

Lauren's eyes grew wide. "Oh my God, what about the store? I need to call Marco, tell him not to—"

I kept my hand on hers. "Don't worry! Rafe and I have the store covered."

She set the glass on the nightstand, her eyes opening wider. "You do?"

I smiled proudly. "Yeah, we opened at regular time, and we've had good traffic. All is well. Rafe talked to his dad, and he's bringing the sunflowers for tomorrow, and I'll pick up the baked goods this afternoon."

Lauren's shoulders relaxed. "Oh, honey, I'm so thankful for you!"

It was weird to have my aunt look at me so gratefully. I squirmed as I sat on the bed beside her, feeling uncomfortably warm. She wasn't ill, but the room had that "sick room" feel. I fetched Lauren's phone from between the covers and handed it to her. "Would you like to see if there's any news from the sheriff?"

Lauren inhaled sharply, tapped the phone, and scrolled. "No, nothing. I'm not sure how much more I could take anyway." She stared out in front of her. "I shouldn't be surprised by this news, but I held out hope…" Her voice trailed off as she chucked the phone away. Buried deep in the covers, Peppercorn screeched and jumped.

"Whew, she scared the life outta me!" Lauren gasped, hand to her heart.

I grinned. "Crazy cat." I leaned over and gathered the kitty to my chest. "You suspected Uncle Michal may have—y' know?" Sweat formed along my hairline. I hoped she wouldn't start crying again.

Lauren pushed her tousled hair back over the crown of her head. "I ruined everything. Michal was despondent after Pops fired him. Humiliated. He was a proud, proud man. I should have fought for him, for us, but the miscarriages, the fights, and building a business. I didn't have anything left to give."

I set Peppercorn next to her and gathered the soon-to-be stale scone from her lap. "You could only do what you could. Uncle Michal had fifty percent of the responsibility." I trailed a finger along the duvet. Should I ask? "I was thinking about our talk the other day."

Lauren stroked Peppercorn and nuzzled her nose in his fur. "Yes?"

"You mentioned something about Nan and Pops liking a different guy you had dated." Please don't get mad or start crying or throw me out of the house.

She chuckled. I couldn't believe it. Whew. "Oh, yes." The corner of Lauren's lips went up. "They loved Mr. Perfect. God, I haven't thought about high school in ages."

My attention could not have been more rapt. "Who was he?" I'd been tapping my foot but stopped when I realized it.

Lauren continued to pet Peppercorn. "My high school boyfriend, Scott Foster. In fact, I did think of him when you mentioned that girl, Hattie." She looked from the cat to me. "I wonder if they're related. Foster is a common enough name—"

"They are," I blurted out.

Lauren flinched at my outburst. "Oh?"

I had to calm myself down. "Hattie made a big deal out of her Dad being the DA."

"Yes, yes. That's Scott. Come to think of it, he helped us keep Michal's arrest and disappearance quiet." She nodded her head, obviously thinking back to the sad events. "That time is such a blur, now. I remember being surprised at how kind Scott was to me during that time."

I was so intrigued; I thought I might levitate off the bed. "Why were you surprised at that? You'd been close, right?"

Lauren sighed. "It was so long ago. Scott was, and I guess still is, an ambitious man. I didn't do, say, or want the same things in life. We had a horrible breakup. These days people would say he stalked me—calling at all hours, showing up places he wasn't wanted." She shuddered. "Even after he helped us with Michal's issues, I was wary of trusting his motives. Anyway, I'd stay away from that family, Ivey. I think you already know that."

"I sure do. What a creepy thing." I stammered. "I had no idea. I'm sorry I brought it up."

Lauren patted my hand. "No, no. Thankfully, time has lessened that wound. I'd like to believe he's moved on, as I have."

I nodded, then added the juice glass to a pile for the kitchen. Lauren didn't need any more questions. "Rafe and I have a quick errand, but we'll come by and check on you after we close up."

"Okay, you go on. I need a shower, and Peppercorn will keep me company."

"Do you promise me you'll try to eat something?"

Lauren rubbed her belly. "I'll try, but my stomach feels like I swallowed a stone."

I went for the door. "I'll get you some water and leave it by the bed."

"Ivey," she said.

I turned. "Yeah?"

"Thank you for being here."

"I love you, Lauren. Everything's going to be okay. I just know it." I hoped I was telling the truth.

Chapter 52

Ivey

Once I returned to the Sunnyside, Rafe and I handled customers (mostly me), restocked from the storeroom (mostly Rafe), and we cleaned and straightened for the next day. Running the store was, for sure, a three-person job, but we got it done and made a decent profit. I was about to ask Rafe to text his father about the next day's flowers when Mr. Torres walked in. Some people have remarked on how much I resemble my father, but wow! He was Rafe in about twenty-five years.

Mr. Torres was an inch shorter than his son, and stockier. He had the same wavy black hair, cut closer than Rafe's, and intense brown eyes. His resting face was harder than Rafe's, but I guess that happens. I had seen that same hardening (if that's the right word) in my father's face through the years—especially after Afghanistan. I remembered everything Rafe had shared about his brother and felt a sudden rush of empathy for his parents.

"Good afternoon!" Mr. Torres said, his face perking up. "You must be Ivey. I'd shake your hand, but I've got a bundle here." He glanced down at the container of sunflowers in his arms.

Startled out of my (probably moronic) staring, I rushed forward and tried to take the flowers from him. "Oh, I'm so sorry! Yes, I'm Ivey. Let me help—"

"No, no, dear," he replied. "I'll bring them back, um, behind the curtain?"

I backed away and stuck my hands in my back pockets. "Yes, right back there. Rafe's—" but Mr. Torres was already through the curtain. "—back there," I muttered to the air.

Once he and Rafe unloaded the flowers, Mr. Torres sought me out to offer his support for Lauren. I was standing behind the counter, looking through the day's receipts on the iPad.

Mr. Torres folded his arms across his chest. "My wife, Gabby, and I want you to know that we are here for you and Lauren—whatever either of you may need."

I nodded. "Thank you so much, Mr. Torres. Lauren's hanging in there. A lot of emotions are coming to the surface." I clicked the iPad off. "Did you know my uncle?"

Mr. Torres seemed surprised. His eyes scanned the store, then came back to me. "Oh, no, no. He was already out—um, he and Lauren had already split before I took the job at Corbett Farm."

I palmed my forehead. "That's right! Rafe mentioned that—three years, right?"

He smiled with closed lips. "Yes."

"But you've lived here longer than that?" Was I some sort of investigative idiot? Why was I grilling this man?

Thankfully, Mr. Torres didn't seem bothered. "True, we moved to Walloon ten years ago, but we didn't meet your family until I took the job."

Rafe joined us from the storeroom. He crossed behind his father and leaned on the open side of the counter. "We're all set, Ives."

I glanced from father to son. Their dynamic felt brittle, like something could splinter between them at any moment.

Rafe stiffly addressed his father. "Ivey and I are gonna hang out for a while, but I'll be home for dinner." I could see the heat rising on his face, a bit of perspiration at his hairline and upper lip. "Thanks for bringing the flowers, I can come to pick them up tomorrow if that helps."

Mr. Torres placed a hand on the counter. "Let's see what my day brings tomorrow. A few minutes away from the office isn't a bad thing. Text your mother, so she knows when to expect you, please." He turned to go, then stopped abruptly, and squared on Rafe. "Have you spoken to Tonio in the past few days?"

Rafe stepped back, rubbed his neck, then sidled toward me behind the counter, his body tense. "Uh, no. Why do you ask?" He shoved his hands in his pockets and looked down.

Mr. Torres' gaze bored into Rafe's forehead. "I was out by the shed yesterday and noticed a cigarette butt. Your brother's the only one who smokes, so I thought maybe he came by the house for some reason."

The tension between the men was absurdly obvious. Rafe kept looking down while his father glared. I gathered the paper receipts, shivering a bit and unconsciously stepping away from Rafe.

"Weird. Why would Tonio just stand in the backyard and smoke?" Rafe's voice was tinny.

"Good question, son. Good question," Mr. Torres blinked, and his penetrating gaze softened. He tapped the counter twice with his thick gold ring. "Make sure you text your mother, and Ivey—good to meet you."

Rafe and I watched his father leave, then we turned to each other simultaneously.

Rafe spoke first. "Laid back guy, right?"

I grinned. "He's a bit more formal than most."

Rafe took the receipts from me, laid them on the table, grasped my hands, and pulled me toward him. "That's the sweetest description of my father I've ever heard." He bent to kiss my cheek.

I moved closer and laid my head on Rafe's chest, feeling his breath flow over my scalp. We stood soundlessly entwined for a minute or two when I looked up. "Why did Tonio come by your house?"

Rafe flinched but didn't break our embrace. "You're scary perceptive," he said into my hair.

I pulled away slightly and studied his expression. "Your brother's not in trouble, is he?"

He sighed, "He's okay, just checking on me. He knew Dad would be mad if he came to the door." Rafe took his phone from his back pocket. "One sec. It's Morgan."

I nodded. Family crap is beyond complicated—I wouldn't want to talk about it either.

"He's just leaving work, so we better get going. Let's talk more in the truck, okay?"

"He's just leaving work, so we better get going. Let's talk more in the truck, okay?"

Chapter 53

Ivey

Once we settled in his truck and on our way to meet Morgan, Rafe asked me, "So, how'd you know I wasn't totally honest with my dad?" He tapped the steering wheel in time with a song playing low.

I grinned slyly. "Not totally honest?" I crooked an eyebrow.

Rafe gave me a sidelong glance. "Okay, okay, not honest at all! I admit it."

I chuckled. "I can just tell."

"You can?" He fully turned his head this time.

I pointed out the windshield. "Hey! Keep your eyes on the road!" I settled back into the passenger seat, stupidly proud of my perceptive abilities.

The truck bounced and jerked when Rafe turned onto a pock-marked road. "So, how can you tell?"

I gripped the car door to keep from flying out of the seat, then shook my head. "Nope, a girl doesn't reveal her secrets." I flashed him a wide smile. How did he not realize that he rubbed his neck and looked at his feet when he was nervous?

Rafe snorted. "You sound like Arya."

"Who's that?" An icy spark of jealousy crept through my bloodstream.

"She's a character on *Game of Thrones* who was in this religious group. She referred to herself as 'a girl' in a few episodes."

I'm such an idiot. I fiddled with my seat belt. "Wow, that is incredibly geeky."

He kept his eyes on the road but poked out his lip. "Gee, thanks. You're really not gonna tell me?"

"Nope, don't even try the lip." I laughed. "I'll keep the upper hand, thank you very much." The truck lurched forward when we hit a pothole. "God! This road is sketchy." I said, taking in the now dirt-laden path. It was full daylight, but sinister-looking trees hung over the road as if we had entered a forgotten forest; a trash-strewn side path led to a parking lot with tufts of weeds poking through the pavement.

"It sure is creepy," Rafe added. He took his foot off the gas and coasted, peering outside the windshield.

A few seconds later, the navigation system sounded. "You've arrived at your destination."

The Wheelhouse itself wasn't as rundown as we had expected, considering the dilapidated parking lot. Morgan's black Honda Fit was parked out front, the latest model car by at least ten years. Rafe pulled up alongside, then turned to me. He paused before speaking.

"Ives, I'm worried about you coming inside 'cause who knows what kinda shady dudes come to a place like this." He gestured toward the building. "Are you sure you want to do this? The news might not be too great either."

If any other guy had made this little speech, I'd have given him a healthy dose of eye rolls and derisive sighs. But I could tell that Rafe was sincerely concerned.

I took hold of his hand and squeezed it. "I get it, I don't like the looks of this place either, but I need to know what the owner can tell me about my uncle."

He clutched my hand in return. "Yeah, yeah, but—" Rafe's eyes narrowed. "Let's be ready to make a quick exit."

I nodded then we both looked out the windshield at the shabby beige exterior of the bar. Whatever rebranding or renovation done recently didn't help much. I could see its last name, Walloon Saloon, burned into the wood above the new neon letters spelling out The Wheelhouse. My mind flashed to my dad's tirades about paint primer.

One of the double screen doors opened, and Morgan waved us in. "Come on!" he mouthed.

Rafe and I glanced at each other. We shrugged and exited the truck. As I rounded the front of the F150, Rafe grabbed my hand.

No one in the bar looked up from their afternoon drinks when we walked in, which was a relief. I was a bit concerned about the bikers, but I wanted to appear unfazed for Rafe's sake.

Eighties music played loudly in the background, and the air smelled of stale beer and weed. Dark walls, streaky windows, and ancient black lacquered tables and chairs made up the dining area. Shelving above the windows held scattered trophies, Detroit and Chicago sports memorabilia, plus old liquor bottles. There were two pool tables in a room to the right. Both stood empty.

Morgan took the lead as we followed him toward the bar. "Mr. Habibi'll be right with us." The bar itself was shiny black with a stainless-steel countertop—startlingly new, compared with the rest of the décor.

Rafe pulled out barstools for each of us. "How long have you been here?"

Morgan shrugged, then perched himself in front of a tiny soda glass. "Not long. Maybe ten minutes."

I clutched my cross-body purse protectively. "Thanks so much for meeting us, Morgan."

"No prob!" Morgan looked toward a light coming from a dark hallway to the bar's left. A slim, compact gentleman greeted him. "Hey, Mr. Habibi. These are my friends, Rafe and Ivey."

Peter Habibi extended his hand first to me, then to Rafe. "Nice to meet you." His English was heavily accented, possibly Pakistani. (I knew this because Clara's mother's family was from Pakistan.) Mr. Habibi's smile was genuine, and his dark eyes were bright. "Would you care for a drink, either of you?" He chuckled. "Only soda, though!"

My stomach flip-flopped, eager to hear what this man would say about my uncle. "Nothing for me, thanks." My voice was shrill with anticipation. I glanced at Rafe, but he waved off a drink too. "Mr. Habibi, Morgan said you remember my uncle, Michal Lyska." I hoped I didn't sound too demanding, but a quick look at my phone reminded me that Lauren was home alone and grieving—it made my chest tighten.

"Yes, I do!" He talked with his hands, pointing his fingers at no one in particular. "One moment, please." He went down the bar, spoke quietly to a bartender, and then returned. "Come, come to my office. I have some photos to show you."

The weight in my chest lifted, replaced with an adrenaline surge. "Really?" I squeaked. "Photos, that's awesome!" I beamed at the guys and hopped off the barstool.

We followed Mr. Habibi down the hallway, past the restrooms, then into an office with Persian rugs hanging on the walls. There was an ornate desk but no chairs. Large poufs covered in South Asian-looking fabric were strewn about—it was quite the spectacle of color and texture. I plopped onto a pouf. He went behind the desk, opened a drawer, and pulled out an overstuffed scrapbook. He riffled through the pages, balancing the enormous book on a slender palm. He resembled a child looking through a giant leather-bound Bible.

He ran his finger across and down the page. "Ah! Here we are." He handed the book to me.

I took the book from him and balanced it on my lap. "Thank you," I said. Each page had four Polaroids labeled "Annual Dart Tourney" in loopy, feminine handwriting. As I concentrated on the photos, Mr. Habibi told us about the scrapbook.

"My wife put this book together." He paused, then cleared his throat. "She died two years ago."

All three of us offered our sincere condolences.

Mr. Habibi waved us off, but his misty eyes betrayed him. "When Morgan called, I remembered the book right away." He bent over to point at a specific photo but stopped himself. "Do you see your uncle in the photos? I can help you."

How incongruous was the gentle kindness of this man who owned a rough and tumbled back road bar? I learned something that day about not making snap judgements.

I smiled. "Yes, please. The last time I saw my uncle I was just a little girl."

Mr. Habibi moved closer and pointed at the tallest man in several photos. I squinted and studied the images. Yep. There's my uncle Michal standing at a polaroid's edge; I remembered his height accurately. Uncle Michal wore a red flannel shirt and jeans; his long dark hair pulled back, with strands framing his unsmiling face.

Rafe and Morgan came up behind me and leaned in to look. "Wow, he's a big guy." Rafe commented, looking intently at the photos.

Morgan asked, "Who are the other men in the photo?"

Mr. Habibi scanned the page and spent a moment studying the photos again. "I'll be honest, the only reason I remembered Michal Lyska was that he left a rather large unpaid tab. His employer settled it, eventually." He stroked his chin.

I cringed. "That was my grandfather, Paul Corbett."

"Oh, yes! A good man, very good man," Mr. Habibi looked back at the photos. "I see some of our regulars, but many of them have moved on," his voice trailed off as he appeared to be searching his memory. "Ah! This man, I do not remember his name—" He settled himself on the nearest pouf and pointed at the page. "He was a friend of Mr. Lyska."

I peered at the crazily familiar face. Dark, almost black hair. High, sharp cheekbones and scarily black eyes. The guy was younger than Hattie's father, Scott Foster, but this man could be his brother.

Chapter 54

Ivey

Rafe, Morgan, and I stood outside The Wheelhouse and excitedly discussed the information Mr. Habibi had given us. I clutched a Ziploc bag holding my uncle's photos protectively to my chest.

Morgan scratched his buzz cut scalp. "Did Hattie ever mention her dad having a brother?"

"Nah." Rafe dug his hands into his pockets. "She talked about her little brother, Adam, but no one outside her nuclear family. At least, not that I can remember."

An idea popped into my head. "Hey! If this mystery guy lives around here, maybe the phone directory app might link him to Mr. Foster."

I handed the photos to Rafe and pulled out my phone, quickly finding the White Pages app and typed in Scott Foster's name. There were several people with the same last name, but only one listed a Charlevoix County number.

"Hmm." I scanned the list of possible relatives.

"Anything?" Rafe asked impatiently.

Morgan jingled his keys, so I looked up at him. "Do you need to get on?" I sighed, then stuffed the phone into my crossbody. "I didn't see anyone listed other than Aliyah, Hattie, and Scott Foster, Sr."

Morgan nodded. "Yeah, I need to get home. I'll see what else I can find later tonight. Would you mind if I took one of the photos to scan? I might be able to run a Google image search; it's a long shot, but you never know."

I grabbed the Ziploc from Rafe, fished a photo out, and handed it to Morgan. "Great idea! I can't tell you how much I appreciate it." I hugged him.

Morgan squeezed me back. When he pulled away, his face was bright red. "No promises though." His sneakered foot pawed at the dirt. "It's hard to get a good image from a polaroid."

Rafe clicked on his key fob. "If anyone can do it, you can, Morg." The guys' fist-bumped each other. "Talk later."

I nodded at Morgan. "Drive safe."

Chapter 55
Hattie

Hattie always wished her family had a house on the lake like Stace's, but hanging at Stace's house had to do. Her mind, full of the morning's revelations, whorled around like Adam's little Brio train going round and round its wooden tracks.

Stace Millikin, her Barbie blond hair braided and pulled off her tanned face, adjusted her coral-colored bikini top as she turned to her front on the lounge chair. "So, you think your dad has some sort of ongoing feelings for Ivey's aunt?" She settled back into the lounge cushion and tilted her face to the sun. "You don't think they are having affair, do you?"

Hattie bolted upright from the neighboring chair, her knees up and feet planted on the cushion. "Oh my God, Stace, that is completely disgusting. You know, everything isn't about sex!"

Stace reached for the can of La Croix on the teak table between them. She popped the top and sipped. "Okay, walk me through it, Hats." She made a rolling gesture with her other hand.

Hattie looked at her pale pink toenails and picked at a cuticle as she told Stace about finding her dad's yearbook, the connection to Lauren Corbett, and this morning's events.

When she finished, Hattie stared at Stace intently. "Well?"

Stace responded automatically. "Oh, yeah, crazy. What does your gut tell you?"

"I don't know." Hattie laid back on her chair and inhaled deeply.

The girls lounged quietly, sipping their drinks, and fanning their sweaty bodies.

Finally, Stace yawned, then changed the subject. "So, how are things going with Hank?"

"He's fine. We're fine." Hattie nibbled on her thumbnail, realized the bad habit then pulled her hand away.

Stace kept her eyes closed. "That doesn't sound like an exciting romance, babe. Do you want Rafe back?"

Hattie waved a hand. "Eh, I can't think about Hank or Rafe right now. That's boring."

Another few minutes passed in silence. They could hear a faraway woodpecker and the glub-glub of the pool's water filter.

Stace spoke first. "Do you think Ivey knows anything about your dad and her aunt?"

Hattie sat up again, her lips now stretched into a wicked smile. "You've given me a fantastic idea!"

Stace grabbed the corner of her towel and wiped her forehead. "How on earth did I do that?"

Hattie scrambled up from her lounger feeling perfectly chill in a simple black string bikini. She paced around the tiled pool surface nibbling the edge of her thumbnail again. "Yes! I think we need to have a party."

Stace gazed at her own lengthy, lacquered nails. "Well, that's a change of subject," she dead panned.

"Not at all, I know just who to hit up." Hattie's voice trailed off. She strode over and stood over Stace, raking her fingers through her hair. "We'll invite everybody, and I have a special someone I'm sure Miss Priss Ivey would love to meet."

Stace glanced up at Hattie looming above, then shaded her eyes. "That sounds ominous."

Hattie waved Stace off. "Me? Ominous? I'm all about bringing people together."

Stace crooked an eyebrow. "Oh, yeah, Hattie Foster—humanitarian extraordinaire!"

Hattie ignored her friend's sassy comment, tiptoed to the pool's edge, then waded into the refreshing water satisfied that she had everything back under control.

Chapter 56

Ivey

Back in my room, I checked in with my parents by text—no response from Dad, but that wasn't strange. During military exercises, his schedule was erratic, and often he would text me late at night. I appreciated it because I worried about him. Dad could be a loner. Maybe being the only male in our household fostered that.

Mom did text back. I was relieved she didn't bring up my ill-fated talk with Pops. Worrying about that conversation only increased my overall anxiety. I mean, what girl wants to hurt or piss off her grandpa? Certainly, not me. I continued to wonder whether stirring up my family's raw emotions was worth it. But, the truth needs to come out.

As I curled up on my bed, I listened to the frogs and cicadas while fading sunlight filtered through the shutters, I pondered the inevitable upheaval if the police definitively identified my uncle's remains. How would Nan and Pops react? Would it harm their health? I'm sure Mom would freak out and Dad would be stoic. I have no idea what my sisters would do—they could be super supportive or completely distant.

Lauren believed that Uncle Michal was dead; that the DNA test would confirm the dental records. Would I feel that way in her position? Or would I hold out hope? I know she's emotionally tapped out.

Earlier, when Rafe dropped me home after our trek to The Wheelhouse, Lauren was out of her room. She appeared to have bathed but was buried under several blankets on the couch.

I knelt beside her. "How're you doing?"

She yawned and rubbed her eyes sleepily. "I'm all right. It felt good to take a bath."

I lowered my butt onto the carpet. "Did you eat anything?"

She grimaced. "I don't have any appetite." She messed with her slightly damp hair. "I'm sorry."

I tried not to look worried. "You don't have to apologize to me. I feel kinda useless, Aunt Lauren. I want to help you. Would you like me to call Mom?"

A teardrop squeezed from the corner of her eye. "No! No, I can't deal with any other people." She took my hand but kept her face forward toward the muted television. "I know they love me, please don't think I'm—"

"Again, you don't have to say sorry to me. I'll do whatever you need."

We both stared at the soundless *Friends* episode; it was the one about a blackout.

I thought about telling Lauren what we had learned about Uncle Michal today, but I was sure that our investigation would stress her out; or worse, she'd want me to stop asking questions. We didn't really learn anything that helpful anyway. Uncle Michal had played darts with a guy that looked like Scott Foster—big deal. I also felt like she'd disapprove of my having been at a bar.

"How about I make us some chicken noodle soup?" I asked. "I'm pretty much starving,"

She nodded but remained focused on the television.

I puttered over to the kitchen, opened a few cabinets looking for the canned soup, then retrieved a pot. I'd never cooked on a gas stove before this trip, but I loved the click-click-click of the starter. It made me feel like a Top Chef. I popped two pieces of whole wheat bread into the toaster while the soup warmed, then I scooped out and mashed a ripe avocado. I knew that warming soup and making avocado toast was not technically cooking, but I enjoyed the routine of it—not having to think.

My brain had been on perpetual overdrive since visiting The Wheelhouse. My body was so heavy, but not in that good way, like after a workout. It felt more like I'd gone a few rounds with a UFC guy. Despite that, I fixed the two bowls and diagonally sliced the toast, setting everything on a large melamine tray with utensils and napkins. I shuffled back into the den, then placed the tray on the coffee table.

Lauren swung her legs off the sofa and reached for the toast; she nibbled it slowly, so I was satisfied with her effort. We watched another *Friends* episode, and I assured her that Rafe and I had the store set for the morning. She stretched and yawned, rose from the sofa, and slumped back into her room.

Before I went to my room, Rafe texted.

Rafe: Hope Lauren's ok - cu tomorrow!

Ivey:

Chapter 57
Ivey

Rafe and I had gotten to know most of the other vendors at the Walloon Market, and for good reason. When we were both helping customers, we needed someone to simply stand in our space while we were in the back or out in the parking lot. I think some of the ladies who frequented the Sunnyside relished Rafe toting their packages to their cars—I didn't blame them one bit.

Our little beverage thieves Reynie, Patton, and Ben came back, but now we paid them five bucks each to sort flower stems and stack merchandise in the storeroom. They turned out to be good helpers. Ben's mother thanked Rafe and me for giving her son something to do during the summer other than video games.

I smiled at the thirtyish, brunette mom who was accompanied by her angelic two-year-old named McKenna. "Ben's a hard worker, Mrs. Eisner. Since my aunt is under the weather" (that's the party line so far) "we're glad to give the boys something to do." The tiny girl toddled around the shop, clutching a purple and white unicorn purse. Unlike her brothers, McKenna never touched anything on the tables or shelves. It killed me how cute she was—white-blond hair pulled severely to the top of her head with a sequined clip and pink light-up sneakers.

Mrs. Eisner, casually chic in a beige boat neck top and matching knit capris, corralled McKenna and grasped her chubby hand. "You have my cell number, Ivey. I'll be back to pick up the boys in an hour."

I waved. "Sounds good! See you then." I returned to filling the greeting card display rack.

Morgan told me yesterday that he had tried to identify the guy in the polaroid photo using Google photo search, and some other programs I can't remember, but no luck.

It was a long shot anyway.

After I'd studied the photos more closely, I realized there wasn't any reason to believe that my uncle knew this one man any better than the other five guys in the group. No arms were draped over shoulders like guys do when they're friends. We were only going on Mr. Habibi's recollection that Uncle Michal and this man even hung out at all.

Rafe came back into the store with Reynie trailing behind. "Man, how many bunches of sunflowers can one family need?" Rafe wiped his brow.

"Yeah, man!" Reynie shouted, his eyes shining and gazing up at Rafe like he was Ironman.

I wagged my finger. "No complaints now! People like Mrs. Grayson keep us in business.

Rafe winked. "Yes ma'am, boss lady."

I stopped organizing the card display and feigned a thoughtful look. "Boss lady? I like that! From now on—"

"Oh, no! I shouldn't have said that!" Rafe's big laugh made my stomach do flip-flops.

Reynie giggled too. "Boss Lady, boss lady!" He danced around, his sandy brown hair flopping in his cherubic face.

Ben and Patton flew out of the storeroom.

"What's going on?" demanded Patton. He was Reynie's older brother and sported the same shaggy light brown hair, dressed in camo cargo shorts and a tee-shirt with a surfer on it. Reynie was definitely his older brother's "mini me."

Reynie spun like the Tasmanian Devil grazing a table with Stassi's watercolor display before Rafe caught hold of him. "Ivey's the boss lady!" Reynie chanted.

Why do kids like to chant? Is it some primeval need from caveman days?

I couldn't help but be charmed by Reynie's silliness and how darling Rafe looked holding the boy around the stomach about a foot off the ground.

I raised my voice a decibel or two. "Okay, okay. Let's calm down and get back to work, guys. Ben's mom will be back before we know it. You'll each get to pick a bag of sunflower seeds if you get all of tomorrow's stems sorted!"

Three sets of athletic shoes thump-thumped back into the storeroom. Food was a bigger incentive than money for those rascals.

Chapter 58

Ivey

Rafe and I sat on Lauren's porch stairs after work, talking about what to do over the upcoming weekend. "Are you sure about this party?" I asked, projecting my uncertainty onto Rafe. Lauren and I had planned a Saturday girl's night—watching a rom-com and ordering veggie pizza. I was relieved that she felt up to quasi-socializing, but I felt guilty for wanting to hang with Rafe.

He looked down at his phone, scouring the class Reddit thread for details about a big get-together at some guy's lake house. "Yeah. Tucker Bostic's family has one of the sickest places in Walloon. He's had this party for the last two years, but it was right before school started. Seems he's gonna have it early this summer." Rafe returned the phone to his back pocket and turned to me. "We could leave early if it gets boring, but it's been a blast in the past."

I giggled. "You're a poet," I said, even though I was obviously entirely dorky.

Rafe scootched toward me, his jeans melded with mine, soft and warm; his arm curled around my waist pulling me closer. He buried his lips into my neck and made a low growling sound as his kisses sent lovely waves of excitement up and down my spine.

A purr escaped my throat as I draped my arms over his shoulders and tilted my head giving him more surface area to kiss. I had become way too used to "kissing at will."

I pulled away, but our faces stayed close together. I had to ask. "I guess Hattie'll be there?"

Rafe glanced down, but he didn't pull away from me. "Maybe." His eyes gently lifted. "There'll be tons of people though. I haven't seen her around the Market lately—have you?"

"Nope, thank God." A little bead of sweat formed at my hairline. "I'm not scared of her or anything." I fanned myself.

It sure is warm today.

"I know," Rafe assured me. "Hey, we really don't have to go if you don't want to." He rubbed my back. "We could go to a movie or just hang out here or at my house."

I shook my head and breathed in deeply. "I'm being a baby. I want to go—it'll be fun!"

"Cool!" Rafe let me go and crawled off the steps. "We'll talk more tomorrow."

I took in the totality of this amazing, kind, and talented guy standing at the foot of Lauren's stairs gazing at me like I was the most important girl in the world. His perfectly worn-in jeans and grey tee shirt looked so good. He ran his fingers through his hair like a dang supermodel, then said, "Y'know, I think we should bring those photos to the party."

My head snapped back, reflexively. "Why?"

"Maybe someone at the party could identify your uncle's friend?"

I stood up and joined Rafe at the foot of the porch stairs. "You think we should ask Hattie?" I, honestly, didn't know how I felt about his train of thought. It was risky. She could spill the beans to her father.

He stepped back and raised both hands. "Only if it's okay with you—totally, your call."

Rafe Torres, the calmer of nerves. I smiled, reached out, and squeezed his hands. "I'll think about it."

Chapter 59

Ivey

After watching Rafe's truck pull away, my mind drifted to what I could possibly wear to the party. I climbed the steps, then reached for the painted-over handle.

Lauren shrieked.

I yanked the screen open, pushed the front door aside, and sprinted in when a deeper, more pitiful wail came from her bedroom.

"Aunt Lauren! I'm coming!" I screamed. The distance to her room seemed to expand, like in that horrible dream I had weeks ago.

I found Lauren crumpled beside her bed, her cell phone loosely held in her right hand, her head hung low on her chest, hair matted and falling forward. Lauren's greying nightgown hung off her shoulders making her look like a character from *Les Mis*. Her wail devolved into a whimper as I knelt beside her.

"Aunt Lauren, what's happened?" I whispered, my neck hair prickled.

She didn't answer but inched her phone toward me. I plucked it out of her hand, then held it to my ear. "Hello?" My voice cracked.

A male voice answered, "Hello, hello? Lauren?"

My heart pounded hard enough to make me gasp. "No, this is Ivey. Who's this?"

"This is Sheriff Preston, Ivey. Is Lauren alright? She—"

I slid to the floor next to Lauren, my back up against the bed's edge. "She's safe but not all right. Is this about my uncle?" The carpet felt like bristly Florida grass on the slim strip of skin above my waistband.

I heard the Sheriff take a sharp inhale. He paused before responding. "Yes, I'm so sorry, but the DNA test came back, and the remains we found earlier are, indeed, Michal Lyska."

"Oh my God," I stammered. This monstrous news was not a surprise but overwhelmed me as if I were pressed down by a giant hand. Then, I got pissed, really pissed. "Sheriff, why would you tell her this on the phone?" I knew I was being rude, but my poor aunt was gut-wrenched.

The sheriff cleared his throat. "I understand how upsetting this is, but Lauren called *me* for an update." His voice was oddly reassuring. "I owed her the truth."

"I'm sorry, of course," I said, humbled.

"I'm in my car. I'll be there in just a few minutes—sit tight." He disconnected.

I threw the phone down and snuggled my head on Lauren's shoulder. "It'll be okay, I'm here," I assured her as she dissolved into another torrent of tears.

Chapter 60
Ivey

"I'm so glad that Lauren agreed to have that grief counselor come over and talk," said Rafe, as we drove over to Tucker's party.

"Yeah." I'd worn a dent between my eyebrows from pressing into my forehead over the past two days. I clasped my hands together on my lap to keep from doing it again. I was completely conflicted about leaving Lauren, but she and the grief counselor urged me to take a break and go to the party.

Rafe glanced over at me, then touched my thigh, reassuringly. "Hey, she'll get through this."

I looked at him skeptically. "How could you possibly know that? Has anyone in *your* family up and disappeared, then turned up dead? Probably murdered?"

Wow, that came out way bitchier than I intended.

Rafe had been utterly sweet and supportive since we'd heard from the police; even asking loads of questions about the crime scene and what the Sheriff himself had concluded, thus far.

He took his foot off the gas, pulled over, then shifted the vehicle into park. Rafe disengaged his seat belt and then turned to me, his eyes full of compassion. "Come 'ere," he whispered.

I unbuckled and melted into Rafe's embrace, my tears ruining the makeup I'd meticulously applied. "I'm sorry for snapping at you. I don't know what to do. Lauren talked to my parents this morning and they are completely freaked out. I guess I don't blame them." I gritted my teeth to keep from becoming hysterical. "Dad can't leave his post, so Mom wants both Lauren and me to go to Arizona and stay with my grandparents!"

Rafe flinched when I mentioned my leaving Walloon Lake. "What did Lauren say about that?" His voice stayed measured and calm, but I could feel his body go rigid.

I settled back in my seat, then fetched a tissue from my purse. "Lauren insisted that she was okay, and she wanted to stay here while the police investigate." I flipped the sun visor's mirror down and dabbed at my puffy eyes. "This whole thing scares me, but I'm sure my place is here—

helping Lauren. Mom doesn't understand, of course. She thinks I'm useless."

Rafe's eyes lowered like he was contemplating what to say next. I couldn't imagine what he would say—the situation felt out of control. Adults would, yet again, swoop in and take over, and I'd end up with no say.

"Listen," Rafe's voice shook. "I thought going out tonight might be a good distraction, but maybe I should take you back—"

I'd freaked him out.

"No, no!" I practically jumped out of my seat. "I do need to get out of the house. Besides, we told Morgan we'd meet him—he's been such a help."

"Man, I'm sorry about your parent's reaction." Rafe hung his head, then peered at me side eyed. "Did the Sheriff talk about the case at all? Leads or suspects?"

I stuffed the tissue back in my bag and smoothed the hair off my forehead. "The sheriff said that there'd be an article in tomorrow's paper and online, asking for any information anyone may have. Maybe that'll help…" I thought back to what Sheriff Preston told Lauren after the DNA confirmation. "He said that the cause of death was blunt force trauma. Most probably someone came up behind him, and Uncle Michal didn't even know it was coming. Oh!" I grabbed Rafe's hand. "This is weird—" I got a wave of adrenalin thinking back to the details. "Get this. His body was moved recently to the location mentioned by the anonymous caller!"

The color drained from Rafe's face. He clutched at his neck. Wait—they're putting an ad in the paper? Won't that alert the, um, bad guys?" His voice sounded high, and nerve rattled.

"Yeah, I thought that was weird too. They don't mention names or specifics, just that a body was found and is there anyone who saw or heard anything strange."

Rafe nodded but he was clearly shaken.

I cupped his sweaty face in my hands. "I didn't realize this would make you so upset." I kissed him on the cheek and noticed his usually warm skin had turned cold and clammy.

He tugged my hands from his face, wiped his brow, put the truck back in gear and pulled back onto the road. "No, no. That's not it. I probably ate something that's not sitting well." He cleared his throat, rolled his head in a small circle, then plastered on a smile.

I sat back, confused. "I appreciate your empathy, I really do."

"Of course." He said quietly.

We drove in silence, winding through leafy streets on our way to the other side of Walloon Lake.

"Morgan said he'd bring the polaroid he's had tonight, but we don't have to talk about anything." Rafe sounded normal again. "Up to you."

I stared out the windshield at the purply pink sky. "Okay."

I heard the party before I saw the house. Rafe slowed as we passed Chargers, Lincolns, Corvettes, and one of those boxy, hulking Mercedes SUVs. There were a few regular cars and various trucks like Rafe's. We pulled behind a tricked-out Ram truck. I swung open the door, hopped out, and landed on top of a prickly bush that scratched up my ankles. "Son of a—" I said, under my breath. I looked up to heaven, wondering what other blood, real or imagined, I'd shed tonight. Stop being so melodramatic, Ivey.

Rafe came around the back of the truck and caught me dabbing at my ankles with yet another tissue. "Oh, no! I'm so sorry! I didn't see those shrubs." He kneeled and took the tissue out of my hand and gently wiped the remaining blood off my left ankle. I gazed down at him, being such a gentleman. My already weary heart melted even more.

He helped me crawl out of the bushes, and we walked, hand in hand, toward a gigantic house, lit up like a Hollywood premiere. I half expected a red carpet as we approached the front door, but instead, there was a vast expanse of white steppingstones each framed with perfectly tended grass. I don't know anything about architecture, but Tucker's house was all angles, glass, and chrome—very modern. Rap music blared and echoed off the lake making it sound like the vocals were fighting each other.

There were people everywhere in various states of dress and sobriety, dancing, drinking, and splashing around in the backyard pool. When we made it up to the industrial-looking sliding glass front door, my jaw dropped. We could see through the front all the way to the rear glass doors that lead to the lake.

I turned to Rafe. "This is the most amazing house I've ever seen in my life!"

He chuckled. "I know! It's freaking sick. Tucker's mom is a surgeon, and his dad is some sort of investment banker. They have three other houses, too!"

We crossed the threshold entering the living room, slash, dining room, slash, bar, which was bigger than our entire house. Tons of people were inside, sitting and chatting within the sofa clusters sprinkled around the space. I looked up at towering white beams that crisscrossed the raw wood ceiling.

"Hey, Rafe! Glad you could come," said a deep voice that halted my ridiculous staring, at least for the moment.

Rafe shook hands with a nice-looking boy in a polo shirt and wild madras shorts. "Tucker! Great to see you. This is Ivey." His hand was possessively placed on my lower back.

I waved at Tucker lamely. "Hey. Your house is beyond!"

Tucker flipped his longish brown bangs back and smiled. "Thanks! So, you're the famous Ivey."

I winced. "What?"

Rafe echoed me. "Yea, what?"

Tucker wrang his hands together. "Oh, shit. No reason, really. I just heard your name a few times. Listen, I gotta check on the beverages. Come get a drink!" He dashed across the floor and ducked behind an enormous marble bar.

Rafe glanced at me. "Well, that was weird."

I nodded. "Yeah, I could use a drink though." I grabbed Rafe's hand and led him to the bar. I'm not that into alcohol, but I've learned (all credit to Kelli) that sipping on a hard cider keeps the peer pressure at bay. Behind the bar were four Igloo coolers filled with every possible canned beverage, and Tucker crouched like he was playing hide and seek.

Rafe leaned against the marble countertop with an amused expression on his face. "Um, Tuck, could we have two hard ciders while you're down there?" He tapped on the bar like an anxious customer.

Tucker dug through a cooler and grasped two cans in one hand. "Here ya go," he said, sheepishly. "Have a blast."

Rafe popped both cans and handed me one. "Seriously, where'd you hear Ivey's name? Don't be shady, dude."

Tucker stood up and wiped his hands on his shorts. "You should know better than anyone *who* knows all the deets about everyone in town."

Rafe and I exchanged glances.

I crossed my arms, settling a hip against the bar counter. "Oh my God, seriously?" Hattie Foster certainly had a lot of influence around here—at least with people our age.

Tucker pursed his lips. "Sorry, she's kinda co-hosting tonight. She hit me up a couple of days ago and told me that I should have the party early." He plunged his hands into his pockets, looked at his feet, then back at us. "She can be very convincing."

Rafe clicked his tongue, then sipped from his cider can. "So, where is she?"

"Out by the pool last I saw." Tucker fetched himself a Budweiser, cracked it open, and took a swig. "Oh, and Ivey, good luck."

Chapter 61

Ivey

Rafe guided me to a white leather sofa. We sat down and sipped our drinks. I looked around at all the people I didn't know. No one was staring at me, yet I still felt like a fish in a bowl.

With a tiny lift of his head, Rafe acknowledged some swimsuit wearing guys who walked by. "You wanna hang here or go outside—maybe get talking to Hattie out of the way?"

I sighed. "I don't know." Was I ready to engage with Hattie? Bring up all this emotional business?

Talking with Hattie was even more daunting now that we were here. I rubbed between my eyes, then placed my hand on my stomach. The cider was disgusting. Several of Rafe's classmates made their way over to our couch, and he made introductions. Everyone was super nice, so I forgot about Hattie for a moment. I enjoyed meeting people my age. Other than Rafe and Morgan, I'd spent most of the summer with tourists and older folks.

We talked and laughed and even danced to some songs that weren't my personal favorites, but Rafe was a good dancer. I clomped around like a llama in Steve Maddens, but it was awesome to feel part of the group, like I belonged in some small way.

Morgan finally showed up, and he motioned for us to join him in a cabinet-lined room just off the kitchen. I had seen rooms like it in magazines—a butler's pantry. (If there was ever a house that would have a room called a butler's pantry, it was this one.)

He hugged me and elbowed Rafe. "How are you guys doing?"

I smiled. "We're good. Rafe's introduced me to a bunch of people from your school. Not that I'll remember anyone's name."

Rafe squeezed my hand. "Ivey's been great—not sure I'd want to meet so many random people."

Morgan glanced around, then removed the polaroid we'd received from Mr. Habibi from his cargo shorts pocket. He handed it to me. "I'm so sorry I couldn't find anything useful."

I took the photo and tucked it in my cross-body bag's front pocket. "It's okay. Rafe said he texted you the latest from the police, right?"

"Yeah, that sucks." His angular face softened. "How's your aunt doing?"

I distractedly opened a nearby cabinet to see what people might store in a butler's pantry: dishes, a silver teapot, and little matching cups, more dishes. "Lauren's not good." I told him. "She's hardly left the bed since the Sheriff confirmed my uncle's identity. Oh! And it seems that his remains were moved recently."

Rafe started coughing, then choking, intense enough that Morgan pounded on his back.

"Relax, man. Try to breathe." Morgan edged back to give Rafe some air. We both inspected Rafe's splotchy and sweaty face.

Rafe laughed weakly, then cleared his throat. "A-hem, I'm okay." He excused himself to get water.

Morgan and I chatted in the pantry for a few minutes. "Maybe I should go help him." I muttered.

Just then, Rafe strode back, looking better, but loudly cleared his throat. "Sorry, guys." He wiped at the sweat along his hairline. "I don't know where that came from."

I turned my attention back to Morgan. "Lauren met with a grief counselor earlier today who prescribed some sleeping pills. Before she took them, Lauren insisted I go out and have some fun," I reached for and then squeezed Rafe's hand, which was clammy like earlier in the truck. "But I'm thinking we should go check on her soon."

Well, after I talk to Hattie.

Rafe took out his phone and noted the time. "It's about nine- thirty. How about we aim to leave in thirty minutes?"

I grinned. "That's great. Hey, wonder where's the closest bathroom? There must be about ten around here." I walked out of the pantry scanning the great room. "I think I see one."

A girl with brunette spiral curls, a lacey tank, and bike shorts had just vacated a nearby restroom. I scooted past her and shut the door behind me. I was in the most ornate powder room I'd ever seen. The floor was marble; it matched all the floors in the house, but the walls were, literally, ivory silk. At least, I think they were silk. I did my business, washed my hands, then dried them thoroughly so I could safely touch the fabric. Wow. It was like the walls were lined with someone's wedding dress. I turned to the mirror to check the probable trainwreck that was my makeup, when I got an overwhelming chill. Rafe was acting weird—shady, even. I mean, I appreciated that he cared about Lauren and me, but his reactions appeared personal in a strange way.

Someone banged on the door, so I smoothed my hair, adjusted my crossbody and exited the bathroom. Rafe, Morgan, and several people I'd recently been introduced to were gathered near the open doors leading to the pool. As I walked over to meet up, a flash of black hair and bright pink flew by. Despite the loud music, laughing and screaming, and the general roar of people talking, I heard a high-pitched voice call out, "Rafey! Oh my God! You're here!"

I got to Rafe's side just as Hattie flung herself at him.

A very annoyed looking, extremely buff guy trailed behind her, crossing his arms at the scene. The guy said, "Hattie, get off him, will ya?" His voice was squeaky and pitiful.

Hank Purcell. I remembered Rafe mentioning him when I first met Hattie. Poor guy.

Rafe turned bright red and pushed Hattie away. "Hey, Hats, what's up?"

Hattie wore a barely-there magenta string bikini. She looked good; I had to give her that.

I tucked my hand around Rafe's elbow and glued myself to his side. "Hi, Hattie, so nice to see you again." I plastered a smile on my face. I probably looked like the Joker.

Why so serious, girlie?

Hattie winced at the sight of me. Her shiny lips curled to a sneer. Her fingers spread over her bony hips. "Eh, oh, hello, Ivey. I didn't know you'd be here."

My eyes bored into hers. "That's weird, because everyone I've met tonight seems to have expected me."

"Well," she huffed. "I wouldn't know anything about that."

Hank came up behind Hattie and wrapped his beefy arms around her waist. She slapped at him. "What are you doing?"

Hank's face fell. "You can be a real bitch sometimes, you know that?" He turned and marched toward the pool.

Rafe's body tensed. "You should really go hang with your boyfriend, Hats, I think you hurt his feelings."

Hattie took her ravenous eyes off Rafe long enough to locate Hank, who dove into the pool. "Oh, he's fine. Such a baby."

I stood there taking in the exchange between Rafe and Hattie. Before I thought it through, I blurted out, "Hattie, could I talk to you privately?"

Chapter 62

Ivey

There was an honest to God gasp from the people around us.

I crinkled up my face and scanned the crowd. "Seriously? I didn't invite her to dual at dawn, guys!"

"You may as well have!" yelled one of Hattie's minions—not sure which one.

Hattie crossed her arms and studied me before calmly answering, "Sure, why not? Follow me." She waltzed into the house like she owned it, pushing people out of the way as she went.

I started to follow when Rafe pulled me back. "What the hell? Ivey, this is *not* a good idea. I should come with you."

I patted Rafe's chest reassuringly. "It's okay, don't worry." I sprinted to catch up to Hattie.

She led me to what turned out to be a home office. I would have expected dark wood panel walls lined with leather-bound books and a massive desk with coordinating brass lamps, but this office stayed with a modern theme. The walls were stark white with a Lucite desk right in the middle of the marble floor. The most advanced-looking Apple computer monitor was the only thing on the desk—no keyboard. Hattie pulled the silver ergonomic office chair out and sat down, her skinny elbows placed on the desktop with her hands folded under her chin.

I took a seat in one of the roundish chairs facing the desk.

"Okay, what do you want to talk about?" Hattie tilted her head, almost curiously, sat back in the chair tenting her fingers as if she presided over a courtroom.

I pulled a polaroid from my cross-body bag and slid it over the Lucite surface toward her. I pointed to the unknown man. "Do you know who this is?"

Hattie leaned forward and picked up the photo. First, she looked puzzled, then a shroud of confusion or anger or hurt came over her. She didn't say anything for a few seconds.

Finally, she looked up, the shroud gone, replaced with her typical "annoyed by the world" expression. "Where did you get this?" She dropped the polaroid on the desk like it had lice.

"The photo was taken at a bar that used to be called the Walloon Saloon." I pointed to my uncle. "This is my uncle Michal Lyska. He disappeared about five years ago. I'm asking because you alluded to 'criminal' activity when you came by the store the other day—you do remember that, right?"

"Of course, I remember," she snapped, gesturing toward the polaroid with a bony, red tipped finger. "But I don't know anything about that photo or some skeezy bar."

I stood up and made my way around the desk and planted myself next to Hattie. I put the photo back in front of her and pointed at the mystery man again. "When you mentioned your father being the District Attorney, of course, I googled him. So, when I saw this photo, I couldn't help but notice a certain resemblance."

She looked up at me with fury in her eyes. "Are you implying my father had something to do with your uncle going missing?" She shot up and the office chair went flying back against the wall with a smack, her fists clenched at her sides. It was tough to take her seriously in that pink bikini.

I held up my hand, hoping she'd calm down. "Hattie, I know you've taken an instant dislike to me." I paused, wondering if I should mention Rafe. "For whatever reason, but my aunt and I just found out that my uncle is dead—"

Hattie recoiled. "What?"

My shoulders sagged. "Yeah, the cops are pretty sure he was murdered."

Hattie started pacing around the room. That strange, difficult-to-pinpoint look on her face again. Was she sad? Mad? Psychotic? She chewed on her thumbnail.

I started to say something, but she held up her hand. "No, don't say anything else." Her voice was cool and calm. "I don't know who the photo man is. I agree that he bears a passing resemblance to my dad, but that's all it is— a passing resemblance. My God, it's freezing in here!"

I pursed my lips. "Well, you aren't wearing much."

Hattie looked around the room, then at me with a clenched jaw. "It is a pool party, y'know." She rubbed her upper arms.

A crowd of partygoers gathered outside the office's floor-to-ceiling window, and one guy had his nose pressed against the glass. I gestured toward the window. "We have spectators."

Hattie turned, dropped her arms to her sides like dead weights, and rolled her eyes. "Christ."

"Thanks for looking at the photo. Really," I said, crestfallen that Hattie legitimately didn't seem to recognize photo man. "I thought maybe we had a lead 'cause—"

She blinked then moved toward me. " 'Cause what?"

I sat down again. "Because I found out that your dad and my aunt went out back in the day."

Hattie plopped into the other chair, then put her head in her hands. "Did *she* tell you that?" Her voice was muffled.

"No, I found her yearbook." God, this girl is prickly. "Lauren acknowledged that they dated, but that they haven't had much contact since—except…"

Should I tell her about her father's role in hiding my uncle's disappearance?

Hattie laughed. She lifted her stupid perfect black bob and started laughing.

My back stiffened and I clenched my fists so hard that my stubby nails dug into my palms. "You know what? Hank's right. You are being a bitch. I thought you might be able to shed some light on things but to laugh at my uncle's death—"

She rubbed her nose. "No, no, I'm not laughing about that. I'd never do that." She went quiet, her lips flattened, suddenly calm and collected again.

"Okay, then what's so funny?" I pressed between my eyebrows to squelch a coming headache.

Hattie told me about her similar discovery of our family's connection and her confrontation with her father. She admitted that she didn't buy her father's explanation as to why he and my aunt behaved like they existed on separate planets.

I shook my head, sure that Hattie didn't know about her father's having stalked my aunt. "I'm not sure I believe your dad either."

Chapter 63

Ivey

Hattie and I sat in silence for a few beats when someone knocked on the office door.

"Yeah?" we answered, simultaneously.

Tucker stuck his head in the room, a pinched look on his face. "Everything okay in here? Um, my mother can be very picky about her—"

"Oh, shut up, Tucker!" Hattie snapped. "Everything's fine. Bring me a towel or a blanket—it's freezing in here!"

Tucker tucked tail and disappeared just as Rafe walked in, followed by Morgan and Hank, who carried a pink sarong like an offering to baby Jesus.

Hattie sped toward Hank and snatched the sarong. "Thanks, babe!" She draped it around her shoulders with a flourish.

I was frustrated at the interruption since Hattie and I had finally come to some common ground concerning our families' complicated connections. "Hattie and I are still talking. Can we have a few more minutes?" I asked the guys, looking at Rafe pleadingly, hoping he'd understand that I had the situation in hand.

Hattie disagreed. "I'm done here!" she announced, then singled Rafe out. "I'm assuming my special surprise hasn't arrived yet." She batted her eyes.

Seriously?

Thankfully, Rafe didn't look impressed either. He folded his arms, one eyebrow raised. "What surprise is that?"

A disconcerting smile crept over Hattie's face. "Oh, you'll see!" She dragged Hank out of the office, so I waved Rafe and Morgan further in the room.

Morgan pulled up a chair and sat down with his legs wide like guys do. "You better spill, Ivey!"

I clicked my tongue. "I asked her straight up if she knows who the photo guy is." I made quote marks in the air.

Rafe stood beside me, placing a hand on my hip. "And?"

"She says she doesn't know but agrees he has a passing resemblance to her father." I did the quote thing again.

Rafe grabbed my fingers this time. "You're gonna have to stop doing that." He grinned.

"Okay, okay, no more air quotes. She also found out about Lauren and her dad dating in high school. And she said she had grilled her dad about it, but that he blew her off."

"Hmmm." Morgan scratched at his chin. "You are one brave human being, Ives. Hattie scares the living hell out of most people."

"She's like a rabid chihuahua." I glanced at the door. "But I wasn't in any mortal danger." I watched Rafe as he went toward the window, then joined him. We watched the twenty or so people around the pool, either splashing in the water or hanging out on lounge chairs. This was the first time I'd surveyed Tucker's family's lake view. Bright from the outdoor lights, an enormous boat dock was attached to the property. There was a wood-sided speed boat tied in one slip, and a large pontoon-type craft suspended under a covered hoist. The third slip was vacant.

Rafe told me that Tucker's parents were on an extended trip around the Great Lakes on their sailboat which explained the empty slip. What a life. Being able to just take off on a summer adventure. I wondered why Tucker didn't go, but then I thought about being trapped on a boat, for months, with my parents, and I understood. I guess someone looking at my life might think I was pretty lucky to have a summer adventure.

A wash of realization came over me. I wanted to make my own decisions, be useful. I was kinda doing that right now. It's true that my parents made me come to Walloon for their own reasons, but the things I've done here have been totally me. It was a scary, heavy, but gratifying thought. Rafe and I crisscrossed our arms behind each other. He settled his head on mine which made me tingle and feel warm at the same time.

We stood there for a while until Rafe jerked up his head. "No way!"

I popped out of my calm reverie, stepped back, and stared at him. "What?" I glanced behind us. Morgan had gone, and I followed Rafe's gaze out the window.

"Come on, Hattie's damn surprise is here," he muttered. Rafe was halfway out the door before my feet moved.

Chapter 64
Ivey

Outside by the pool, the music blared. I kept my eyes fixed on Rafe fluidly moving through the crowd—sliding by people and excusing himself as he went. I caught up to him just as he approached a guy standing at the lake's edge. With long black hair pulled into a low man-bun and his back to us, the guy had on a flannel shirt with the sleeves carelessly cut off and well-worn jeans.

Rafe called out, "Tonio, what the—?"

When the guy turned around, I almost fainted. He was Rafe's twin, but with a sad, beaten-down kind of expression. The brothers hastily hugged. Rafe briefly perched his hands on Antonio's shoulders, then pulled him into a whisper.

I stood a few feet away, not able to hear anything, honoring their personal space. They talked furtively, gesturing with their hands when Rafe turned and waved me over. Both smiled as I tip-toed through the black-eyed Susans and Pappas grass that lined the seawall.

I was a bit self-conscious. "Hey." What would Rafe's brother think of me?

"Ivey, my brother, Antonio. Apparently, he's Hattie's surprise." Rafe sighed.

Antonio and I shook hands a bit formally, his eyes darted left and right despite his relaxed posture. "Hi, Ivey, nice to meet 'cha." His lop-sided smile seemed forced.

"Nice to meet you too." His hand was warm, his skin dry.

"Let's go sit on the dock," Rafe suggested, then started toward it.

Antonio and I followed behind. He pulled a pack of cigarettes from his pocket and thrust it toward me. "Smoke?"

I grinned and shook my head. "No, thanks." His desire to share charmed me.

There weren't nearly as many people on the dock as in the pool area, so we clip-clopped down the planks to a couple of built-in benches. Once we all sat down, Rafe started, "Well, I'm sure Hattie thought she was stirring up trouble by inviting you here, but why'd you come—not that I'm not glad to see you." The brothers held each other's gaze for several seconds.

Antonio took a drag off his cigarette and blew it out the side of his mouth. "I figured she was up to something, but I haven't been to an ole fashioned lake party in a while." He rolled his shoulders back. "Plus, I wanted to meet Ivey." He winked at me. I felt a blush coming on.

Rafe laughed. "You're so full of it. You've never liked parties."

Antonio snorted. "That's true, but Hattie's a very convincing person—"

Rafe ran his fingers along the dock surface. "Yeah, everyone agrees with that."

Hattie's ears must have been burning because she ran down the dock toward us, screaming, "Tonio! Tonio! I'm so glad you came!"

Antonio smiled wryly then crooked an eyebrow.

Hattie made it to us and embraced Antonio like he was a long-lost relative. "Isn't it great that Tonio came, Rafe?"

"Yeah," Rafe's face was stoic. "But why did you want him here?"

Hattie's effusive expression fell, replaced by a devilish drawing in of her lips. "I thought he'd have fun." She settled herself beside Antonio and drew her fingers up and down his back. Tonio looked everywhere but directly at Hattie.

Rafe studied the display. "You wanna know why I think you invited my brother?" His voice was deep, almost a snarl. It was like that first day I saw him outside Lauren's house.

A shiver ran down my spine.

Rafe moved menacingly toward Hattie. "I think you wanted to make Ivey uncomfortable and off balance— make her think you know me, or my family better than she does."

Hattie made a fake scared face, then broke into hyena-like laughter.

"You are so conceited, Rafe Torres! Not everything is about you!" She stuck her nose in the air.

I couldn't believe that just a few minutes ago, I almost thought Hattie had some empathy, some compassion for someone besides herself.

I stood up and wiped non-existent dust from my skirt. "Either way, I'm glad to meet Antonio," I said, "but I need to get home and check on my aunt."

Hattie stroked Antonio's arm possessively. "Oh, no, don't go," she said flatly, her attention squarely on Rafe.

"Ha, uh." Antonio shirked away from Hattie with an amused grin. "I'm gonna go, too. Uh, thanks for the invite, Hattie."

Rafe and I scrambled toward the house leaving poor Morgan waylaid by a girl who'd crushed on him since the seventh grade (he'd told me earlier). I turned to see Hattie pounding down the dock toward us, skirting around Antonio.

"Ivey! Hold up," she instructed.

I stopped despite my utter distaste for her bossy ways. "What is it, Hattie?" I folded my arms with a huff.

Hattie looked Rafe up and down. "Um, excuse us, please." She pulled me toward her. "This is private."

"Okay, okay!" I reluctantly marched after Hattie, while Antonio caught up with Rafe. The two started to chat in Spanish.

Hattie led me behind a massive potted tree. She stepped too close for comfort but held my upper arm with a vise-like grip. "I wanted to tell you I'm sorry for laughing before."

You could have knocked me over. "Um, thanks." I glanced at my arm. "Could you let me go now?"

Hattie released me, then backed away. "I'll see if I can find some info on the photo guy," she said, her face was now soft and almost kind. "Obviously, I don't have my phone on me, can I give you my number?"

Still stunned, I unzipped my crossbody bag. As I pulled out my phone, my uncle's polaroid came with it. "It might be easier if you have the photo, but please don't lose it," I said, happy I'd taken several screenshots of the polaroid already. I typed my password in the phone, then handed it to her.

Head bent over my phone, Hattie's thumbs clicked in her number and passed it back to me. When she lifted her face, the clenched jaw and pursed lips were back on. "Send your contact to me." She said brusquely, snatching the polaroid out of my hand. "I can't guarantee anything." She ran off quick as a rabbit, leaving me shocked but hopeful.

I told Rafe about Hattie's surprising offer to help as we exited the house with Antonio sauntering behind. I climbed into the truck and pretended to look at my phone while the brothers stayed outside speaking rapid-fire Spanish. I texted Lauren that I'd be home in a few minutes, knowing that she wouldn't answer. Antonio waved at me, then proceeded up the street while Rafe got in the driver's side.

"Well," he said, hands on the wheel. "That was the weirdest party ever."

"Yeah, it was. I cannot believe how much you and your brother look alike."

Rafe cranked the ignition and chuckled. "Yep."

"What were you talking about just now. Not to be nosy." I fiddled with my purse strap.

Rafe reached over and rubbed my knee, assuredly. "I don't think you're being nosy, Ivey. I filled him in on how Hattie's hassled you before. It was bizarre how she was hanging on him—it freaked him out. He doesn't want trouble with Hank Purcell."

"Yeah, is Antonio doing okay, though? Y'know, with the things you've told me about."

Rafe extended his long arms on the steering wheel. "He's hanging in there. He's got a place to stay and is looking for a job. He's doing some handy man work around the trailer park he's in, but he wants something better." I noticed sweat at his temple.

I nodded. "That sounds good—he's moving forward, but…"

"But?" Rafe stared ahead.

I shivered. "Listen, you've been beyond supportive and defensive of me through all—" I waved my shaky hand. "This."

Rafe turned to me, his eyes stormy. "Yeah?"

I shrunk toward the passenger door but persevered. "I get the feeling that there's something going on with you." My throat clenched and I swallowed hard.

Rafe's shoulders relaxed and his normal sweet, toothy smile appeared. "Aw, nothing's wrong." He cranked the ignition. "I'm still pissed at Hattie for dragging Tonio into this."

I hesitated. "Dragged Tonio into what exactly?"

Rafe pulled the truck onto the street, white knuckling the wheel. "Nothing," he said. "I don't know what I'm saying." He laughed unconvincingly. "I'm tired, I guess. Don't worry about me."

When we pulled up to Lauren's a few minutes later, I unbuckled and slid over to hug Rafe. He buried his head between my neck and shoulder. "You know I'd never hurt you, right?" He mumbled.

I pulled away and scanned his face for any clue to Rafe's thoughts. "Of course, I know that." I kissed his pouty lips. "I'm here for you too, y'know? You don't have to be a superhero all the time."

Rafe chuckled. "Yeah, you're right."

I made for the door, anxious to check on Lauren when Rafe pulled me back into a long, passionate kiss that left me breathless.

"I'll see ya tomorrow, mija."

I could barely remember my name.

Chapter 65
Rafe

It took Rafe twenty minutes to make it to Antonio's trailer. When he got there, his brother had already packed a duffel. Antonio chucked the bag into the bed of Rafe's truck, then returned to the trailer for a portable tent. He got in the passenger seat. "Ready."

Rafe put the truck in gear and headed back to Walloon. "I can't believe Ivey's photo guy is your boss!"

"Yeah. Judd McArthur. He's definitely the guy who told me to bury that effing trunk."

Rafe didn't want to agitate his brother, but things were getting real, and fast. "And you have no idea if this Judd guy has anything to do with Hattie's dad?"

"Nope. I googled Hattie's dad, and they do look similar, but I don't know anything about a connection." He pulled the band out of his man bun, then shook his hair out. "That'd be crazy."

Rafe agreed. "And you never heard him mention someone named Michal Lyska?"

Antonio fiddled with the hair band, then shoved it in his pocket. "I'm not someone Judd bounced ideas off of. I'm an addict who owed him money. I'm nothin'."

Rafe couldn't bear it. "You're *not* nothing. Don't talk like that!"

Tonio smiled crookedly. "Hey, I know, bro. I mean, I'm nothing to Judd and Timmy Hill."

"Timmy Hill?"

"Yeah, he's Judd's muscle. Total douche but he'll do anything Judd tells him. They're both nasty guys."

"Well, now I know what Judd looks like from the photo, what about Timmy?" Rafe frowned, then mumbled, "Seriously, a grown man called Timmy?"

Antonio smirked. "Timmy has the IQ of a ten-year-old, but that only makes him reckless." He went on to describe Judd's henchman in detail as Rafe pulled into a lonely boat launch off the lake. Several old kayaks and canoes bumped and bobbed, tied to the rickety dock. The brothers exited the truck and loaded Antonio's items into one of the canoes.

Rafe shivered, anticipating trouble but helpless to stop it. "You have everything?"

Antonio nodded. "Yeah. You'll make the call in the morning?"

Rafe's voice cracked. "I will. You have the burner?"

Tonio took it out of his pocket and held it up.

"You're sure it'll work out there?" Rafe asked warily.

Antonio tousled his brother's hair. "No, I'm not, but what choice do I have?"

Rafe ducked, then swatted at his brother's hand. "Stop, hey! Text me when you get there to check the signal." He grabbed around Antonio's back and held him close, fighting back tears.

Antonio leaned into the hug for a minute but wriggled away when his emotions took hold. "Hey, it'll be okay, little bro." He patted Rafe's back. "Love you, man."

Rafe stood on the shore and watched his only brother row out of sight, then he drove home, climbed in bed, and fell into a fitful sleep.

Chapter 66

Hattie

The alarm shook Hattie from an exhaustingly repetitive dream where she was running away from something, trying to get someone to help her, and no one would listen.

"Uh, my God," she moaned, then turned over on her back and rubbed her throbbing temples. She'd had a few more drinks than she'd intended at Tucker's last night. Hattie heard the tell-tale thud, thud of Adam's sleeper-clad feet coming down the hall. She braced her hungover body for—

"Hattie, Hattie, Hattie!! Come down for pancakes! Liza's making pancakes!!!" Adam bellowed when he barged into her room and hopped on top of Hattie's stomach. She curled into a defensive fetal position. "Adam! No! You're too big to jump on me!"

Undaunted, her little brother burrowed under the covers and pretended to be a puppy nipping at her feet. She giggled despite herself. "Adam! Silly boy." Hattie reached under the sheets, pulled him up, and kissed his little cheeks. "You're the sweetest, naughtiest little puppy ever."

"I—I can't breathe," he gasped, poking his head out. "Are you gonna come for pancakes?"

She snuggled him again and kissed his forehead. "I'll be down in a minute, don't you eat them all, now."

Adam crawled off her bed and sped down the hall yelling, "I will eat them all!"

Hattie rubbed her temples again, then rolled off the bed and crept wearily to her bathroom. She leaned over the sink and squinted at her blotchy face, hair sticking up, and mascara crusted under her eyes. "This may take more than a minute," she said to her reflection.

Fifteen minutes later, Hattie ambled down the staircase wearing a long satin kimono and fuzzy slippers. She passed by the half-moon table in the foyer on which her mother's Murano vase used to sit. *You'd think Dad would have replaced it by now*, she thought.

Hattie recalled that her mother took the news fairly well, considering. Her father had promised to get a new one. Her parents' stilted conversation about the vase had been interesting. Hattie's mom had remained calm but said the oddest thing. They had been in their bedroom, the evening after the vase had been broken, while Hattie eavesdropped through the thin walls.

"You know how much that vase has always meant to me, Scott." Her mother's tone held none of her usual cloying submissiveness.

"Yes, of course, dear." Hattie's father responded.

"No, Scott, look at me." Her mother paused. "You know what that vase represented, why it's important."

Hattie'd never heard her mother be that insistent about anything. She was proud of her.

Now, Hattie passed by her father's study, then through the kitchen on her way to the back porch where Liza had set out a lovely Sunday brunch: egg and cheese casserole, crepes, fruit and, of course, pancakes. Her family sat at an iron table with floral padded chairs. Liza poured juice for Adam.

"Good morning!" welcomed her mother wearing a flowing lemon-yellow caftan, her hair pulled back severely with a clip.

Hattie tipped her head and pulled out a chair. "Hey, Liza can I have some hot tea—English breakfast?"

"Of course, darling." Liza turned toward the kitchen.

Her father looked over his coffee cup with a wicked arch to his eyebrows. "You got home late last night."

Hattie clicked her tongue. "Is that a statement, or a question?" She took a pancake from the family-style platter, then plopped it on her plate.

He glared. "I guess it's a statement. Where were you?"

"Tucker Bostic had his summer party last night. I was kinda the cohost." Hattie took a bite of pancake.

"Jesus, how much is that going to cost me?"

Hattie's mother fake-slapped her husband's wrist. "Please don't make a big deal."

"Don't worry about it, Dad." Hattie poked out her lip, sarcastically. "I put it on the Amex, so it's not like real money."

"Hilarious," he snapped back.

"Oh, we had so much fun!" Hattie went on. "That girl, Ivey, was there. She's going out with Rafe now. And Rafe's brother Antonio stopped by." She slyly peered at her father.

He flinched. Part of the reason Hattie had broken up with Rafe was her father's constant haranguing about the "bad" element in Rafe's family, namely Antonio. Her father set his coffee cup down with an abrupt clank. "Why would a nineteen-year-old man come to a high school party? I find that concerning." His eyes got crinkled and thin like a snake.

Hattie waited a beat for dramatic effect. "I invited him, that's why."

Her father stared darts at her. "I find that concerning as well."

Adam held up his pancake. "Look, I made a moon!" He had nibbled into the center of his pancake.

Hattie turned her attention to her brother and smiled warmly at him. "Oh, sweetie, that's so cool!"

Her mother gently guided her son's syrupy hand down to his plate. "Great job, Addie, now gobble it up. We're meeting Noah and Mason at the park soon."

Hattie, her mother, and her brother chit-chatted about Adam's friends and what they'd do at the park while her father finished his food in seething silence. He eventually excused himself and skulked to his home office.

After she'd eaten a pancake, some fruit and finished a cup of tea, Hattie decided she needed to confront her dad about the man in Ivey's photo. Last night, she'd fixated on the photo, noting the resemblance between her father and the mystery man. Hattie dreaded the thought of her father, or anyone in her father's orbit having something to do with Ivey's uncle's death. *Could Dad possibly be that sinister?*

She'd tucked the photo into her kimono pocket earlier that morning, so now, Hattie propped herself against the office's open French door, staring at her father as he concentrated on his computer screen. "You really shouldn't work on Sundays, Dad."

He looked up, narrowed his eyes and pulled on his collar. "What can I do for you, honey?" Despite the term of endearment, he didn't sound all that psyched about talking.

Hattie strode into the room, closing the door behind her. "I have a couple of questions."

He leaned back in his chair taking his fingers off the keyboard. "Okay, shoot."

Hattie touched her kimono pocket, as if to assure herself that the photo was still there. "Did you know someone named Michal Lyska?"

His face remained expressionless, but he tapped the keyboard to darken the computer screen. "Why do you ask?"

Hattie rolled her eyes and sighed. "Could you just this once, answer me directly, Dad?"

Her father gestured toward one of the burgundy leather chairs in front of his desk. "Sit down. I'll tell you what I know."

She complied, butterflies churning up her belly.

Her father's tone was matter of fact. No sign of stress or concern. "Since you're asking me, I assume you know that Michal Lyska is, or was, Lauren Corbett's husband."

Hattie nodded.

"Short answer, I did not know him at all, personally. Professionally, I was the ADA on a matter concerning Mr. Lyska—I never spoke directly with him, though."

Hattie squirmed in the seat, making a squeaky sound on the leather. "Ivey told me that her uncle's remains were recently found. That he was probably murdered."

Her father's face finally changed, softened. "Yes, I'm aware. It's tragic for Ms. Corbett but," he tapped a finger on the desk. "Ivey really shouldn't be discussing the case with anyone."

She nodded again, feeling a spark of empathy for Ivey and her aunt. It felt like a weight pushing down on her. "Well, it's a scary situation." *Ironic that I'm kinda defending Ivey now.*

Her father leaned forward, placing his elbows on the desk. "Why are you so interested in all this?"

Hattie's voice came out squeakier than she intended, "Ivey gave me this." She rose and plunked the polaroid onto the desk right in front of her father.

Her father's cheek twitched. He didn't move, just stared down at the photo. "What the hell is this?"

"God, Dad! Ivey got this polaroid at some broken-down bar." Hattie made her way around the desk and pressed her finger onto the photo. "This is her uncle and here—" she said, losing all patience, "is a friend of his who looks familiar, right?"

Hattie's father bolted upright from his seat. "Hattie!" he barked. "This isn't some teenage revenge drama. If what you're saying is true, your friend has valuable evidence in a possible murder investigation."

Hattie trudged back to the chair, feeling more confident in her questions. "Hold on now," she said. "I just wanted to know if you can identify the man I pointed out. I wasn't connecting him to Ivey's uncle's death— what do you know about it?"

Her father blinked several times as if coming out of a trance. "Well, I don't know anything at all about Mr. Lyska's death; I'm simply emphasizing that the police need all information for their investigations."

"Okay." She drew the word out dramatically. "So, you have no curiosity or comment on this guy, who looks exactly like you, being a friend to a possible murder victim?"

Her father tilted his head, as if trying to see the photo more clearly; his tone was now chilly. "I don't think we look that much alike, but I'll check with the sheriff concerning Mr. Lyska's past associates."

"Fine." Hattie stood up, went to the office door, then started down the hallway toward the stairs wrapping her kimono tighter, her blood running cold.

Her father slammed the office door behind her, and she heard him already on his phone.

Chapter 67

Ivey

I raised my voice so Rafe could hear me from the Sunnyside storeroom. "Do we have any more stationery?"

Mrs. Delaney held up a package of stationery decorated with clusters of blooms. "With the single sunflower, dear!"

"One sec!" Rafe shouted back to me.

God, I love his voice.

I smiled. "Should I wrap up your other items while he looks for the stationary?"

"That'd be lovely, thank you, Ivey." Mrs. Delaney had been a repeat customer over the summer and a super nice lady. I snuck a couple of sunflower sticker sheets in her bag. I knew she'd enjoy the freebie. We'd received tons of positive feedback about fun little gifts, like stickers, stamps, or any extra inventory items.

Mrs. Delaney brought a floral doorstop to the counter. "I'm so sad the summer shops are closing soon. It's been fun having all the fresh flowers and decor."

I thanked her for being such a valued customer when Rafe bounded out of the storeroom holding the desired stationary high. "Found the last one!" His grin was wide and toothy.

I waved him toward me. "Excellent, hand it here."

Rafe sidled up and squeezed me around my waist.

"You two are so cute." Mrs. Delaney reached for her purchases. "See you on Closing Day!"

"Thank you! Owf!" Rafe pulled me into a kiss before she exited the booth. "Rafe! Stop, we're working." I wasn't truly bothered at all.

"Mmm." He growled into my neck. "I love your lips, and your neck, and your ears." He nibbled his way up to my left ear.

I giggled and snuggled closer into his chest. "You smell like flowers."

He pulled back and looked at me with faux horror. "Flowers? I smell like flowers? That's what you say when I'm trying to be sexy?"

I laughed as heartily as I had in forever. "But I like it!"

He hugged me closer. "Good, 'cause I'm cool with being a flower guy."

An hour later, we finished the daily closing routine: storing the unsold sunflower stems in the fridge, tidying up the counter, and gathering the small amount of cash we collected (most transactions were done on the iPad). I planned to take it to the bank the following day.

I placed the cash pouch in my crossbody bag, then scooted out of the booth so Rafe could close the shutters, securing the booth overnight.

"You have everything you need?" Rafe threaded a sturdy lock through the shutters' metal brackets.

"I do." I patted my bag.

He grabbed my hand, and we started out of the market.

A stocky man wearing camo pants, a hunting vest, thermals, and a beat-up Cubs cap approached us. He was out of place—not only with his clothing (it was eighty-five degrees out) but, also, in his whole vibe. The man's gait was tense, like he was braced for an attack. "You must be Rafe," he grumbled.

Instinctively, Rafe stepped in front of me but kept a firm grasp on my hand. "Yeah, can I help you with something?"

I peered around Rafe as the man completely invaded Rafe's space. We both had to step back to avoid being crowded, but we were stopped by the adjoining booths behind us. A nasty smirk spread over the man's face as he wiped at his scraggly greying beard.

Rafe balked at being cornered. "What's up with you, man? Back off!"

"Antonio said you guys looked alike." The man sneered.

Rafe shuddered at the mention of his brother. "Yeah, so?"

I clutched at Rafe's belt and looked around; my neck stretched painfully as I frantically hoped someone would walk by—no such luck.

"Where's your brother?" the man demanded, his voice deep, insistent.

Rafe sniffed, his body now quivering with fear or anger. "I'm not telling you anything. I have no idea who you are." He pushed toward the man, trying to intimidate him with five extra inches and shaky bravado. I was clinging to Rafe so tightly that he yanked me along.

I gasped. "Rafe, don't!"

The man was not intimidated. He pulled a gun from the back of his pants and held it across his body, not pointing the weapon, just making sure we got a good long look.

My heartbeat skyrocketed, and I gulped for air. I couldn't stop my body from shaking, so I clung to Rafe as his posture deflated.

The man's hot, sour breath filled the stagnant air around the three of us. "Listen to me." He pushed his gun-laden chest into us. "Your brother knows who I am." Rafe stood his ground. "And he knows why I want to talk to him."

My vision narrowed; black fuzz gathered around the edges of my eyes. I wanted to run, but my feet dug into the gravel. Not that I could go anywhere, sandwiched between Rafe and the booth behind us.

"Okay, okay. I'll tell him! Just back off!" Rafe sounded miles away.

The man thankfully stepped back as Rafe and I exhaled in tandem. The man stuffed the weapon back under his hunting vest. "By tonight," he grunted, then ambled away as if he'd simply asked us the time of day.

It felt like the world had rebooted itself. Rafe swiveled and caught me by the shoulders. "Are you okay?" He was so kind, I could cry. I couldn't speak yet, so I bobbed my head.

We breathed together, holding each other's gaze.

Rafe disconnected from our embrace, then started to pace like a panther.

"We need to call the police," I said, slowing my breath.

"No!" Rafe replied, a bit too quickly. "No, let me think." He rubbed his neck with both hands.

I couldn't believe it. "Rafe, my God, the man had a gun! We need to call the police!"

Rafe took both my hands, his voice steady and low-pitched. "We need to get to my house now."

Dread crept through my veins. The world wasn't making any sense. I looked down at my feet.

Rafe lifted my chin. "Ivey, I'm pretty sure I know who that guy is, and what he wants. Tonio's in real trouble and I need to get to my parents. Please come with me."

I wanted to argue. I wanted to run. I wanted my mom and dad.

Chapter 68

Ivey

We ran the ten minutes it took to get to Rafe's house—me, texting Lauren a flimsy excuse for my delayed return home, and Rafe texting his father. It felt as if we were the only humans in town—like that unsettled feeling when you leave a movie theater when it's still light out.

I tried to get Rafe's attention, to ask him how he knew the man who accosted us, fearing the answer but needing it all the same. I knew there were things he hadn't told me about Antonio, and I was okay with him telling me in his own time. But now, I dreaded the truth, and what it might mean for him and us. Mr. Torres's truck screeched into the family's driveway right as we arrived.

Rafe's father glanced up and down the street, then herded us into the house. "Get inside."

We sunk onto the corduroy couch in the Torres' living room, while Mr. Torres' loomed over us. I felt disgusting with sweat and dust from our run.

Mrs. Torres ran into the room, phone in hand. "The Sheriff's on his way," she said breathlessly. Mr. Torres groaned. "Okay, tell us what happened."

Rafe dropped his head into his hands, shoulders heaving. When he lifted his head to address his father, tears streamed down his crestfallen face. "I think it was a man named Timmy Hill. He had a gun, and he—" Rafe gulped. "He was looking for Tonio."

Mrs. Torres fell onto the couch between us, mumbling reassuring words. "You're safe now. It's going to be okay." The mantra, possibly, to comfort herself as well.

Mr. Torres rubbed his neck, so much like Rafe, it took my breath away. "Jesus, what's Tonio gotten into?" He lowered himself to the vinyl recliner behind him.

I didn't know what to do or say. I sat there like a quivering lump.

When the air-conditioner kicked on and I shuddered, Mrs. Torres rubbed my arm and patted my hand. "Oh, mija, the Sheriff will be here soon." She looked at her husband. "Marco, we need to call Lauren, let her know."

"Yes, we will, but let's wait for the Sheriff to get here," he replied gently.

At that, Rafe got up from the couch and started pacing. "Dad, Tonio told me about these guys. He owes them some money, so he's been working for them."

"My God, all right." Mr. Torres took a deep breath in. "Go on."

Adrenaline pounded through my body. What would Rafe say? I knew he was keeping something from me. A stab of anger pierced my heart.

"Mijo, please, talk to us!" his mother pleaded.

Rafe paused, then looked at me. His eyes were damp and the corners of his mouth downturned. "I'm not a hundred percent sure, but this guy and his boss may have known Ivey's uncle. They may have—"

I gasped. Blood rushed to my ears, making it hard to hear over my own heartbeat.

Mr. Torres exploded off the recliner. "Tonio's involved with a murder? Is that what you're saying?"

Rafe raked his fingers through his sweaty hair. "No, no! Not the murder itself. He was desperate to get away from these guys, Dad."

The men squared off, looking like prizefighters sizing each other up before the first punch. Mr. Torres stood shaking but remained silent. Mrs. Torres and I sat on the couch, stunned and speechless.

My chest burned, my hands and feet went numb, my mouth dried up and the room spun.

A bang on the door broke the dreadful hush. Sheriff Preston cleared his throat loudly. "Marco? Gabby?"

Mrs. Torres rose from the couch, abandoning me in my misery. "Thank God, Ed!" She said, as she flung open the front door.

Sheriff Preston hooked his thumbs on his utility belt, surveying the hot mess before him. "Okay, folks, let's stay calm. Marco, you look like you're about to pop a blood vessel."

Rafe's father snorted. "I might, Ed. A man named Timmy Hill threatened Rafe and Ivey an hour ago at the market."

The Sheriff took his notebook out of his shirt pocket. It stung that I'd seen him do that so recently. "Let's start at the beginning. Ivey, Rafe? What happened?"

Rafe turned to me—like I'd be able to speak after learning about Antonio's connection to all this. I slowly shook my head.

Rafe, then, turned to the Sheriff. For a second, he looked like a little boy who'd shot a bb through a window.

"Ivey and I had closed the Sunnyside when this man came up and demanded to know where Tonio was. He said stuff about us looking alike, then he pulled out a gun."

The sheriff looked up from his notetaking. "And you think the man was Timmy Hill?"

"Yeah, he was about 5'6, heavyset, dressed like he just returned from hunting, Cubs hat, grey beard. Tonio had described him to me. He told me Timmy is Judd's muscle…" Rafe's voice trailed off.

The Sheriff's eyes widened. He shifted his feet. "Judd McArthur?"

"Yeah," said Rafe.

Mr. Torres raised his arms as if surrendering. "Wait! Who the hell is Judd McArthur?"

"Just a minute, Marco." Sheriff Preston held up a finger. "Ivey, do you have anything to add to Rafe's account?"

I shivered. "That's about it."

The sheriff nodded, then detached his walkie-talkie from the Velcro on his shoulder, then spoke into it.

Mrs. Torres returned to the sofa, then encircled me with her right arm. "I'm going to call Lauren," The touch was comforting but also a wee bit invasive.

"Yes, please," I squeaked.

Chapter 69

Ivey

Everyone seemed to talk at once. They went from high-pitched to low grumbles, discussing drugs, money, and violence. And there was Rafe—smack dab in the middle of it.

When I excused myself to head for the powder room, a scuffle ensued. Rafe tried to follow me, but the sheriff detained him with a firm grip. "I need you to walk me through what your brother knows about MacArthur and Hill." Their voices faded when I slid the pocket door closed and turned on the faucet. I stared at myself in the antique oval mirror over the ceramic sink. I didn't look any different than I had earlier in the day, but I felt like I'd become a pod person. I'd been held at gunpoint. Isn't that something that only happens on the news or in a Jason Statham movie?

I'm not sure how long I sequestered myself in the Torres' powder room, but it must have been at least ten or fifteen minutes, because before I knew it, Aunt Lauren knocked softly on the bathroom door. "Ivey, honey. Are you okay?" I'd settled onto the commode lid, dabbing at my face with a damp hand towel.

"I'm okay—be out in a sec." I sniffed, stood up, took a deep breath, and prepared to return to the wretched living room. As I exited the hallway, I heard my parents' voices, and a wave of blessed reassurance warmed my heart.

Lauren conferenced my parents onto her phone's speaker. "Birdie? Honey? Are you okay?"

"Dad!"

My father's commanding voice boomed through the speaker. "We'll be there as soon as we can."

"Don't worry, we're coming to get you," my mom echoed. "I can coordinate flights—"

My dad interrupted her. "Carrie, please, calm down."

"Mom, Dad, I'm okay." I massaged my forehead which helped clear up the lingering fogginess. "You don't have to do that. We have Closing Day coming up, and—"

"You don't have to handle this all alone, honey," Mom replied. "You've been through such a shock. Lauren, will you take me off the speaker?"

I looked at Lauren, mentally willing her to reassure my parents of my safety. She winked at me, then walked to the kitchen with the phone to her ear.

"Hey, Ivey's safe here, Carrie. I know. I'm going to the other room."

It didn't escape my notice that coming to the Torres' home was Lauren's first trip outside since she'd heard about Uncle Michal's death. The fact that she was here, supporting me, warmed my heart. Despite her pain and grief, she'd pushed through it to be with me now. I couldn't let Lauren down—I had to woman up.

Rafe, Mr. Torres, and the Sheriff now gathered around the dining table across from the den. Rafe was hunched over with one hand massaging the back of his neck while his hair hung in his face. The three men spoke in somber tones.

"Here you go, dear." Mrs. Torres handed me a water glass full of sliced lemons.

I took the glass with both hands. "Oh, thank you. I'm sorry I ran off like that."

"It's okay, mija. It gave us time to get Lauren over here." She patted my shoulder. "I'm so sorry for all of this. We had no idea Rafe was pulled into Antonio's problems." Mrs. Torres lowered her gaze. "I hope Lauren can assure your parents. I don't blame them for being frantic."

I glanced toward the dining room. "Rafe looks miserable in there."

She looked wistfully at the trio, wringing her hands. "Yes, he does. I hope he can help the police."

I could feel the worry radiating from Mrs. Torres. "I promise I had no idea that Rafe knew anything about those men," I stammered. "I only just met Antonio. If I'd known—"

Mrs. Torres cut me off. "I know, I know. You haven't done anything wrong." Her face looked so sad. Tears pooled in her eyes.

I chugged the water, set the glass on the coffee table, then we rose and joined the men in the dining room.

Sheriff Preston turned his attention to me. "Anything to add, Ivey?"

I stole a glance at Rafe, who sat there looking like a whipped pup. "Not anything Rafe hasn't already said; it all happened so fast. The man was terrifyingly calm."

The Sheriff nodded. "Sounds like Timmy Hill. Not much ruffles him, but he's as violent as they come." He turned back to Rafe and his father. "So, neither of you has any clue as to where Antonio may be holed up?"

Mr. Torres spoke up first. "I'm embarrassed to say that Antonio doesn't share his whereabouts with me, especially since Gabby and I asked him to move out."

Rafe snorted. "You mean, told him, to move out." His tone was unabashedly bitter.

I nervously undid and redid my ponytail. The tension between Rafe and his father permeated everything and everyone, like a noxious fog.

The Sheriff moved alongside Rafe, looming over him. "Let's keep to the issue at hand. Rafe, you're sure Antonio hasn't given you any clue as to where he may be?"

Rafe's expression darkened. "Honest, Sheriff, he didn't—" He glanced at me—his eyes begged me not to contradict him.

I kept quiet, but thought why would Rafe lie when a gun-toting psychopath is out there searching for Antonio? Wouldn't he be safer with the police? Was Tonio still at his trailer?

Then it occurred to me.

Brother Isle.

Chapter 70

Ivey

I texted Rafe the minute I settled into Lauren's Jeep for the quick drive home.

Ivey: wth?

Rafe: I know ur pissed, I'm sorry

Ivey: yes!! can u talk

Rafe: in 10

Ivey: k

Lauren gripped the steering wheel, squinting at the afternoon sun. "Are you texting your parents?"

I reflexively tilted my phone away. "No, just telling Clara that I'll hit her up later." Lies.

"Are you hungry?" Lauren asked as she guided the Jeep onto Main Street. "Listen to me talking about food when you both could have been killed."

"It's okay." I tucked my phone into my purse. "I'm a little hungry." I was so not.

"It's not okay. I've managed to endanger you without even realizing it."

"None of this is your fault!" I barked.

It was Uncle Michal's fault getting involved with those men, Timmy and Judd.

We arrived at the house and Lauren turned off the ignition. "You are my saving grace. How did you get so wise?" A tired smile flickered on her lips.

I pretended to be calm. "It must be that Corbett blood."

Lauren's eyes brightened. "How about I make popcorn, and we'll watch a dumb romantic comedy?"

"You've got a deal," I said. "But let me call Mom and Dad first."

When I got to my room, I texted Rafe instead.

Ivey: I'm home

I sat on the bed, knees up, phone on my thighs, waiting for a response. 5:35 p.m.

And waiting.

And waiting.

I called my parents and begged them to let me stay in Walloon for the final two weeks of the summer. Mom cried and Dad simmered, but they acquiesced when I gave them the Sheriff's cell number. I couldn't help but wonder if I had tried harder to stay home for the summer if my parents would have backed down. But then I wouldn't be here for Lauren, or Rafe.

5:57 p.m.

The smell of buttery microwave popcorn wafted down the hall.

Lauren yelled from the den, "I've got *50 First Dates* queued up!"

"Be out in a minute!" I shouted back.

I was sure that Rafe had been arrested. I pictured him sitting in a holding cell, scared and alone. Or worse—not alone, with huge, terrifying murderers and psychos.

6:15 p.m.

Finally!

Rafe: Hey

Ivey: what's going on???

Rafe: meet me @morgs pier 10p, going 2 BI

Ivey: really?

Rafe: Ives, I need u, we have 2 warn him

Ivey: k, I'm still mad & freaked out

Rafe: me too

Three hours and forty-five minutes till we would meet up.

I changed into some sweatpants and a hoodie, rolled my shoulders back, then marched into the den for popcorn and a movie.

Chapter 71

Ivey

Time moved like the sloth in *Zootopia*. By the time the movie ended, I'd checked my phone about hundred times. Lauren had fallen asleep three-quarters of the way through, but I inadvertently woke her at 8:25 when I yelped at a text from Rafe.

"Oh, sh—"

Lauren jumped. "What, what?" Her eyes darted around the room in a panic.

"Everything's alright," I assured her. "I thought I felt a bug on me." Lying had become way too easy.

She smiled sleepily. "I did tell you that Sheriff Preston has a cruiser patrolling the area, right? I thought you might have seen something."

I did not know that factoid. "All night?" That could be a problem.

Lauren nodded and took a languorous stretch. "I'm going to bed, hon. Can I get you anything? Will you be able to sleep?"

"I'm fine, really. I'm just worn out." Understatement.

Lauren shuffled out of the room. "Love you!" She said as she disappeared down the hallway.

"You, too!" I texted Rafe about the patrolling police officer.

Rafe: damn, will you be able to get out?

Ivey: don't go w/o me, I will get out

Rafe: be careful

Ivey: wait 4 me

Rafe: 4 ever

I dropped the phone on my lap. The breath caught in my throat. That was the most romantic text I'd ever read.

What am I doing? I thought. I'm a rule follower. I don't sneak out of houses to warn possible felons as police patrol around the neighborhood. Come to think of it, I don't even know what a felon is. Is that what you call someone after they go to prison? Yeah, Ivey. That's what you should be thinking about right now – proper terminology.

My phone vibed and I looked down expecting another text from Rafe. It was Hattie.

Hattie: I found something.

Ivey: what??

My breath sped up, almost hyperventilating, as my thumbs hovered over the phone.

Hattie: I talked to Dad, no help, but he knows something.

Ivey: Does the name Judd MacArthur mean anything to you?

Hattie: It does- Wait!

Ivey: yeah?

Hattie: That's my dad's cousin. Haven't seen him in years

Ivey: wow that's crazy. Hey, thx

Hattie: good luck

Ivey: thx again, really

Judd MacArthur is Scott Foster's cousin. Wow. What does that mean for Lauren? For Antonio and Rafe?

I wracked my brain over the next hour. I did some restorative yoga poses and changed my clothes twice. (The first was too baggy. What if I got caught on something as I sneaked around the house? The second—slick black leggings and a close-cut top.) I was ready.

I went to the window and cranked it open as far as it could go. It was a tight squeeze as I hoisted my left leg, then my right over the sill. I perched there for a couple of seconds, reviewing my escape plan; basically, get out the window without alerting Lauren or the cop driving around, check.

I'd watched the police car for an hour to figure out his route—every ten minutes. He wasn't just cruising by either; he'd slow to a crawl right before he got to Lauren's house and scanned the whole area with a bright flashlight.

I avoided the gravel driveway by running through the grass until I got to the dock behind the Walloon Hotel. Once there, I huddled next to a potted tree to catch my breath. My hands shook, and the blood pumped heavily in my ears. I knew that the patrol cop didn't have any reason to arrest me— yet—but getting questioned now would not look good for Rafe and inevitably, Antonio.

I pushed myself to my feet and tiptoed across the dock, past the Barrelback Restaurant and the grassy area in front of the Square. Morgan's family's boat slip was on the third dock jutting into the lake. We'd strolled by one day after work, and Rafe had pointed the boat out. When I arrived, I saw a flash down at the end of the dock. Rafe! My treacherous heart wanted to rush over and throw myself into his arms, but I didn't. Keep your cool, Ives. I, carefully, made my way down the dock, and saw Rafe crouched next to the Turner's boat.

Rafe waved me toward him. "Come on, we gotta go!" He extended his hand, which I grasped, and he helped me onto the wobbly craft. Then he fiddled with the outboard motor.

"Won't the outboard be too loud?"

Rafe tilted his head, considering. "I hope not. Morgan said his parents like to take the boat out at night, so they bought the quietest motor they could find. That's why I asked to borrow it."

I nodded. "Does Morgan know about what happened this afternoon?"

Rafe kept messing with the motor in a way that did not give me much confidence. "Yeah, but not where we're going right now." He turned from the motor. His eyes were tired, as he looked through those long lashes.

More secrets. We needed to have a long talk.

Rafe tugged on the engine cord, and it chugged to life. Certainly not silent, but it would have to do. We wouldn't be the only ones on the lake, but hopefully, we were the only ones going to Brother Isle.

Chapter 72

Ivey

The journey to the campsite should have only taken about fifteen minutes at a good clip, but Rafe cut the engine about halfway there. I shivered from the humidity and frightful anticipation. "What's going on?"

"I need to tell you a couple of things before we get there," he said. I'd already told him about Hattie's text before we left the dock. We agreed to tell the sheriff the next morning.

"Okay," I said. "Do you think Tonio is armed?"

Rafe looked past me. "No, well, maybe—"

I tried to stand up, but I couldn't get my boat legs. "What!" I plopped back down on the bench seat.

Rafe covered my mouth with a shaky hand. "Shhhh!"

I tasted his sweaty palm and jerked away. "God, okay, what do you need to tell me?"

He hung his head. "It's not such a long shot that Tonio's at Brother Isle."

"That's good, right?" I said hopefully. "We can warn him." I didn't get the problem.

Rafe fumbled with his jacket pocket. "True, but I definitely know he's there because—" he held up a cheap flip phone, the kind you get at Walmart with no contract. "We've been in contact with these."

I groaned. "Is that a fricking burner phone? What is this? Law & Order: Summer Vacay?"

"I guess so." He chuckled. "You're pretty funny, y'know."

I ignored that comment and rolled my eyes. I'd blown through my allotted serotonin for the day, so I sat there on the vinyl-covered bench, the boat beneath me sloshing back and forth, each cell jazzed to the max. "So? Go on."

Rafe rubbed his neck and sucked in a breath. "You didn't hear everything I told the sheriff, so let me fill you in."

I wondered what else he could possibly say. A wave of nausea cascaded over me.

Rafe spoke quickly. So much so, that I tuned out most of it until I heard him say, "Bottom line, I helped Tonio bury the trunk with what turned out to be your uncle's—"

My jaw dropped.

Rafe put up his hands. "Hold on, hold on. Before you flip out, please let me explain."

I grasped my seat, my nails grinding the underside. "Okay…" I muttered.

"Tonio came by the house in the middle of the night. He told me that he'd been doing odd jobs for a guy, so he could pay money he owed. I didn't ask him why he owed money—I knew it was for drugs. Anyhow, Tonio has managed to get himself clean since my parents kicked him out. He wants to get a legit job or possibly go back to school." Rafe wiped his forehead. His hand shook a little bit. "The guy, who we now know is Judd MacArthur told him just one more job and Tonio'd be square on his debt."

"My uncle's body," I whispered.

Rafe nodded and took my hands. "That's why I fell asleep at work the next morning. I'm so sorry I lied." He looked down. "Your hands are freezing."

I looked past Rafe's anxiously beautiful face, into the clear, dark night. "I'm just…" My poor uncle, whatever he did, he didn't deserve to end up in a trunk, disrespected, tossed away like garbage. My grieving aunt, thinking he abandoned her. Having to wait years before she learned the truth. Now, this. More people dragged into this mess by these terrible men.

"You're just?" Rafe scooted closer to me.

I shook off my obsessive thoughts. "Nothing, go on. Please."

"Okay, Tonio tried to do what they asked by himself, but he busted up his arm digging up the trunk. He felt like he had no choice but to ask me to help."

"And you had to," I said, touching his cheek.

Rafe sniffed and wiped his nose with his sleeve. "I couldn't believe it—Tonio was sure he was out. Then, Judd wouldn't let him go. He threatened to kill Mama and Dad. He threatened to kill me."

We sat quietly for a minute or two, the boat rocking from side to side, breathing in the cool, humid air.

I let Rafe's admission wash over me. I leaned forward and laid my head on his sagging shoulder. "I've been so selfish to think that Lauren and I were the only people suffering. I'm sorry you were forced into all this."

Rafe brought his hands to my face. He gazed at me with sweetly damp eyes and kissed me. His lips were salty and smooth. He pulled me closer and closer until we fused like smoldering coals slowly turning to ash. A breeze cut through our embrace, scattering the heat away.

My chest muscles relaxed. "I just had a brainstorm. Maybe this wasn't dumb luck or bad luck. Maybe it was what needed to happen to uncover the truth about Uncle Michal and to help Tonio get out from under this man's thumb."

Rafe crooked an eyebrow. "You think?" Hope sparked in his eyes.

I leaned close and said, "We need to get Tonio to turn himself in."

Chapter 73
Ivey

Rafe shoved his hair back from his face while revving up the outboard. "Tonio's never gonna go for that."

When we approached the shoreline leading up to Brother Isle, Rafe cut the engine, then we drifted toward a small patch of sand surrounded by whitish-grey boulders. The moon reflected eerily off the stone surfaces.

Righteous enthusiasm flowed through my veins. I said, "I admit it's risky going to the cops, but realistically, how can he expect to run from this?"

Rafe's head drooped, muted in thought.

I could not imagine how conflicted Rafe must be about his brother. I wanted to shift over to sit right beside him, put my arms around him and assure him, but I stayed put to keep the boat balanced.

Rafe's voice sounded quaky. "Do you have any idea how much jail time he and I could be facing?"

I tilted my head. "I don't."

"Five to ten years."

I looked down at my shoes, feeling deflated. "Wow, how do you know that?"

"Googled it. And that's with a great lawyer, which my family can't afford," he responded.

I was useless—weak and braindead. Suggesting that Tonio turn himself in had come from my gut—not based on any authentic experience.

Rafe focused on the front of the boat. "But you're right, we do need to consider all our options." Rafe said encouragingly. His phone vibrated loudly. He held up a finger. "Okay, yeah, we'll do that... yeah, bye." Rafe pocketed his phone and cranked the outboard, steering the boat backward.

I gripped my seat again. "What now?"

"Tonio wants us to land somewhere else. Shhh," Rafe placed a finger to his lips.

Our boat sloshed side to side reacting to a faraway speedboat's wake. Rafe expertly worked the outboard, so we headed west of Brother Isle. We came to a tiny inlet so low profile I thought we were floating right into a thicket of bushes. Rafe cut the engine, ducked his head and I followed suit. We glided under soft willow vines like luggage on a conveyor belt.

There on the bank was a well-worn canoe and Antonio Torres.

Tonio was bedraggled. A filthy t-shirt hung off his shoulders; his jeans sagged on his bony hips. It'd only been hours since I'd met him, but he managed to look skinnier, skeletal. The front of our boat bumped the rocks lining the shoreline. The water stayed deep. I wondered how we would get out of the boat without getting soaked.

That turned out to be the least of my worries.

The brothers locked eyes as Rafe tried to hand Antonio the tow line. Tonio shook his head slightly, his eyes blazing.

Rafe reared back. "Wha—?"

I gasped so sharply that I choked and screamed at the same time.

Tonio jerked his head toward the bushes and mouthed, "Go back."

Behind him, the tangle of vegetation parted, and out came Timmy Hill holding the same pistol he threatened us with earlier.

"Nice to see you both again." He cackled like a creepy movie villain.

Tonio's body deflated. "I'm so sorry."

My breath caught in my throat. I knew this expedition might be dangerous, but it never occurred to me (and I assume Rafe) that Timmy Hill knew about Brother Isle. Maybe we can gun the engine and back out of the inlet. My brain flipped through dozens of escape plans.

"Rafe?" I looked at him, stoic, his hand still on the motor.

Timmy moved forward and placed the gun barrel against Tonio's temple. "Don't even think about leaving. We have a few things to discuss with all three of you."

We?

As if on cue, another man pushed his way through the bushes. Tall, dark slicked-back hair and bone-white skin. He wore a tracksuit that was so new, it sparkled in the moonlight. He wore ridiculously white trainers that were now caked with mud along the edges.

Judd MacArthur in the flesh.

Rafe and I were hoisted out of the boat, and none too gently. Judd grabbed me and dragged me over the rocks onto the muddy shore. He stepped back and pulled out another gun. My phone jostled in the front pocket of my hoodie. My skin was hot as the blood rushed to my limbs. I fought to breathe; fear strangling me.

While I laid there catching my breath, Rafe had shaken Timmy off and started to bargain. "Listen, let's just—"

"Shut up." Judd barked, his voice deadly calm. "Walk." He turned into the bushes as Timmy Hill gestured for us to follow.

The pitch black descended as we trudged through the trees, but my eyes adjusted. Rafe grabbed my left hand and Tonio shuffled along my right. None of us said a word. A million cop-show scenarios flashed through my head.

Don't get taken to a second location, echoed through my brain. I'd heard that at a self-defense class at school. I remember the sweaty instructor who had asked me to pretend to be a victim while he showed us some ways to get away from an attacker.

A kick to the groin.

Scream and run—most people can't hit a moving target.

If he tries to sexually assault you—gouge out his eyes.

None of these things applied to our current situation. Our phones were our only hope. We arrived at Rafe and Tonio's old campsite. There was a shabby tent, and glowing embers in the firepit.

Judd MacArthur propped himself against a tree, then waved his weapon indicating for us to sit. Timmy guarded our backs.

Tonio moved toward MacArthur. "Judd, please."

One of these men had killed my uncle. The thought made me so nauseated that I gagged.

Judd's snake eyes turned to me. "What the hell is wrong with you?"

I gagged again, sour saliva coming up. "I—"

Then, I had an idea.

Chapter 74

Ivey

Rafe tried to put his arm around me, but Judd thrust the gun at him.

"Hands to your sides!" Judd's teeth glimmered viciously.

"She's scared, man," Rafe shouted back.

"It's okay, I'm okay," I made my voice tremble. "I need to" I choked—grunting and groaning as dramatically as I could.

Judd gestured with his weapon again. "Oh, for Christ's sake, if you're gonna puke, go behind a tree. I don't want to see that."

Rafe tried to grab my hand again, but I pulled away hoping he'd understand, and comply, while I executed my plan.

Once free from the cluster of males, I scrambled behind a thick tree trunk. I made a big production of coughing and gagging. I knew I only had a few minutes—if that. I whipped out my phone and Hattie's contact info popped up. Seeing her number enhanced my original idea.

My first thought was to text 911, which I did, then I shakily sent Hattie a location pin with the word "help". I coughed and gagged some more for effect, then I tossed the phone under a leafy shrub. Sweat poured into my eyes. I swiped at it when Timmy bounded over. "That's enough," he growled. "Pull yourself together." He wrenched my arm so hard that it felt like it dislocated.

"Stop!" I screamed, trying to yank my arm from his beefy grasp. But he didn't stop. He dragged me back to the creepy campfire crew.

Rafe was frantic, more agitated than I'd ever seen him. I dropped down next to him rubbing my arm. I wiped my face with my sleeve. I hoped my wide eyes might telepathically reassure Rafe that I was okay for now.

Judd instructed Timmy to go and hide our boat. "And make sure there aren't any nav devices on it!" He yelled after him. Judd turned his attention to Rafe and me. "Antonio, search them."

Thank God I threw my phone away. But will Judd believe I didn't bring one?

Tonio rose from the ground like a robot and flatly asked us to stand. His defeated, hangdog expression made me want to cry. Rafe handed over his phone and the keys to the boat. When he got to me, I shook my head. Tonio tilted his head with surprise and disbelief. I glanced toward the bushes where I "vomited."

I saw a flicker of acknowledgement in Tonio's eyes, then he turned to Judd and gave him Rafe's items. "She doesn't have anything on her."

Judd narrowed his eyes. "Yeah, sure. What teenage girl doesn't have a cell phone?"

I panicked, so I started blabbing. "My parents are really strict; they won't let me have one." I looked at him up through my lashes, trying to be pitiful. It seemed to work.

"Whatever." Judd blew it off and settled on a nearby flat-topped rock. He ran his non-gun hand through his super-jelled hair. It sprung forward so he smoothed the lock back over his skull. It was disturbing how much he looked like Hattie's dad. "I don't like this situation any more than either of you." He waved the gun around recklessly. "I'm a businessman. I don't like threatening people, but when folks like our Antonio here don't follow orders—people get hurt."

We all turned instinctively when Timmy stumbled through the bushes, back to the campsite. "No nav. It's just a fishing boat."

"Alright, Tim, sit down."

Tonio spoke up. "Judd."

"No," Judd aimed the gun. "I've heard *your* story." He looked at Rafe. "Little brother, what did *you* tell the cops?"

Rafe glanced at me, straightened from a slump, and addressed Judd as confidently as he could muster. "I told them that your sidekick here threatened me and my girlfriend."

I was so proud of Rafe's bravery. Please, God. Help us. I teared up thinking about my parents—how devastated they'd be if something happened to me. Sure, they're uber-parental, but they love me, and my sisters. God. Dee and Rose. They could be so bossy and annoying, but… my friends, Clara, Kelli. Please, Lord, get us out of this.

Rafe kept his eyes on Judd. "I didn't say anything else 'cause I don't know anything else."

A super creepy smile spread across Judd's face. "Now why don't I believe you, little brother?"

I knew I had to stall for time, and I needed to know, to understand, why they killed my uncle. "Why did you kill my uncle? Michal Lyska."

Judd recoiled. His eyes shot over to Timmy. "Pat her down again." His voice was cold as steel.

Rafe stood up and blocked me, his arms spread wide. "No. Don't you dare touch her!"

Judd stood as well. "Little brother, here's your choice. Tim pats her down or—" he walked around the smoldering fire and whispered in Rafe's ear. "Or she takes her shirt off to prove she's not recording anything."

I shuddered and put my hands in the air, ready to be searched. "It's okay," I said. "I'm not recording anything."

Timmy didn't seem all that interested in spending that much time frisking me, thankfully. He stepped back and shook his head.

Judd settled back on his rock perch. "Well, Ivey, is it? Your Uncle Michal made several poor decisions. We were good friends for a while." He looked up at the still, starry night. "I thought he'd be a good addition to my team, but instead, he became an enemy."

I tried to keep my wits about me, but tears forced their way out. "How?" My voice cracked.

Judd MacArthur looked me up and down. Was there sadness in his eyes? "Michal didn't take the hint when we framed him for the hardware store robbery."

I narrowed my eyes. "Why frame him?"

Judd pondered for a few seconds. "Let's just say that a government official needed Michal out of the way, for personal reasons."

Rafe and I turned to each other, and he whispered, "Hattie's dad—"

Judd stood up and paced around the dying fire. "Oh yes, I almost forgot! Your little Scooby-Doo investigation at the saloon. Scott mentioned that." He scratched at his ear.

The wind had picked up. I hugged myself to stay warm as I shivered uncontrollably.

Judd was on a roll. "Scott was pissed off when he heard I'd killed Michal. He only wanted him out of town, or, out of the country, even better."

My limbs dissolved, tears and snot ran down my face. "Why would Hattie's dad want my uncle gone?"

Judd stopped pacing and smoothed his shiny hair again. "I haven't seen Hattie since she was a baby girl." He mused. "After the mess with Michal, Scott pretended I didn't exist. It hurt my feelings—" Judd patted his heart, mockingly. "But he made it worth my while. I hadn't heard from him for years when he called me earlier this summer. Scott was hysterical that a friend of Hattie's was asking questions about Michal." His smiled directly at me. I shuddered. "I guess that was you, Ivey. Scott threatened to turn me in, but I beat him to it by having our Antonio here move the body." He laughed to himself. "Then I placed a call to the police tip line."

"You set up your own cousin?" Rafe asked.

Judd's voice dripped with rancor. "You probably think Scott is a superhero public servant like everyone else. Well, he's not."

I felt like I had to keep Judd talking; it felt like it was our only chance. "I know that Hattie's dad went out with my aunt when they were in high school."

Judd cackled, and I winced at his cruelty. "Ivey, you get the gold star! Before Adam came along, Scott had planned to leave Aliyah and pursue your aunt. I have no idea how he thought he'd get away with it, though. What an idiot!" Judd waved his weapon around again. "The first step was to frame Michal, then deport him, while comforting your aunt through the whole thing—the stupidest plan I'd ever heard."

Antonio spoke up. "What a minute. Why are you admitting to all this?"

Judd's icy gaze slid to Antonio. "Maybe I'm unburdening myself."

Timmy Hill snorted as he stood up behind us. Then he and Judd cocked their guns. Everything went hauntingly still, like an old-time movie projector just stopped.

I pictured my uncle, even though he was just a fuzzy memory. I remembered a quiet, friendly, and gentle person. He wasn't a criminal. I thought of my aunt, and how she didn't know the truth. Maybe she'd never know. I grasped Rafe's hand on my left and Tonio's on my right and closed my eyes.

We inhaled all at once.

A startling wind whipped up and raced through the campsite. The firepit coals flickered with the rush of oxygen. We all frenetically looked around while blinding beams of light flooded the campsite, spastically bouncing around. Six heavily armed figures rushed out of the surrounding trees, guns drawn, their deep, guttural shouts telling us to get on the ground. Rafe threw himself over me, and Tonio landed alongside. I tasted rich dirt, burrowing my head down, then froze in place.

Rafe, Antonio, and I huddled together and prayed.

Chapter 75
Aftermath

My room was oppressively warm. The ceiling and walls hung over me, ready to squeeze me between their plastered jaws. The room was nothing like the colorful and cheerful version I had discovered seven weeks ago. I laid on the bed and stared up at the ticking ceiling fan. I reminded myself that the room was exactly as it was when I plopped on this same comforter, texting with my girls, just about to meet Rafe for the first time. I was the one who'd changed.

After last night's terrifying events, the stress hormone let-down had rendered my bones achy, exhausted. Keeping my eyes upward, I frantically felt around the sheets for my phone. When I found it, I brought it close to my face: 11: 47 am.

Last night came back to me in flashes. The police spotlight on Brother Isle had felt like the sun coming to rescue us. It turns out, Hattie had indeed received my text and location pin. She notified the police immediately, who had mobilized the SWAT unit. Two of the armed officers had pulled Rafe, Antonio, and me up off the ground and whisked us through the trees onto a police boat. Before we were taken away, I saw Judd MacArthur and Timmy Hill prostrate, their arms bound with zip ties. Relief had washed over me, dampening my overburdened synapses. The bad guys were caught, and we were safe, at least physically.

Once Rafe, Tonio, and I had boarded the police boat, they swaddled us with tinfoil blankets. The gesture contradicted the brusque attitude of the officers, but I was thankful for the warmth.

Sheriff Preston appeared and seated himself opposite the three of us. "Are you kids, okay? Do you need some water?"

We all shook our heads, no one seemed ready to speak.

The Sheriff nodded. "Just take it easy. It'll be a few minutes to shore. Then your guardians will meet us at the station."

We looked back and forth at each other. Of course, our guardians. There was no getting around my parents coming to get me now. It was just as well.

Once we had docked, we rode to the station, still silent. Rafe and I slumped together, our heads joined while Tonio stared out the window, his breathing ragged and clouding the glass. I took his hand and squeezed it. He half-smiled, "You saved us, Ivey." Then he closed his eyes and leaned his head against the glass.

We arrived at the brilliantly lit police station; I winced at the glare. They seated us in separate rooms, which initially freaked me out, until Lauren breezed through the dingy grey door and joined me at the metal table. She held me as I finally let myself cry. Lauren stroked my ratty hair. "It's okay," she cooed. "It's over now."

I smelled the gardenias on her.

Eventually, the Sheriff came in and asked me tons of questions. I told him everything that happened that night and all summer, for that matter. I begged him to tell me what would happen to Antonio and Rafe, but he would only say, "We'll see."

Lauren and I left the police station at 2:26 am without seeing either Torres brother.

"Ivey! Are you going to come get breakfast?" Lauren's voice cut through the gloom.

I sat up. "Lauren? You're serious?"

And there she was—showered, dressed, with her hair pulled back. She had flour on the tip of her nose and a dishcloth between her palms. The scent of bacon, eggs, and biscuits wafted in from the kitchen.

Lauren laughed. "Of course, I'm serious!" God, I'd missed her sunny personality so much. She walked to the bed and settled on the end. "I figured it was time I started taking care of *you*."

"But how are you doing?"

She set the dishcloth aside and took my hand. "I'm good, honey. It's not been easy, but I know the truth now. Michal was a complicated man, a troubled man, but now I know he *didn't* abandon me." She looked past me, full of thought, her blue eyes bright. "I never realized that I could forgive just about anything but that—thinking he could up and leave me." Lauren looked back at me. "I'm so thankful that you're safe and those awful men are in custody."

I flashed back to the two of us leaving the police station barely nine hours earlier. I hadn't seen Rafe or Antonio, but I had seen Scott Foster being escorted into the station. He had his hands in front with a jacket draped over what I assumed were handcuffs. His wife trailed behind talking a blue streak to Sheriff Preston. Poor Hattie. No one deserves the pain of their parent being arrested. She had truly come through for us —we owed her our lives.

I yawned so deeply that my jaw popped. "I got some sleep, but I feel hollowed out, like, emotionally." I told Lauren. I stretched my heavy arms and legs. "I'm so worried about Rafe and Antonio."

"I completely understand, " Lauren said soothingly. "I'll see what I can find out while you get ready."

I smiled. "Thanks. I love you." I meant it with my whole being.

"I love you too, sweetheart. Now get your butt up!" Right on cue, Peppercorn leaped onto the bed and rubbed against me. "See, even Peppercorn is up and about." Lauren laughed as she left the room.

I swung my legs over the side of the bed. My head was swimming and fuzzy, but I rose and followed Lauren's instructions. I made my way to the restroom, splashed water on my face then grabbed a sweatshirt from the closet, and started down the hallway.

I heard Lauren whispering with someone, and my heartbeat quickened. I rushed the last few feet and there he was.

"Oh, Rafe! You're here!" I gushed and wrapped him in my arms. He snuggled his head on top of mine, so we fit like puzzle pieces.

"I'm okay, baby."

I gazed up at him, so filled with joy that I couldn't say another word.

Chapter 76
Epilogue

The day after the Sunnyside closed for the summer, Mom and Dad came to get me from Walloon Lake. Who knew that I'd get my parents' attention by simply surviving a kidnap and a murder attempt, plus solving a cold case?

Easy, peasy.

It was tough leaving Lauren, but she promised that she was going to be fine. She reconnected with the counselor she'd seen after Uncle Michal's disappearance, which gave us all some comfort. We made plans to visit with her over Christmas, even flying in Nan and Pops to celebrate.

A few weeks later, Daisy, Rose, and I lounged on bean bag chairs in the tv room back home in Florida. *Legally Blonde* played in the background while my sisters pelted me with questions about my summer. It was odd being the center of their attention. Odd, but fairly satisfying.

Rose could hardly stay in her spot. "I can't believe how brave you were! How did you think to fake being sick?"

I paused. It was hard to get back into my headspace from that night. "I was more desperate than brave, but since I already felt sick to my stomach; I went with it."

Daisy set a bowl of pretzels on the floor, then scooted forward in her bean bag chair. "I can't imagine how terrified you must have been. I've never even seen a gun, let alone had one pointed at me. Your quick thinking saved everyone!"

I could get used to all this praise. "Well, I could tell that the older guy, Timmy, didn't like fussing with me, so, I took a chance that he'd leave me alone long enough to send a text or two, especially if I was sick."

Daisy leaned toward me and rubbed my shoulder. "You are a freaking boss!"

I took a sip of Diet Coke, then licked my lips. "I appreciate y'all coming home from your conference early—you didn't have to do that."

Rose waved me off. "Of course, we did! Our little sis was almost killed! And poor Aunt Lauren, finding out all that horrible stuff about Uncle Michal. You saved her too."

Okay, I changed my mind; all this adulation was kinda weird.

Daisy's face turned serious; her shoulders tensed. "I'm sorry I gave you crap about talking to Pops."

I shook my head. "No prob. The police had asked Lauren and I not to discuss the investigation, so how could you have known?"

Daisy seemed to relax. "True, I get that, but it almost got you killed!"

Rose waved a hand to get my attention. "So, more importantly, what's going on with Rafe? He is such a hottie!" She twirled her blond braid, her blue eyes sparkled. My sisters truly were profoundly identical.

I grabbed the pretzel bowl off the floor. Clara and Kelli had grilled me about Rafe the week I got back from Michigan. I'd shown them about a thousand pics from the summer and we'd talked all night.

"We're in touch, and we'll see." I arched an eyebrow, enjoying my sisters' curiosity.

"Chicken!" my sisters said, simultaneously.

I giggled and nibbed a pretzel chip. I wanted to keep Rafe and my relationship private, at least for now.

We finished the movie and chit-chatted some more when Daisy's phone chirped. She looked at the screen, paled and brought a hand to her mouth. "Oh my God!"

Rose and I moved over to her and peered down at the phone. Daisy held it up, then burst into tears.

Brandon High School Teacher of the Year, Jackson Moultrie, found dead after a faculty party, screamed the website's headline.

Mr. Moultrie was not only the most popular teacher at Brandon High, but he had singlehandedly gotten Daisy and Rose into their summer Leadership Conference.

Huddled together around Daisy in her bean bag chair, we all took a moment to let the horrible headline sink in.

I stood up, rubbed Daisy's back reassuringly, then said to Rose, "I'll be right back."

Rose nodded, so I made my way up the short staircase that led from the basement tv room to the kitchen. I took my phone from my back pocket, planning to text my mother but my fingers had a different idea though.

Ivey: You will **NOT** believe what just happened here.

Rafe: Tell me, baby.

— THE END —

Acknowledgments

I'm overwhelmed with the enthusiasm, know-how, and guidance I've received from Wild Ink Publishing. Thank you so much Abigail Wild, Brittany McMann, and S. E. Reed for taking a chance on me and *Sunflower*. An enormous amount of thanks to my editor Laura Wackwitz. You've not only read *Sunflower* a million times, but you've championed the story from the beginning.

I also want to thank Southern New Hampshire University for facilitating my Master of Fine Arts and my thesis instructor, Angie Smibert, for her insight and constructive criticism. There is no way I would have stuck with writing without SNHU's fantastic program. It toughened my skin and taught me how to navigate the publishing landscape.

Thank you to my first developmental editor, Eve Porinchak. Your helpful comments and professional experience truly enriched my manuscript.

Many thanks to the multi-talented Myra McElhaney for taking the time to counsel me about social media, publishing, and marketing. You inspired me to keep going! Thank you to my fellow wine enthusiasts, Stephanie Allen, Joyce Messer, and Denise Cardo for connecting me with Myra, along with encouraging my writing from the start.

The inspiration for *Sunflower's* setting, Walloon Lake, came to me on a visit to my dear friends, Gayle and Paul Sherlag, and their home state of Michigan. Driving from the Traverse City airport (just like Ivey and her Mom) I saw miles of sunflower fields and was hooked on Michigan's Lower Peninsula. I can't believe it took me over fifty years to visit this incredibly beautiful part of our country. Big thanks to Andi Fron, Mary Lou Jansen, Susan Fron, and Andrea Disner for reading *Sunflower* at various stages, and being constant supporters of my work.

I appreciate Corporal Michael Ricks, Gwinnett County Police Department, for taking time to talk with me about the ins and outs of police investigations. Any inadvertent inaccuracies are completely mine.

I believe firmly that all writers are readers first. In that vein, all readers need their posse. Thank you to my book club gals: Sherri Wright, Nikki McGlamery, Margaret Harrison, Julie Mills Watson, Lisa Garmon, and Leigh Ann Herrin for your enthusiasm and support.

Thank you also, to: Jeannie Briggs, Amber Parra, Karen Loftin & Anne Bruno for taking the time to read *Sunflower* and give feedback.

Special thanks to my friend of over forty years, Bonnie Evans, and the best sister-in-law in the world, Sheri Broom, for reading early manuscripts and being uber cheerleaders!

Thank you to my amazing family, starting with my mother, Joanie Doorley, who brought me up with books and fostered my love of reading. It's possible that Mom is even more excited about *Sunflower's* publication than me! Also thank you to my brother, George Doorley, and my niece, Carly Doorley, for your love and encouragement. I want to thank my mother-in-law, Connie Broom and my incredibly supportive brother-in-law, Matt Broom.

My husband and I lost both our fathers, Bill Doorley and Jim Broom, in 2013. Throughout my writing journey, I've wished they could be with me to celebrate. I do feel their encouragement from their heavenly home. Thank you, Dad and Pop.

Many thanks for my undeserved blessings, my sons, Clay and Max Broom, and my wonderful daughter-in-law, Jen Broom, for their constant love, support, and encouragement. You've all read early manuscripts, and I hope you love the finished product!

Last, but certainly not least, my husband of thirty-eight years, thank you Ward Broom for being a steadfast support system for me throughout this crazy journey. There was not a moment where you weren't confident in my ability to not only finish my manuscript but see it through publication. There is no way I could have achieved this dream without you. I love you!

To my readers, I cannot tell you how honored I am that you've chosen to spend your hard-earned money on *Sunflower*, and taking the time to read. I hope you love Ivey like I do and that you look forward to more adventures with the Des Jardins family.

Love,
Donna (D L) Broom

About D L Broom

DL Broom is a debut Young Adult author, retired educator, and mother of two grown sons. She enjoys reading thrillers and mysteries and writing contemporary and historical fiction (her flash fiction, *Ellie*, was featured in *The Penmen Review*). DL received an MFA in Creative Writing (2022) with the Young Adult mystery, *Sunflower*. She loves bringing multidimensional characters, fascinating settings, and intriguing storylines to her readers. DL lives in Georgia, with her husband and their crazy dog, Starbuck. Her author's website is: www.dlbroomwrites.com